continued . . .

"Smart, dangerous, and sexy as hell, the witches are more than a match for the warlocks and demons who'd like nothing more than to bring hell to earth and enslave mankind. Always an exhilarating read."
                                                            —*Fresh Fiction*

"*Witch Heart* is a story that will captivate its readers. It will hook you from the first few pages and then take you on a wild ride. It is a fast-paced story but it is also a story that will make you feel emotion. Anya Bast uses words like Monet used paint. It's vibrant. It's alive. Readers will be able to see the story come to life as it just leaps out of the pages."
                                                            —*Bitten by Books*

WITCH BLOOD

"Any paranormal fan will be guaranteed a Top Pick read. Anya has provided it all in this hot new paranormal series. You get great suspense, vivid characters, and a world that just pops off the pages . . . Not to be missed."
                                                —*Night Owl Romance Reviews*

"Gritty danger and red-hot sensuality make this book and series smoking!"
                                                            —*Romantic Times*

WITCH FIRE

"Deliciously sexy and intriguingly original."
                                —Angela Knight, *New York Times* bestselling author

"A sensual feast sure to sate even the most finicky of palates. Richly drawn dynamic characters dictate the direction of this fascinating story. You can't miss with Anya."
                                                            —*A Romance Review*

"Fast-paced, edgy suspense . . . The paranormal elements are fresh and original. This reader was immediately drawn into the story from the opening abduction, and obsessively read straight through to the dramatic final altercation. Bravo, Ms. Bast; *Witch Fire* is sure to be a fan favorite."
—*ParaNormal Romance*

"A fabulously written ultimate romance. Anya Bast tells a really passionate story and leaves you wanting more . . . the elemental witch series will be a fantastic read."   —*The Romance Readers Connection*

"A terrific romantic fantasy starring two volatile lead characters . . . the relationship between fire and air makes the tale a blast to read."
—*The Best Reviews*

MORE PRAISE FOR ANYA BAST AND HER NOVELS

"Had me sitting on the edge of my seat from page one."
—*The Road to Romance*

"A lovely erotic tale . . . This unique and passionate story is filled with humor, fire, and heartwarming emotion."
—*Romance Reviews Today*

"Anya Bast pulled another winner out of her pocket."
—*Night Owl Romance Reviews*

"An entertaining erotic romantic suspense tale."
—*Midwest Book Review*

Titles by Anya Bast

THE CHOSEN SIN
JEWELED
JADED

WITCH FIRE
WITCH BLOOD
WITCH HEART
WITCH FURY
WICKED ENCHANTMENT
CRUEL ENCHANTMENT
RAVEN'S QUEST

Jaded

ANYA BAST

HEAT
NEW YORK

THE BERKLEY PUBLISHING GROUP
Published by the Penguin Group
Penguin Group (USA) Inc.
375 Hudson Street, New York, New York 10014, USA
Penguin Group (Canada), 90 Eglinton Avenue East, Suite 700, Toronto, Ontario M4P 2Y3, Canada
(a division of Pearson Penguin Canada Inc.)
Penguin Books Ltd., 80 Strand, London WC2R 0RL, England
Penguin Group Ireland, 25 St. Stephen's Green, Dublin 2, Ireland (a division of Penguin Books Ltd.)
Penguin Group (Australia), 250 Camberwell Road, Camberwell, Victoria 3124, Australia
(a division of Pearson Australia Group Pty. Ltd.)
Penguin Books India Pvt. Ltd., 11 Community Centre, Panchsheel Park, New Delhi—110 017, India
Penguin Group (NZ), 67 Apollo Drive, Rosedale, Auckland 0632, New Zealand
(a division of Pearson New Zealand Ltd.)
Penguin Books (South Africa) (Pty.) Ltd., 24 Sturdee Avenue, Rosebank, Johannesburg 2196,
South Africa

Penguin Books Ltd., Registered Offices: 80 Strand, London WC2R 0RL, England

This book is an original publication of The Berkley Publishing Group.

Copyright © 2011 by Anya Bast.
Cover art by Tony Mauro.
Cover design by Rita Frangie.
Text design by Tiffany Estreicher.

PRINTING HISTORY
Heat trade paperback edition / June 2011

Library of Congress Cataloging-in-Publication Data

Bast, Anya.
    Jaded / Anya Bast. — Heat trade pbk. ed.
        p.   cm.
    ISBN 978-0-425-24109-7 (trade pbk.)
    1. Triangles (Interpersonal relations)—Fiction.   I. Title.
PS3602.A8493J33 2011
813'.6—dc22
                              2010036501

PRINTED IN THE UNITED STATES OF AMERICA

10 9 8 7 6 5 4 3 2 1

For my readers.

Thank you for buying my books. Thank you for spending time in the worlds I've created and for opening your hearts to my characters.

I love receiving your emails, and your comments on Facebook and Twitter. I deeply appreciate your reviews and am always excited to see your lovely faces at my book signings. I am profoundly grateful for every last one of you.

It's only through your support that I'm able to tell the stories that crowd my mind and to live the dream of being a writer, the dream I've had since I was seven years old.

Thank you.

One

The problem was expectations.

Lilya Orensdaughter sat in an outdoor café in downtown Milzyr, sipping a cup of black coffee and watching a family at another table. The man held a small child on his lap while laughing and talking with his wife. They looked happy, in love.

Even though Lilya had long since put aside such expectations, once in a while they reared their heads. For a moment, watching the young family, she was swamped with a wish and woeful longing—a partner with whom to share her life. Just that. No more. She knew better than to add a child to her yearning. Children would never be for her.

Neither was a man. Not like that. Not one who loved her the way she loved him, wholly, completely, and reciprocally, the way that couple seemed to love each other.

She turned her face and mind away, looking down the crowded

street of Milzyr. The city had changed so much since the revolution, yet in many ways remained the same. Pleasant autumn weekends still thronged the cobblestone streets with milling couples who spent the afternoon window-shopping and talking with each other as they strolled. Unless one of the odd contraptions that was meant to replace the horse-drawn carriage rumbled past belching smoke, one couldn't see any difference now that the Edaeii and their royal court had been toppled from power.

Yet the differences were there. The Jeweled, or those magicked ones who'd been formerly called such, were mostly in hiding now, afraid to face a populace that had murdered them on sight just a few short years ago. Every face that Lilya gazed upon made her wonder: Where were the magicked? It was a sore in her heart that they hid from the world. Things were better for Milzyr apart from that lack—the country needed its magick back.

A hand touched her shoulder. She looked up, smiling into her best friend's face. Evangeline's belly was round as a ball these days. Grimacing from the effort it took to move in such a condition, Evangeline lowered herself into a chair opposite Lilya.

Lilya's smile widened. "I'm surprised Gregorio and Anatol are letting you out of their sight these days."

"It was a fight, let me tell you." Evangeline caught the eye of the waiter and ordered a cherry sugar water. "I told them I'd had a child once before, could do it again just fine, and they needed to act more like my husbands and less like my jailers."

"Good for you. When is this one due?"

"Soon. Within the next couple weeks. It can't come soon enough for me. I feel like I'm twice as heavy as I was with Nicoli." She smoothed her hand over the expensive fabric of the light green day gown that covered her stomach.

"Maybe you truly are twice as heavy. Maybe it's twins."

Evangeline's eyes widened and her face blanched for a moment. "The thought has crossed my mind. Twins. *Egad*."

Lilya smiled and took a sip of her coffee. "Good thing you have two able-bodied fathers to help you out."

She smiled. "They can't wait for this one to get here."

"I know they're crazy for Nicoli. That little boy seems to be the light of their life alongside you."

The waiter brought Evangeline's pink-colored sugar water. "I'm lucky to have them."

"Didn't I tell you so?"

She nodded. "And you were right. You always are." She sipped her water. "How are you doing, Lilya?"

"Wonderfully, as usual." Lilya took another sip of her coffee. Indeed, as long as she kept her expectations low she couldn't ask for a nicer life.

Evangeline offered her a conspiratorial grin. "How many men have offered to whisk you away from your sordid life this week?"

"Only two." She pouted. "And one of them is a man who offers at least once a month. The number is rather low. I may be losing my touch." She had plenty of men who adored her, who stared at her with puppy-dog eyes and offered her the moon on a silver-plated dish, but she didn't love any of those men back. Not the way they deserved.

If she'd been a gold-hunting sort of woman, she'd have been married a long time ago. It wasn't that financial stability didn't matter to her. To a woman who'd grown up impoverished, money was very important—but other things were more so.

Evangeline laughed, her blond hair curling around her face. "I highly doubt that."

Lilya reached into a bag on the ground near her feet and pulled out a frilly baby gown. "I brought you a gift for the impending little one."

"Oh, it's beautiful," said Evangeline, taking the gown into her hands. "Truly, it's gorgeous. It's also very, very pink. Do you know something I don't?"

Lilya leaned forward a little. "I am very good at predicting the sex of babies. I say yours will be a girl." She shrugged a shoulder and smiled. "Maybe two girls. If so, I'll have to buy a second dress to match."

Evangeline blanched again.

Lilya laughed. "You'll be fine."

"Says the woman who is footloose and completely free."

She shrugged. "Ah, well, I am that."

"One day you'll meet a man who wants to whisk you away and you'll *want* to be whisked away by him, Lilya. You'll be in love."

Lilya rolled her eyes. "Perish the thought, Evangeline. I'm happy where I am, doing what I'm doing." *Really*, she reminded herself firmly. It was wrong to hope for anything else.

Evangeline smiled and shook her head. "Just as I thought I was happy in the palace as a J'Edaeii. I had no idea how sweet life could be until all that was taken away. Listen to me, Lilya; you never know what might be around the corner. Stay open to the possibilities."

"You know my stance on love, Evangeline."

She nodded. "It interferes with your work."

"Kills it, actually."

"Maybe that wouldn't be such a bad thing."

Lilya smiled gently. "I know you mean well—"

"I want only the best for you. I owe you a lot, after all."

"I love my life the way it is, Evangeline. Really."

"I know you do." Evangeline smiled, reached across the table, grabbed her hand, and squeezed. "And I love you. I just want you to have someone to share your life with. I never understood how wonderful it could be until I had it for myself."

Lilya squeezed her hand back and smiled. Maybe, but it would never happen. Not for her.

Lilya headed back to the Temple of Dreams a while later. These days she didn't get to see her friend Evangeline very often, and she saw Gregorio, one of Evangeline's husbands, even less. Gregorio had been a frequent visitor to the Temple of Dreams before he'd met Evangeline. He'd never been Lilya's client, though he had been her friend. Now he never visited. It was a testament to the love he shared with his wife. Lilya knew quite well—it was not always so. Many were the husbands who frequented the temple.

Quite regularly so-called happily married men visited the temple in search of liaisons beyond the marriage bed. When Lilya knew that to be the case, she refused them, as was her option. True, deep love—love in which both partners remained faithful . . . it seemed rare. Yet Evangeline had found it with not one but two men. Evangeline was the luckiest of women, and Lilya couldn't help but feel a little envious.

Lilya entered the Temple of Dreams, stepping into the parlor. It was a lavish room, brimming with only the best that the considerable money of the Temple of Dreams could buy. Business was good. In a society that put very little shame on the act of physical lovemaking, she'd put aside quite a large sum of money, even apart from the help she'd had long ago from a friend. She was an independent woman, able to take care of herself. If she chose to leave this life tomorrow, live in her own house, have her own carriage, and live idly for the rest of her days, she'd be able to do that.

And, maybe, one day she would.

Ariana approached her from the entrance adjacent to the foyer while Lilya was taking off her gloves. "Wilhem is here. I showed him up to your rooms."

She frowned, laying her gloves on a small table. "He's not supposed to be here until tomorrow."

"Should I send him away?"

Lilya thought about gentle, shy Wilhem for a moment. That would crush him. "No, that's fine. I'll see what he wants."

Ariana nodded, smiled, and walked away.

The heavy skirts of her blue gown swishing with her movement, Lilya headed up the stairs to her apartment. Wilhem was one of only three clients she had at the moment. She'd amassed enough of a fortune by carefully selecting her men. Rich. Gentle. Nonthreatening. Broken. Unattached. Men she could trust when alone with her. Men who paid vast sums for the opportunity to occupy her bed. Men who needed her.

The only problem was sometimes they needed her too much.

Wilhem was a scholar, a gentle man with fluttering hands and a kind disposition. He was awful with women and awful in bed as well. But he was an easy client and Lilya felt that their arrangement was mutually beneficial. He paid her well, and she offered him the female companionship he seemed unable to procure for himself. It was so with all three of her clients.

She entered her apartment and Wilhem stood immediately

from where he sat on her divan. "Lilya." His hands jerked, his fingers threading, and his kind, homely face split into a smile.

"Wilhem." She crossed the room with a bustle of her skirts, took his long, narrow hands, and kissed his dry lips. She smiled into his face. "I was not expecting you until the morning. Why have you come to me today?"

He blinked and fidgeted, then glanced at a bunch of beautiful flowers that had obviously been raised in a city greenhouse. "I came to bring you these. I think they're as lovely as you are."

"Oh," she breathed, as though she didn't receive flowers every day, and scooped them up from the table. "Wilhem, they're gorgeous. Thank you so much." She wouldn't put them over by the two other bunches sitting in vases on a nearby table. No need to point out his weren't the only ones she'd received lately.

He wrung his hands. "I think of you often, Lilya. Every day. Every night. I want you with m-me always." He fidgeted again.

She struggled to keep a smile on her face. Oh, no. Here it came. She knew these lines in all their forms, and was more than familiar with the nervousness that preceded the declaration. If he spoke the words she assumed he was about to utter, it would probably be the end of their arrangement. What a pity.

"I think I love you." He swallowed hard, his gaze darting away from her. "I had hoped you might consider making me more than just a client. I have money, you know. I could offer you a good life."

Yes, they all thought they could do that, give her a "good" life. As though the life she had now wasn't good. As though she hadn't chosen it. As though she wasn't a property owner with a considerable amount of money in the bank and didn't have the ability to walk away when she chose.

As though she needed them.

He fumbled with something in his pocket. An offering ring, she was certain. She had an entire drawer filled with them. A fortune in offering jewels. She couldn't bear to sell any of them, however, because of the sentiment in which they'd been given to her, and the men almost never took them back. Instead the rings lay in a jeweled and glittered heap in a drawer she tried to never open.

Before he could pull out the small ring box, she put her hand over his to stop him. "Wilhem, please sit down."

She sank into the couch with the flowers in her lap. He sat next to her, his pale face flushing. He pushed his spectacles back up onto the ridge of his nose.

Swallowing, she pretended to choose her words carefully. In reality, they were the lines she always used. "I am very flattered that you think of me this way, but I am not the right woman for you."

He started to protest and she set her fingers to his mouth. "Let me finish." He fell silent and she let her hand drop into her lap. "I am happy here, doing what I do. You must accept that our relationship can be no more than what it is right now." She paused and looked hopeful. "Can you?" There was always the chance the arrangement could be salvaged.

His gaze dropped into his lap and he pulled the small box from his pocket and opened it. Inside was a beautiful sapphire ring. "But I wish to marry you."

Ah well.

She reached out and closed the box. "No, Wilhem. I care for you greatly, but these deeper feelings are ones I do not share. I cannot marry you."

He sat for several long moments and she held her breath. Here was the moment where she would either lose Wilhem as a client or keep him under uncomfortable circumstances. She would not turn him away. The choice was his to make.

Finally he stood stiffly. "I cannot remain only a client to you, Lilya."

Letting out the breath she'd been holding, she relaxed and stood. "I think that's a very wise decision, Wilhem."

"There's no chance you will reconsider?"

She smiled kindly. "You are a wonderful man, but you are not the man for me."

His face went wooden. "I want you to have this to remember me." Without meeting her gaze, he pressed the ring box into her hand and hurried toward the door.

Lilya stood in the middle of the room with the box clasped loosely in her hand, watching the door close behind him. With a sigh, she walked over and carefully placed the box in the drawer that held so many more. Her heart felt heavy at the loss of Wilhem. He'd been a nice man and she wished him well. She hoped he wouldn't be lonely.

A knock sounded at her door. Immediately she walked over and opened it, wondering if it was Wilhem, perhaps having decided he didn't want to leave her. She hoped not. Under the circumstances, it was better he left. There was nothing worse than the uncomfortable relationship between two people when one knew the other didn't love as much.

Ariana was on the other side. "There's another man here to see you."

She frowned. Goodness, she hadn't even had a chance to take her coat off yet. "I'm not expecting anyone. Who is he?"

"I don't know." Ariana shrugged. "He showed up and asked

for you. I gave him something to drink and put him in the blue receiving room. He's not one of your regulars and doesn't look like your type. Should I send him away?"

She chewed her lip and shrugged her coat off. Ariana had said he didn't look like her type, yet perhaps he was a potential client. She was very selective in whom she agreed to see regularly, but she gave all men an equal chance. "No. I'll go see what he wants. Thank you, Ariana."

The Temple of Dreams was quiet this afternoon. Normally their clientele didn't start arriving until the late afternoon or evening, though she had no appointments for the day. She reached the blue room and entered to find a large man sitting at the small table, seeming to dwarf it.

"Can I help you?"

He turned.

Her breath caught. *It couldn't be.* She took a step closer, examining his face. "Byron?"

He smiled and her heart skipped. "Hello, Lilya."

Two

She blinked and her face flushed, emotion rising to clog her throat. She was certain she'd never see him again. He was from another time, another life. "How did you know where to find me?"

"I left Milzyr, but you never left my mind. I have been inquiring about you over the years, so I knew right where to locate you."

He'd been keeping tabs on her? Inquiring about her? She wasn't sure what to do with any of that information. His very presence was more than she could process at the moment. Her legs shook as she walked into the room. "It's been a long time." Her voice sounded as shaky as her legs felt.

"Yes, and you look even more beautiful than before, Lilya. More sure of yourself. Confident. Happy. Healed?" He smiled again, and her whole body warmed. "It's been six years."

She sat down on a nearby chair and stared at him. "You disappeared. After you helped me, left me the deed to the house, you just . . . *left*. I didn't know how to get in touch with you, then I discovered who you were and . . ." She trailed off. "Well, then I suppose I was too nervous to contact you."

This man had been her salvation. He'd literally saved her life when she'd been young. He'd lifted her out of the mess she'd made of her existence, set her on the path to making her own decisions, controlling her fate, and then one day she'd woken up and he'd just been . . . gone.

He spread broad hands that she remembered fantasizing about when she was younger. He'd never touched her, though. Not sexually. Not more than a kiss. Not even when she'd wanted him to. One night, right before he'd left, she'd begged him to put those big, rough hands on her and he'd refused. She'd always wondered if that had been why he'd left. Had she scared him away? "You made it plain you didn't want anything of me but superficiality," Byron said.

She looked down, controlling her emotions. Once she had them in check, she looked up at him. "Can you blame me after what I'd been through? It was not a good time. I wasn't ready for any sort of deep emotion when I was simply dog-paddling to keep my head above water."

"I know. How are you now?" He gestured at the room with his hand. "Are you happy with the decision you made? Knowing what I know of you, this is not a life I would have predicted you would make for yourself. I left you well off. You didn't—"

She cut him off. "I've made a very good life for myself here. This was my choice and I don't regret it."

"Ah. Your choice." His pupils darkened and he went silent for a long moment, considering her. "Maybe in time I'll come to understand your motivations."

"In time?" She frowned. What did that mean? She couldn't imagine he would want to spend any time with her. Not now. She'd been a project of his long ago and, like any new project of a rich man, she'd assumed he'd eventually lost interest in her.

He ignored her query, his gaze skating over her, warming her from head to toe. "You look, as usual, beautiful."

She felt herself flush. Men told her she was beautiful all day long, but this was one of the few who could bring color to her cheeks when he said it. "Thank you. You also look well. The years have treated you kindly."

He studied her for a long moment, his dark blue eyes seeming to go even darker and bluer. "Such a polite thing to say, Lilya. I think we know each other fairly intimately. We don't need to observe all the social niceties."

"You're right." She smiled, studying him.

He was not a particularly handsome man, not in the classical sense. His features were a little too rough and craggy for that. His nose looked like it had been broken a couple of times. He appeared more like a thug than an heir to a fortune. His lips were full and sensual, though, and there was a whole ocean of emotion and keen intelligence in those blue eyes.

Byron Andropov was a mystery to her. A man who had found her in the worst part of her life and pulled her out of her misery with a single motion of his moneyed hand. He'd set her on the path to salvation back then and hadn't taken advantage of her vulnerable state even though she'd begged him to. Then he'd disappeared one morning and she'd wondered about him ever since.

She swallowed hard, her brow knitting. She didn't know what to do with her hands, so she threaded her fingers in front of her.

Suddenly she realized she felt a little like Wilhem must have felt minutes ago. "Byron, why did you leave?"

"My father died," he answered. "I had to return home to see to the arrangements and take care of his businesses. By the time I left I knew you were back on your feet and wouldn't miss me." He grinned. "Did you miss me?"

"Of course I did. I wondered for months where you'd gone. You never left a word. Never sent a letter—"

"Whole months?" His eyebrows rose. "Incredible."

She smiled. "You know what I mean. You could have at least said good-bye. Of course I missed you. I owed—*owe*—my life to you."

"No, you never owed me that. Your life is yours to live. I always admired your wildness and freedom. I guess I also thought that if I stuck around, I'd fall in love with you and you'd break my heart. Thus, I broke our relationship off clean." He studied her for a long moment. "I guess maybe I couldn't bring myself to say good-bye."

That coaxed a smile from her. "You're such a charmer. A man like you can have any woman he wants. I know better than to think you'd want me for more than just a couple nights. You're probably married to a beautiful woman by now, with several children running around."

"Ah, my Lilya, ever the jaded one. No, I'm not married. I never took a wife." He grinned. "As far as I know, I've never sired any offspring."

That was hard to believe. The man exuded potency from his very pores. No, he wasn't handsome, but he was the kind of man that women fantasized about. "Now really, Byron, why are you here? Have you just come to visit? Catch up on old times?" She doubted that. Their "old times" hadn't been very enjoyable, not until the very end of the year they'd spent together, anyway.

"No, I'm here on business of a sort. How many clients do you have right now?"

"Three. Well, two, as of five minutes ago." She sat back and pressed her lips together, not wanting to give out more information before he did. Did he want to be her client? That didn't sit right with her. Not Byron. She couldn't do it. He was too different from the other men she took into her bed. Too . . . special.

"Only two?"

She nodded. "I see them about once a week, sometimes twice."

He frowned. "I'd expected you to have more."

"*I* choose my clients, not the other way around. These men suit me. They're not cheating on their wives, they're gentle, and they seem to need me."

"Need you?" His voice held a note of insinuation.

"Sex isn't always about the physical act, Byron. In fact, it very often isn't about that at all. Oh, it's nice, the orgasm, but it's more about connecting with another person, feeling their smooth skin, the heat of their body, the sensation of their lips on yours. My clients are usually men who are socially awkward, incapable of procuring a wife. They're lonely. For just a little while my clients feel less alone in the world. They feel as though someone cares about them, and I do care about them. Very much."

"But you don't love them."

"Not in the classical sense. That sort of love would ruin me."

"Of course, I can see why you would think that." His voice came out a deep, gentle rumble that stroked over her skin and deep into places her mind didn't like to travel. There was a world more in those words than the obvious.

She directed her gaze into her lap, suddenly unwilling to meet his eyes. This man knew more about her than anyone in the Temple of Dreams, more about her than anyone did. Of course she believed love would be her ruin when once it had been. Experience bred wisdom.

He rubbed his chin. "Only two clients. Are you taking more?"

Her blood turned icy for a moment at the implication. She couldn't take Byron as a client for reasons that seemed impossible to examine at the moment. Having him pay for the privilege of being in her bed was something she couldn't bear.

She shook her head, still unable to meet his gaze. "No. I don't want or need to take on any more."

"Are these three . . . *two* men in love with you, Lilya?"

She examined her hands clasped in her lap, thinking of Wilhem. "Some of them think they are, but they only need to see that I'm not the right woman for them. Some of them ask me to marry them. I have a whole drawer filled with ring boxes from their proposals." She raised her gaze to him. "But my clients know my nature. They know not to expect . . . more. At least, they *should* know."

"You have a cruel and dangerous nature."

Her face twisted. "What did you say?" She leapt to her feet. "You haven't seen me in six years! You don't know me at all! How dare you come here and insult me—"

He stood, holding out his hand. "Please, Lilya, I didn't mean to insult you, but you know what I'm saying is true. You weren't born this way; you were made to be this way by what happened to you. You can't help it." He paused, clearly searching his mind for the right words to explain himself. "You're dangerous in the way of a lion. Beautiful to look at, irresistible to touch, yet if someone gets too close, they're going to get hurt. It's simply your nature to draw men, let them fall in love with you, and never reciprocate. That's why you have an entire drawer filled with rejected romantic dreams."

She didn't know how he knew so much about her inner workings, but he was right.

There was something broken in her.

It had started to break when she'd been younger, when she'd been on the streets of Milzyr. Living on her own had made her hungry for love, protection, a companion to share her life with. When all that had come to her, or she'd *thought* it had come, she'd leapt at the opportunity, been betrayed, and her body and mind had shattered into pieces far too tiny to ever pick up. She might secretly wish to find someone to spend her life with and be just a little jealous of women who'd found it, but she lacked the ability to achieve it for herself.

It was simply not in her. Not anymore.

He continued. "It's what I find so beautiful and fascinating about you. Woe be to the man who falls in love with you, and all of them do."

"Maybe I should let all my clients go," she snapped. Her voice held a note of scorn, hating that he'd told the truth about her. The truth hurt. The tone of her voice clearly said she had no intention of quitting, however.

He took a step forward. "Yes. Let them all go and come with me."

She looked up at him, eyes wide. Something hot and painful momentarily caught in her chest. She supposed it was natural she cared about this man more than she might others, considering their past. He'd done so much for her. *"What?"*

"I want you to take myself and a friend on as clients. Come with me to my house in Ulstrat. It would just be for a couple weeks."

She'd been hoping he wouldn't ask. Now that he'd said the words she found they stung like nettles. Her heart shredding a little, she sat down with a thump. "That's very irregular." How could she decline him while masking the fact that his request cut her deeply.

Never could she sleep with this man as a business arrangement. Never could she share him with another woman either, not even if she were being paid.

He sat next to her. "Irregular to entertain two men at once? I would assume you would have that request frequently. In any case, I'm not asking for what you think I'm asking for."

She let out a slow breath. When he'd mentioned his friend, she'd assumed it was a woman. Requests for her to join in threesomes with a man and another woman were very common. Requests for her to join two men were less common, but not infrequent. She very rarely said yes to either arrangement, instead passing them off to the women she knew enjoyed them more.

"Not that. I meant going away from the Temple of Dreams." She searched for a way to deny him without revealing her true reason for saying no.

"I assume that's because it's a safety issue. Yet, you know me. You know I would never—"

She laid her hand on his. "That's not even a question."

He looked down at her hand and she drew it away. "In any case, I'm not requesting sexual services from you."

This was very odd. "What do you mean? You do know what I am, don't you?"

"I want you to come with me to my house for a couple of

weeks and meet my friend. You will be a visiting guest. Pretend it's a vacation for you, one I'm paying you to take. No sex will be expected unless it is something that grows organically between you and Alek." He paused. When he spoke next his voice was low and rough enough to send her skin into gooseflesh. "Or between you and me. Sex only if you choose it."

"I *always* choose it, Byron." She licked her lips, her gaze darting to the side as she remembered things best left to shadow. "I simply don't understand the rationale for this."

"Trust me, there is a purpose. You said it yourself—a courtesan's value isn't necessarily sex, it's companionship. Alek needs your companionship."

She looked at him. "Byron, I don't know if this is a good idea." He sat very close to her, his body heat radiating out and warming her through her clothing. She'd always wanted him and, apparently, nothing had changed where that was concerned. Looking up at him, she gave him a half smile and spoke with a playful lilt she didn't feel. "After all, you'll probably fall in love with me and, as you've pointed out, I'm dangerous. Your heart will be broken by the time the two weeks are up."

"I was immune to you once and feel certain I can manage it again. In any case, while I admit to selfish reasons in choosing you for this, this is not for me. This is for my friend Alek. He needs the experience of a woman like you."

"All right. And why does he need the experience of a woman *like me*?"

"I don't mean in your capacity as a courtesan. I just mean *you*, everything you are. Your charm, intelligence, and ability to enthrall a man. You're perfect to do this job, perfect without even trying and I'm *not* referring to your sexual abilities. Just your personality. As to the specifics of Alek's situation, they're not mine to reveal. Alek will have to tell you."

"That's very flattering." In fact, those words coming from him made her heart race. "May I ask what your selfish reasons are?"

His proximity to her seemed to be in direct correlation to how fast her pulse sped. If he moved any closer she feared she'd have a heart attack. She'd been with many different men, but only rarely did they affect her this way.

Her breath caught in her throat as he leaned toward her, mouth growing closer to hers. "Can't you guess?" he murmured. "Six years ago I could never have taken what I wanted and still respected myself. But now, after so many years have passed . . ."

"You want the one that got away."

"Every which way I can get her." His voice rasped against her skin and tightened her nipples. "If, of course, you wish for the same. I know you did back then. I remember."

His lips found hers and brushed them softly. A shiver ran through her body at the touch. His hand came up to cup her nape as he rubbed his lips slowly across hers once, twice. Then he crushed against her mouth, parting her lips and easing his tongue within. He kissed her in a way few men did; with total control and determination. His lips and tongue were not tentative, gentle, or weak. He knew what he wanted and how he wished to make her feel.

Once, long ago, right before he'd left, he'd kissed her this way. Since then it had been the measure she'd used to judge all other kisses.

Her body reacted immediately, her nipples going hard and sensitive against the bodice of her gown. Her sex became warm. His hand found her skirt and bunched it up, finding the bare skin of her thigh and slowly moving up. The heat of his broad palm made her body flare to life and beg for the touch of him.

His hands on her made her wish he would push her back against the cushions and take her right here and now. She wasn't sure she had the willpower to push him away if he wanted this from her. She could all too easily imagine his big fingers working the buttons of her bodice free and her bare breasts falling into his hands, could envision her skirts pushed up, panties down, and him between her spread thighs. . . .

This was dangerous.

When he reached the lace edging of her panties and tried to push beyond it, she wiggled away from him, breathing heavy. He'd made her sex plump with arousal and her nipples pushed against the fabric of her dress. She took a deep breath and a moment to compose herself. He'd made a mess of her in no time flat. Apparently she wanted the one who'd gotten away too.

When she felt she could look at him without jumping on him, she turned her face to his. His eyes were darker and his face had a lean, hungry set to it. He was not the only one who was having problems resisting the chemistry they'd always shared. The expression he wore let her know that he might have come here for his friend Alek, but it was clear he was here for himself too. That pleased her.

His voice came out a barely restrained growl. "So you agree?"

"No," she managed to push out. "I haven't said yes yet."

His eyes grew darker. Byron usually got what he wanted. This wouldn't be easy. "What will make you say yes? You know I have enough money to pay you anything you wish—"

She shook her head. "It's not about money. I have plenty of

that." Taking a calming breath, she met his eyes. "I haven't met Alek. I don't know him. Usually if I agree to any arrangement, I have interviewed and researched the potential client to my satisfaction."

"I would never lead you into a situation where you would be in danger and, as I said, sleeping with him is not required."

"Yes, of course. It's just . . . you say no sex is expected, yet you're giving me mixed messages." Mixed messages that still made her body tingle. She sighed. "If you put a paid courtesan in a house with two men, sex is always implied. And I'm rather picky about whom I share my body with, Byron. Before I allow a new man into my bed, I talk with him at length, investigate his background. I don't just jump between the sheets with anyone. I control every aspect of the relationship, right down to the sexual activities performed and the duration. *Everything*."

"I understand." He rubbed his chin, looking at her with eyes that saw too much. Then he murmured to himself, "I think I truly *do* understand."

Annoyance flared. He didn't know her anymore; he couldn't understand anything. "What do you th—?"

He interrupted her flash of temper with an even tone that sapped her anger. "Then come with me to my house and meet him. I'll pay you for an extra week to get to know Alek and make your decision. If you don't like Alek and cannot bear to spend three weeks in his company, we'll forget it. I'll have you on a transport back to Milzyr the moment you wish to leave."

She pressed her lips together, considering him. There was much she'd do for this man. This situation was highly irregular, yet . . . it was *Byron* asking her to do it. Her clients could be notified that she might be gone several weeks. Honestly, maybe the break would be good . . . for all of them. Byron's words had given her pause. Perhaps she wasn't helping her clients the way she'd always assumed. Maybe she was causing them pain, keeping them from finding suitable companions they could enjoy for the long term. Maybe she was just helping herself.

Maybe she was making men pay for what had happened to her so long ago. Perhaps part of her enjoyed the fact she could hurt them emotionally. The thought chilled her blood, but it wasn't the first time it had crossed her mind.

Cruel indeed.

"All right, I agree, but I refuse to accept payment from you."

"Refuse? Lilya, I don't think—"

She held up a hand. "Not after all you've done for me."

He shook his head. "You don't owe me anything."

"Byron, I have more money than poor old dead Czz'ar Ondriiko ever did. I don't need any more." She considered him, remembering that the man in front of her was heir to a fortune of unimaginable magnitude. "Actually, I *will* require that you pay. I will double my fee to boot, since there are two men involved, sex or no sex. However, you will not pay *me*. Your money will go Angel House in Milzyr. Is that agreeable?" Angel House was the poorest orphanage in the city.

A smile broke his craggy, compelling face. "I will certainly agree to those terms. Angel House knows my pocketbook well."

"Fine." She swallowed hard and smoothed her skirts to mask her shaking hands. She'd just agreed to spend the next three weeks with *Byron*. Fear and anticipation warred within her.

He considered her for a moment. "Come with me right now. Pack a bag and let's go. I want your company for the next three weeks and I want it to start immediately."

She grinned. "Do you always get what you want?"

The light smile he wore faded. "Yes, Lilya, I do."

Something in his voice made her feel heavy. "I'll go pack my bags."

"I'll be waiting outside in my carriage."

Three

After Lilya packed, she told Ariana where she was going and deflected her well-meaning concern with a quick explanation about her history with Byron. Then she left instructions with a messenger to send word of her absence to her clients.

Of her two remaining clients, Edgar would be the most affected by her absence. He was a gentle, soft-spoken man without any family and few friends because of his shyness. A wealthy banker, he didn't have much in his life besides her and his work. Her hand shook as she wrote the note to be delivered by the courier.

She stopped for a moment to more deeply consider her relationship with him. Perhaps it was time she impressed upon Edgar just how inaccessible she was to him in any way beyond the bed. Perhaps it would force him to look for a wife. He deserved a good woman to love him for the wonderful, warm person he was. At the end of her note, she added as much.

Orrin was her other client. He was a nice man, with nice hands and a nice way about him, a solicitor with no family or friends to speak of. She was his only real companion in the city, though she didn't think he would take her absence very hard. Orrin was a natural loner, happy enough to spend his free time in the company of a good book.

Taking her bag in hand, she stepped out of the Temple of Dreams and was met with the view of a gleaming black-and-gold carriage with a matching set of four ebony horses. Byron never did anything without style—even if it was a hired carriage. At least it wasn't one of those metal contraptions that belched smoke and was more and more frequent on the streets of Milzyr now that the royal family had fallen and the inventions they'd suppressed were in common use. Horses might leave mounds in the middle of the street, but at least they didn't smell of burning oil. Plus, the sound of horse hooves on the ground was far more pleasing than the bone-grinding noise of gears.

The carriage driver opened the door for her and helped her in. Byron sat half in shadow, wearing a hat that she wanted to take off so she could run her fingers through his thick dark hair. Her hands practically itched to do it. If she was able to bed this man, taking Byron's offer would be no hardship at all.

Her cheeks touched with a little pink at her thoughts as she settled down opposite him. "I understand we'll have to take the steam transport to your home."

"Yes, but it's not a long ride. Only a couple of hours. We could take a carriage the whole way, but the transport is a much smoother and shorter journey. I take the transport into Milzyr at least weekly these days, since I'm working closely with Gregorio Vikhin and the university to institute a magickal intervention and studies program."

Her head snapped up so fast at Gregorio's name that her hat slipped to the side. She righted it. "You are? You know Gregorio?"

He nodded. "I understand you are friends with that family."

"I only just met with Evangeline this afternoon at a café."

His eyes went darker. "I admit I've asked after you several times."

So that's how he had such insight into her current life. She wasn't sure how she felt about that. "I didn't know you had any connection with them at all."

"It's relatively recent."

"Why do you have anything to do with the magickal intervention and studies program? Are you funding it?" It was a new initiative from the government to draw out the former J'Edaeii who had gone into hiding during the revolution and draw them in to study and apply their magick in the real world.

He held her gaze. "I do fund it, but I also have a secret."

"A secret?"

"It's not something I could have told you before, but I have a bit of magick. Only a bit. I never would have been a candidate to be J'Edaeii when the royals were in power."

Before the revolution three years ago, those citizens of Rylisk who were known to possess the ability to wield magick had been taken—sometimes forcibly—to Belai Palace and trained. When the magicked had reached the age of majority, they'd been tested on the strength of their powers. If they'd passed, they'd become J'Edaeii, and were jeweled. A precious gem had been set at either the base of the spine or at the back of the neck, depending on their genders. It meant they were "good enough" to marry into the royal family.

Basically, it had been a way for the royals to correct centuries of inbreeding that had leached the magick from their once-powerful genetic line. The J'Edaeii had been considered sanitized of their common birth, their genes fit for inclusion into the royal line. During the revolution most of the royals had been executed. The rest were now exiled. In the chaos of what was now referred to as the Bloody Winter, many of the J'Edaeii had also been rounded up and sent to the guillotine.

Most of those who had escaped were living in secret, afraid to make themselves known to the general populace. It was only now, three years later, that the previously jeweled members of society were daring to step out into the light.

It was a shame, in Lilya's opinion, since the magicked were a national treasure. Rare and as precious as the gems that nestled in their skin. Evangeline was a former J'Edaeii, as was one of her husbands, Anatol.

She sat up in her seat, studying his face. She never would have guessed Byron to hold such abilities. "Magick? What kind of magick you do you have?"

He snapped his fingers and a blue flame appeared in the center of his palm. He walked the flame over his knuckles the way another man would walk a coin. Soon it sputtered and died. "It's little more than a cheap trick. All the same, my parents kept my magick hidden from the royals when they were in power. They worried I would be forced to go to Belai for training. I hid my power for so long I nearly forgot I possessed it. I assume it's a throwback to the royal blood in my veins."

She understood that Byron had been distantly related to the Edaeii, but it wasn't common knowledge. His father had been considered part of the merchant class with a business of mining elusian crystal, a substance that powered lights and other small devices. The Andropov family gave much charity to their town of Ulstrat and was loved for treating their elusian miners well, so the family had been safe during the revolution. During the uprising and the beheadings of the nobles that had followed, she'd worried incessantly about Byron. Anyone without that telltale *son* or *daughter* attached to their last name, marking them as low-born, had immediately been pegged as noble and targeted.

Byron continued. "Alek also has magick, though his is much stronger than mine. In fact, that's why I want you to spend some time with him. I think you can help him with his abilities."

She frowned, trying to track what he'd just said. "You mean you think *I* can help him develop his magick? I have no magickal ability, Byron, and even if I did, I wouldn't be able to help anyone with theirs. You do understand what I am, don't you? I'm a paid companion. Nothing more."

"I disagree, my beautiful."

"Byron, really—"

"You'll understand better when you meet Alek."

She studied him, wanting to ask more, but he'd turned his attention out the window and seemed unwilling to elaborate. Silence reigned for several minutes before she finally tried to press him a little more. "Is there anything I need to know that you're not telling me?"

"There's not much I can tell you myself. I can say that Alek thinks his magick means nothing and I think it means everything.

I'm hoping you can open him up to the possibilities of the world beyond logic. He's locked down, tight in everything he does. There's a reason for it, one he needs to get past. You have some experience in getting over traumatic events and carrying on with your life."

Ah, a kindred spirit, then. Or so Byron thought. She still doubted she could help this Alek, but she was impressed that Byron was going so far out of his way for him. "Why do you care so much about this man?"

His gaze met hers and held. "He's a very good friend and I have known him since childhood. He has no family, only me. I have no family left either. I want everything good for him—the best. Therefore, I want *you* for him for three weeks. Long enough for him to enjoy you." He grinned. "Perhaps long enough for him to fall in love with you. He needs a jolt to his heart. I think you will do the job nicely."

She smiled and looked down into her lap. "You flatter and you're unrealistic. I don't understand how being around me will unlock the magick in him. I have no special powers. I'm just a woman."

He slid closer beside her, caught her chin, and guided her gaze to his. His eyes looked heavy with arousal. "Then you don't know half your worth, Lilya." His voice was low and rough. It sent a tremor through her.

"You overestimate my value. I may disappoint."

His face drifted closer to hers. "I knew you then and I know you now. You've aged, grown wiser, more sure of yourself. It's made you even more beautiful than you were before. No, I will never undervalue you, Lilya. I never have and I never will."

That was true enough. It was seeing her value in his eyes that had saved her life, had put her on the path to seeing value in her own eyes when she looked in a mirror. Without him she would have died in a dirty alleyway years ago.

His lips brushed hers, just the slightest, softest of touches. Her body went malleable, her blood heating. Just the mere prospect of his hands on her turned her insides to jelly, frightened her with the intense desire it lit within her. It was irresistible, so new and different. She wanted more.

She reached up and cupped his cheek, his jaw warm and prickly against the skin of her palm. His gaze met hers and the expression in his eyes—*need tightly leashed*—reached in and squeezed emotion in her chest. Tilting her head to the side a little and enjoying the feel of his breath on her lips for a moment, she pressed her lips to his.

He made a low sound in the back of his throat and slanted his mouth over hers. The action made a thrill of anticipation run through her, set her heart to pounding. Her hand found its way to the nape of his neck, and his arm snaked around her waist. He pressed her into the seats and parted her lips, slipping his tongue into her mouth.

Her body hummed with need. She couldn't remember the last time she'd wanted a man this way. If he asked her she would allow him to take her right here and now in this carriage on the way through Milzyr. The time and place didn't matter—only their bodies and the promise of mutual ecstasy mattered.

The carriage jolted to a stop. Outside the sounds of the transport station filtered in through her pleasure-drugged senses. Desire faded to disappointment. They'd arrived.

Byron pulled himself away from her reluctantly, his eyes heavy-lidded and hungry. She swallowed hard, forcing herself to breathe, and arranged her mussed skirts.

The carriage door opened, letting sunlight stream in. "Steam transport station," announced the narrow-faced driver in a heavy East Milzyrian accent.

She looked out the open door to the long, sleek black transport beyond, steam puffing from its engine. With Byron at her side she suddenly had the sensation that her world was about to change forever. Her stomach fluttered and, stepping out of the carriage, she had an inexplicable urge to bolt. She wasn't sure she wanted her life to change.

Her steps faltered and she looked away from the transport, back toward the city. Maybe she should turn him down, go back to the Temple of Dreams, and forget this ever happened.

"Are you all right?" Byron asked, placing a hand at the small of her back.

"I'm . . . fine." This was nonsense. She needed to get a grip on herself. She'd been 100 percent in control of her life since the moment Byron helped her regain it. There was no reason to suddenly feel as though she'd lost it all again in his presence. It was simply her past rearing its head. If she knew what the trouble was, she could face it—defeat it. She looked up at him and forced a confident smile onto her face. "I'm fine, really."

She just wished she fully believed it.

"Good." He guided her toward the transport. "This way. I rent a private car because of all the trips I take into Milzyr."

Allowing the carriage driver to take care of their luggage, they mounted the steel steps that led into the transport and traveled down the narrow walkway to the car that Byron rented. He shut the sliding door behind them while she sank onto the cushioned seat near a large window and looked out at the busy platform. People hurried up and down the narrow walkway, suitcases in hand and, in some cases, children trailing behind.

"It's amazing," she murmured. "So full of activity."

The steam transport was one of the few inventions that the Edaeii family hadn't suppressed during their reign. She supposed its usefulness outweighed the threat they'd perceived it to be. Still the transport was relatively new and Lilya had never had any cause to ride it. She'd only ever seen the station from afar.

He took the seat across from her and gazed out the window. "It's a marvel of the new age. The Tinkers' Guild is a wonderful organization. I can't wait to see what they come up with next." His words held more than just a hint of wonder.

Soon the conductor blew a shrill whistle and called for any remaining passengers. Then the doors closed and the transport jerked from its place and began to roll slowly down the tracks. They passed out of the city and soon the rolling green countryside became their vista.

She tore her eyes away from the beautiful scene. "So, you know what I've been doing these past six years, but what have you been doing?"

"Taking care of my father's business, playing crossball, dabbling in philanthropy, dodging the revolution. Now I'm working with Gregorio. It's been an eventful few years." He paused. "You never left my mind, Lilya. Not ever. Not even for a day."

She felt her cheeks heat. "Charmer."

"I'm telling the truth."

Glancing into her lap, she admitted the truth. "I never stopped thinking about you either." She raised her eyes to his. "Shame on you for never sending word."

"I'm sorry I hurt you, Lilya, but I thought it was better that way. I needed to leave when I did, otherwise I never would have had the strength. You needed me to leave too."

She tilted her head to the side, annoyance suddenly flaring. "How do you know what I needed?"

"Back then you had no idea, Lilya. Admit it."

She inhaled and looked out the window. "No, I probably didn't."

"You definitely didn't need a mooning man whom you couldn't love following you around."

She smiled, but it was bitter. He was missing the irony of that statement. All she'd had since he'd left were mooning men she couldn't love. "You never would have been that to me."

"You were not ready for another relationship back then, Lilya."

"Not a serious one." She met his gaze. "You're right. Not even one with you. Ivan ruined me for life where those are concerned."

A light seemed to die in his eyes. "I know."

Memory threatened to swamp her and she looked down into her lap. "Can we talk of something else? This is not a happy conversation."

Just then a serving woman knocked on the compartment door, there to offer them refreshments. Lilya accepted a glass of iced tea and concentrated on its cool sweetness washing down her throat, forcing down all the darkness their dialogue had dredged up within her. Apparently seeing Byron had brought much of it to the fore.

Four

Byron watched Lilya mount the stone stairs of his house. She seemed unaffected by the size and luxury of the place. Of course, he knew she would be unimpressed. Lilya was not materialistic. She was never awed by titles or the size of a man's savings account, and no man could buy her affection with money or baubles. Not her genuine affection, anyway. Nothing that truly mattered.

He opened the door and led her into the foyer. Their steps echoed on the marble of the entryway.

She turned in a circle, examining the vaulted ceiling. "It's very . . ." She trailed off, her voice sounding hollow in the immense area.

"Large and empty," Byron said.

She turned toward him, peeling off her gloves. "Don't you keep any servants?"

"I have a woman named Mara who comes in to cook and clean, since I lack abilities in both realms. Otherwise, no. I think a man can do most things for himself. I clear the snow off the steps myself, build the fires myself, and so on."

She raised her eyebrows. "Bring up the water for your bath yourself?"

He smiled. "I had heated water pipes installed the moment they became available. All I need to do is turn a spigot."

She peered down a narrow corridor leading to the study. "I'm impressed. I would have thought you'd have a whole fleet of people to wait on you."

"That only proves how little you truly know me."

"Well." She turned with a sparkle in her eyes. "Then I can't wait to get to know you better."

His stomach took an unexpected dip at the look on her face. He'd never forgotten how beautiful she was, but he'd assumed his reaction to her must have faded over the years. It hadn't. He was as susceptible to her now as he'd been six years ago. That meant he was about to get hurt, but if it meant helping Alek it would be worth it. And she *would* help Alek. Not in the way Alek would probably most like, but in the way he most needed. He couldn't think of a woman better suited.

They held each other's gazes for several long moments. He didn't know what she was thinking, but he was thinking he was in deep trouble.

Her smile widened. "Also, I can't wait to take a bath drawn from water coming through heated water pipes."

He returned her smile, trying to keep the rumble of need out of his voice. "I'm all for that." Especially if he could watch.

"Byron? Is that you? I've been waiting here for—" Alek

walked into the foyer and stopped short, his eyes on Lilya. "Hello."

"Alek, meet Lilya. Lilya, Alek."

Alek walked toward her, totally entranced. No doubt. Any man would be. With Lilya's thick, curling dark hair, deep, dark eyes, perfect skin and face, she was catnip to any healthy male. Yet she was so much more than just a pretty face, as Alek would soon discover. "It's nice to meet you."

"Lilya comes to us from the Temple of Dreams in Milzyr."

Alek stopped short, his smile fading.

Lilya rounded on him. "You didn't tell him?"

Byron grinned, pushing a hand through his hair. "If I had, he would have never come."

A muscle twitched in Alek's jaw and his brown eyes flared with anger. "What is going on here? Byron, why have you brought a . . . a . . ."

Lilya smiled sweetly. "We prefer the term *courtesan*. I'm a very *selective* courtesan to boot." She gave him an undisguised head-to-toe.

The culture of Rylisk was very sexually free, far freer than neighboring countries. In most circles courtesans were respected, but there were always those who judged people for selling their bodies for money. Byron was sure Lilya had never thought of it as selling her *body*, really. In her mind it was probably selling companionship, an ease to unrelenting loneliness, maybe a little caring sentiment whereas her clients would have none. In Lilya's mind she offered a therapeutic service, no doubt.

Byron had no problem with any type of courtesan. It was their choice how they used their bodies and he was not one to judge. He thought he knew Alek very well and he was surprised by

Alek's reaction to Lilya. He'd thought Alek was more open-minded than this.

"I brought her for you, Alek. To distract you a little, loosen you up a bit, maybe even free up your magick."

"Byron, I'm not interested in being distracted or loosened up. I'm especially not interested in freeing up my magick."

"You have a gift, Alek. It's not right to suppress it."

Alek's jaw locked. "It's not your place to say what I do with it."

"As your best friend, it is."

Alek stormed out of the foyer.

Lilya turned toward him with a small, tight smile on her lips. Displeasure sat in the lovely lines of her face. "I think he's angry."

"I knew he was going to be angry." *But not so antagonistic.* "I can handle him. The more important question is—are you angry?"

The smile tightened a degree. "You should have told him what I was."

He raised his eyebrows. "A beautiful, fascinating, intelligent woman?"

Her eyes grew colder and he made a note to watch himself. "You know what I mean."

"I do, but I also think you're beautiful, fascinating, and intelligent."

Her pretty mouth split into a wide, warm smile, chasing away the frigid set of her lips and the displeasure in her eyes. "And I think you're a sweet-talker."

His stomach did another slow flip. He helped her remove her coat, and then started down one of the corridors that led away from the foyer. The carriage driver had set their bags inside the door. He'd deal with those later. "Come into the library, sit down, have something to drink."

"What about Alek?"

"I've known Alek since we were both seven. He needs a little time. His natural fascination with you will win out and he'll be talking to you by tomorrow, I'm sure. Maybe sooner."

"Doesn't he have a home to return to? Won't he just leave? He seems very angry."

He shook his head. "He's staying here for the moment, as he often does. It's closer to the university and his life is *only* the university." He led her into the library.

The library was his favorite room in the house and, therefore, was the most used. It was a large arched chamber with huge windows and shelves of leather-bound books. An enormous gray stone fireplace dominated one wall. Alek had started a fire in it that crackled and snapped. Alek had also made coffee. Byron walked to the carafe, found it still hot, and poured both himself and Lilya cups and they settled into comfortable chairs. They both needed to warm up. Winter was coming upon them fast.

"Do you read a lot?" she asked, eyeing the shelves with a hungry expression on her face.

"Me? Not really. My father was the reader. Still, this is my preferred room in the house. Occasionally I can still smell the pipe he used to smoke in here." He took a sip of his coffee. "I miss him."

"I can see why you love this room. It's beautiful." She picked up a book from a nearby table and paged through it. It was a history book, undoubtedly one of Alek's. History was his passion. Or, perhaps, more a refuge.

"Feel free to read any books you find here. My library is your library."

She looked at the spine of the book she held. "*History of Rylisk During the Meteo-Orusian War of 1230.*" She raised an eyebrow and looked at him. "I think I might go more for some of the literary classics I missed during my nonexistent schooling."

"That one is Alek's."

"He's getting a degree in history from the University of Milzyr? He's a little old for college, isn't he?"

"His third degree, actually. He keeps going back for specializations."

"I see. And you, in your high-handed way, have decided he studies too much and pays attention to his magickal abilities too little." She set the book back down.

"Yes." He paused. "Except without the high-handed part."

She raised her eyebrows. "Not from where I'm sitting. Why not leave the man alone to live his life the way he sees fit?"

"Because I care about him and he's wasting himself. He's caught in the past, afraid to face the future. The future for Rylisk is magick and those talented few who can wield it. The future of our country lies in harnessing their abilities and setting them free, not caging them and monopolizing them for the selfishness of the royals, used like broodmares and studs." As he spoke, he found himself leaning forward in his chair and fisting his hands. "Letting them be free in the world to use their abilities for the advantage of our nation, to teach, to procreate, to live among the rest of us without fear."

Lilya sat staring at him for several moments without replying. "You really care deeply about this. I can hear it in your voice and see it on your face."

"I do. I always have. I was a follower of Gregorio Vikhin before the revolution because I hated to see what the Edaeii had done to the jeweled. I know that I was only a twist of fate away from joining them. When the revolution occurred, I was thrilled, although, like Vikhin, wished it could have been accomplished with less chaos and bloodshed."

"Idealists, the both of you. Of course there is chaos and bloodshed when the lower class throws off years of poverty and oppression."

"What's done is done. Three years later and it's time to rebuild. Rebuilding our country the best we can is my primary concern. That means convincing men and women with magick as powerful as Alek's that it's time to shine."

"May I ask what Alek's magick is?"

"He's a healer, Lilya, and I suspect a very strong one. But the magick is locked down and pocketed away. He had to keep it secret while the Edaeii were in power, but now he has no interest in developing it. Yet I don't think it's because he doesn't *want* to develop it. I suspect he's afraid of it. All he does is bury himself in history. History is safe."

Her brow wrinkled. "But, healing? He could help so many people."

"*Yes.*" The word came out reinforced with the frustration he felt. He leaned toward her, his leather chair squeaking. "*Yes*, Lilya, he could. Yet no amount of conversation can convince him of this. Words do nothing."

She leaned back in her chair and pressed her lips together, studying him. "I'll be truthful, after I saw the way Alek reacted to me, I was going to tell you I was leaving. Now that you're telling me he has powerful healing magick locked away inside him, I'm compelled to stay. I still don't know what I can do to help Alek, but if you think there's something, I'll do my best."

Relief washed through him. He stood, walked to her, and pulled her to her feet. She was much shorter than he was, the top of her head only coming up to his shoulders. He smoothed a tendril of her dark hair behind her ear. "You are the only woman I could think of who would have the effect on him he needs."

She shook her head. "I still—"

"You can make him care about someone outside himself. The last time he did that, he was hurt very badly, but in order for his magick to be set free, he must learn to do it again."

She let out a slow breath. "You're giving me too much credit. I can only be who I am and do what I do."

"That's the beauty of it. You don't have to do anything but be yourself and he will love you."

She drew a deep breath. "Byron, really—"

"Hush."

Pressing her lips together, she wrinkled her brow and looked up at him. "I think you're insane, you know."

"I think I'm right."

He knew his reasoning was sound. His reason for tracking her down after all these years had ostensibly been for Alek's benefit, but the act had been selfishly motivated at the heart of it. Six years ago when he'd found her in Milzyr, he'd fallen in love with her. Back then, fresh from an ordeal that would have broken anyone else, an ordeal that *did* break her for a time, she hadn't been ready and hadn't wanted a relationship with anyone. Even though he'd thought—maybe in his "high-handed" way—that a loving relationship had been exactly what she needed.

So, now, six years later, he'd thought perhaps she'd be different, more willing to enter into a serious, loving relationship with him. But, clearly, she was still the wild, independent woman she'd always been and always would be. Though under the strength she

displayed to the world, he sensed vulnerability. Still, she was just
a little broken.

Was he a bad man for wanting to touch that vulnerable part
of her? Were his intentions dark when his goal was to make her
see him as something more . . . someone to care for, maybe even
someone to whom to bind her life? Maybe it was bad and dark
because in a way it would be like trying to cage a beautiful, wild
animal. That was never right.

And perhaps he'd been wrong. Maybe what she had endured
truly had ruined her for love.

Time would tell.

Movement caught Lilya's eye. Alek had entered the room. She
already stood very near to Byron, but she took an additional step
closer to his body, setting a hand on his waist. If she was going to
do this, she'd really do it. She knew how. Men weren't that hard
to understand—they always wanted what they couldn't have, or
what another man had. Jealousy was a useful tool.

She studied Alek as he wavered in the doorway, looking am-
bushed and ready to bolt. Clearly he hadn't realized she and
Byron would be in the room. He was a scholar, so one would
expect him to be pale, weak-limbed, perhaps wearing glasses. Yet,
he defied that pigeonhole. Well, he was a bit pale and he did wear
glasses, but that's where it stopped. Weak-limbed he definitely
was not. Byron was one of the tallest men she knew, but Alek
rivaled his height. Broad shoulders melded into a leanly muscular
body, hard, as if from regular and vigorous exercise. His reddish
blond hair was thick and had a slight curl to it, making it look

wavy and a little tousled. His face had the handsome quality that Byron's lacked and his eyes were a deep, compelling shade of chocolate brown.

She was actually surprised that Alek was as immersed in his studies as Byron claimed. Women had to be throwing themselves at him. She'd known enough men in her life to understand that some of them were oblivious to such things, but they were rare as unicorns, mostly myth, unless they were actually interested in men instead.

Yet, from the heated look in Alek's eyes when his gaze took her in, she figured the latter was not the case. In fact, she sensed a pent-up sexuality in him. That was good. If she was serious about seducing him, that would make it easier. She could use his attraction to her to draw him out. As a courtesan, she was definitely not above doing such things.

"Alek, come in." Byron's arm snaked around her waist and he pulled her up against his side.

"No." Alek stepped back into the corridor. "I'll go up to my room."

"Alek," Lilya called. "Don't be afraid of me. I won't try and seduce your virtue away." There, a nice prick to his manly pride should engage him.

"I'm not *afraid* of you; I'm just not interested in talking to someone who sells her body for money."

Byron's voice growled out of him. "Alek, this woman is very dear to me and I didn't bring her here to be insulted. You don't know her story. Stop being so blindly judgmental."

Lilya forced a smile. "At least you're honest about your feelings." His words pricked her a little, as comments like those always did. Such sentiments weren't often thrown in her face and rarely so blatantly. "But I wasn't brought here to have sex with you and Byron is not paying me. He's an old friend and I came here at his request because I respect him and I owe him much."

Byron's arm tightened around her waist. "How many times do I have to say you don't owe me anything?" he murmured. Then he said louder to Alek, "She's my guest and you're being abusive to her."

Alek took a deep breath and entered the room, coming closer to them. "Why do you owe him?" A note of heavy curiosity flavored his voice. Was the scholar in him coming out?

She considered Alek. At the moment, she didn't like him very much. However, she cared deeply for Byron and trusted his cause where his friend was concerned. Could she bear to share this story with Alek? She supposed she could, for Byron.

Lilya looked up at Byron. "You never told him the story?"

He shook his head. "Alek, do you remember the year I spent in Milzyr? I went for business just for a few months at my father's request, then ended up staying longer. I came back only when my father died."

"I remember."

Lilya stepped away from Byron and motioned to the carafe. "Why don't you share a cup of coffee with us and we can tell you all about it?"

He hesitated a moment and Lilya marshaled her tongue with effort. Deciding to reveal this story was a huge decision for her. She'd told only her closest friends at the Temple of Dreams about what had happened to her, because every time she was forced to speak the words, they opened up wounds she'd long ago forcibly closed.

Finally Alek nodded and moved toward the table where the carafe sat.

Grief already beginning to clog the back of her throat, she returned to her seat and took a fortifying sip of her cooling coffee. It had been a long time since she'd walked these dark roads of remembrance.

Alek found a cup, filled it, and sat down. He held her gaze for a long moment. "I apologize for my rudeness earlier. I spend too much time with books and not enough time with people these days."

"Byron thinks you do."

"Maybe he's right. I'm looking forward to this story. Byron never explained why he lived in Milzyr for those many months."

"Settle in because it's a long one." Lilya took a shaky breath, preparing to tell her story.

Byron found a seat by the fire and gazed into the flickering flames with a brooding expression on his rough face. He likely wasn't looking forward to reliving this either. A part of her loved him for that.

Lilya began, "I was born into a poor family. My mother died during childbirth and my father contracted an illness that took him from me when I was fourteen. I had no other family and was forced to live on the streets of Milzyr, staying alive by my own wits. I survived that way, remained miraculously unscathed—mostly, anyway—for three years until I met a man named Ivan. I think I fell in love with him the day he offered to make me soup. No one had offered to make me food of any kind since my father had passed. So when Ivan offered to make me soup, I was done for. But Ivan wasn't always so kind. . . ."

Five

van had been the most charming and handsome man she'd ever met, Lilya mused, touching her fingertips to her split lip. She'd never suspected the monster the beauty masked. How could she have been so blind? He roared at her, looming over her like some demon from a child's nightmare. . . .

She flinched away, covering her head from his wrath. Anger flared inside her, pushed her to lash out at Ivan, defend herself. Yet she weighed half what this man did and the room was filled with his henchmen. Any damage she managed to inflict upon him would be revisited upon her tenfold. It was a lesson she'd learned on the streets quickly.

Before this day, just yesterday, she'd loved him. Oh, she'd loved him with everything she was. Yesterday seemed like a century ago and her heart lay smashed under every second of that imagined period of time. Why had she given herself to him? He'd bent her to his will so easily, took away all her free will. He'd done it from the beginning, done it through love.

Never again.

He'd been like no man she'd ever met, buying her clothes, taking her out to dinner, showering her with compliments and small gestures of his affection. In Ivan's eyes she'd felt like the only woman in the world. She'd been so young and, while she'd had a rough few years that had made her seem older than she should have been, still very impressionable. He'd smiled at her and the entire world had stopped. He'd spoken to her and her heart had swelled with warm pleasure.

That love meant everything to a girl who'd spent the last three years of her life living hand to mouth as a sometime street vendor and beggar, living in a dingy rented room when she could afford it and on the streets when she couldn't. For all those years she'd managed to avoid most of the violence that could befall a young girl with no family or protection. Not all, but most of the truly bad stuff.

That was, until she'd met Ivan. He'd been a predator in kitten's clothing. Once she'd realized that, it had been too late.

She'd landed a good job as a flower seller, mostly because she'd been pretty to look at, with her long, curling dark hair and dark eyes. The flower-stand owner had cleaned her up and watched her closely for theft. When she'd earned his trust, he'd left her alone on a street corner to hawk his fresh-cut lilies and carnations. It had been the best job she'd ever had. Ivan had spotted her one day, bought a rose, and then handed it to her. She knew right then her luck, and her life, was about to change.

So it had begun.

A month into their relationship and she'd smiled and blushed when he'd look at her. Two months into their relationship and she'd been head over heels. Three months and she would've done anything for him, even though she'd begun to get the first hints that Ivan was not the businessman he'd told her he was. Or at least if he was a businessman, the business was shady. By that time she was far too gone on Ivan to care very much. He treated her like a princess.

Four months into their relationship was when he'd asked her to live with him. Could marriage be far behind? Lilya said yes and spent the next few days walking on air. She would be safe. She would have food. Love. Children? She'd hoped for it.

She quit her job selling flowers and moved into Ivan's apartment. There were always various men there, men who worked for Ivan, but he wouldn't tell her what they did. They were hard men, who looked at her like she was a piece of candy.

That's when things got bad.

Almost immediately after she'd moved in, Ivan became controlling, dominating, yelling at her over the smallest things. Once in a while he hit her for spilling the tea or incorrectly ironing his shirt. But every time he hurt her, he made it up to her, said he was sorry, that it would never happen again, and bought her something pretty. It had been hard and she'd been disappointed, but she'd stayed.

But today things had gone from bad to hellish.

That afternoon one of Ivan's thuggish men, one of many who lingered around the apartment, had trapped her in a hallway. He'd blown his garlic-scented breath on her and squeezed her breasts. She screamed and fought him.

Ivan had run to her rescue, or so she'd thought. Instead of blaming the man who'd trapped her, Ivan flew into an insane rage. He knifed the man who'd cornered her and he'd slumped to the floor, dying.

Then he'd dragged her out into the main room, accusing her of trying to cuckold him. Beyond reason, eyes crazy, he wouldn't listen to her protests of innocence. He beat her with all the men in the room looking on and cheering. The occurrence had been a swirl of blood, betrayal, pain, and twisted male faces glimpsed through swollen eyes and a blur of tears.

After the beating was done, every part of her body had hurt. Ivan had ripped her dress at the collar and hem. The polished wood floor of the room felt hard and cold under her palms and knees.

Looking up at Ivan through her hair, her split lip burning and her blood thick on her tongue, she vowed that this time she would really leave him. This time she wouldn't let him say sorry, buy her a bauble. This time she wouldn't stay. Even if it meant returning to a hand-to-mouth existence on the streets, she would be out of his residence by sundown.

Then he said the words that would forever change her life.

Ivan shoved her at the men in the room. "She's yours. Do whatever you wish with her. Just take her away and make sure she never comes back here."

Shock had ripped through her veins like a syringe filled with ice water. The men cheered and thanked him, their hands closing over her, pulling her hair, and dragging her backward. She'd screamed and fought, but she'd weighed less than a hundred pounds.

Lilya stopped telling her story, swallowing the ball of emotion that lodged itself at the back of her throat.

Byron was beside her, his big, warm hands on her cold ones. She hadn't even noticed he'd moved to her side. "You're pale."

"Please stop if you need to," Alek added.

She shook her head. "It's all right. I'm stronger than that." She offered a shaky smile to Byron. "You can imagine what happened next. Eventually it ended." Strong she might be, but she said those last sentences quickly, just to get them out of the way. Information given. "They dumped me in an alley of Milzyr, leaving me like a piece of garbage to die alone. . . ."

Every part of her body burned and ached, some parts of her screamed in pain. Her eyes were so swollen she could barely see out of them. For a time during the ordeal she'd left her body completely, giving her numb detachment to what was happening to her. Now her mind offered her no such luxury and she knew she was going to die. . . .

She welcomed it. She wanted it.

Her fingers scratching in the gravel of the alley, she gazed at the people on the street that was too far away for her to crawl to. For a moment she contemplated calling for help, but closed her eyes instead. She curled up in the cold, scraps of her ripped clothing barely covering her, and gave up.

Her thoughts drifted to her father, to the easel and paints he'd once scrounged enough money to buy for her. That was a good memory, a warm one. It was the only thing she could think of that didn't make her feel like vomiting, so she held on to it. Maybe her next life would be better, full of more of those kinds of memories. She couldn't wait to get there.

But life lingered, unwanted.

Darkness took her on and off. Evening came and went. Then day. Night again. Her throat burned from a need to drink water, but she hardly noted it. The pain of her body was too great for that. The haze of her mind was too cloudy for her think straight . . . to care. No, she was far, far beyond caring about what happened to her now. Time itself lost meaning. She prayed to Blessed Joshui that He would end her suffering.

Her eyes closed for what she hoped was the last time, but the muffled sound of footsteps made her open them again.

Black boots met her narrow slit of a gaze. Black boots. Boots kicked. Boots inflicted pain. Boots belonged to men. Men hit. Men hurt her. She looked up into a jagged, rough face. The face of a thug.

Suddenly she found it in her to care.

Some last gasp of a primal desire to survive reared its head. She scrambled back, her body on fire, the dried blood on her body cracking, until she hit the brick wall behind her and fresh pain exploded. Her vision went black, her body went weak, and unconsciousness took her before she hit the ground.

Sometime later she woke again to a bright room, her vision still narrowed by her swollen eyes. Glancing carefully around her, she noticed she was clean; her broken limbs bandaged and set to heal. The walls of the room were painted a sunny yellow. The bedding was a gentle shade of gold shot through with expensive silver thread.

A man stood nearby, perhaps ten years older than she was. He turned toward her. It was the thug. She drew air to scream and terror-filled blackness enveloped her again.

On and off she floated up from unconsciousness. Every time

her eyes opened, the rough-featured man was there. Sometimes he was with another man she took for a doctor because of the way he frowned, fussed, and poked. For those brief times consciousness claimed her, she could see a little more and felt a little better.

Finally she surfaced from the lovely black nothingness she'd come to welcome and stayed aware. Her eyes open, she watched the thuglike man from the bed. His broad back was toward her as he talked to the doctor. They didn't know she was awake and their voices drifted to her on the quiet air.

"How is she doing?" the man asked in a low, gruff voice that fit his face and body.

"Physically, she's healing. Her broken arm and leg will take some time, of course, but her ribs and the lacerations to her face and body are doing well. Luckily I think she'll have minimal scarring. She had some internal damage, but she's been strong enough to endure most of it. However, she'll never be able to bear children."

In the bed behind them, Lilya jolted with a burst of grief. Pressing her lips together, she fought not to make a sound and reveal herself. She'd given up hope of surviving and had even prayed for death, but the cold, hard reality of her infertility still had the power to devastate her.

"Psychologically, I don't know how she'll fare. I have rarely seen such violence visited upon a woman. I suspect she will never fully recover from what's been done to her. However, if she's not been made insane, she might recover enough to live out the rest of her life in some semblance of normality."

The man rubbed his chin, as if deep in thought, and glanced

at her. Her gaze locked with his and his blue eyes opened wide as he realized she was awake. He turned to her, causing the doctor to notice she was aware as well.

The doctor walked to her with a kind smile on his face. He reached her bedside and tried to cover her hand with his. She jerked away. Rationally she understood this man had been touching her in order to treat her, but she didn't like it. Not one little bit. If she had anything to say about it, no man would ever touch her again.

The doctor's smile faded. "Hello there. It's nice to see your eyes open."

She said nothing. She only stared at him, feeling like a wild animal ready to bolt at the first false move he made. She wanted nothing to do with any man. She wanted them all to die. Every last one of them. They should have left her in the alley because there wasn't anything remaining of her to save. She was empty of everything but hate.

"We won't hurt you. What's your name, dear?" the doctor asked. The other man hung back, saying nothing.

She only stared at him in response. She wasn't even sure she remembered how to speak or remembered her own name, for that matter. Either way, she wasn't talking to *him*. Neither of them. She'd kill them, though, if she could.

"All right, my dear. Take your time." The doctor turned, gave a meaningful look to the other man. "I'll be back in a while to check on her."

"Thank you, Nicolai."

The doctor left and the coarse-faced man approached her bed. She remembered him from the alley—black boots. He'd saved her life when she hadn't wanted it saved. Interfering bastard.

She crushed herself backward into the pillows, trying to get as far from him as she could, and glanced around the room for a weapon. This man was huge. There was nothing she could use to hurt him and she couldn't move, anyway. Her arm and her leg were broken.

Again, she was vulnerable.

Again, she was helpless in the face of a man's will. Bile burned the back of her throat. She never wanted to feel this way again.

He held out a large hand. "It's all right. I know I probably frighten you, but you have nothing to fear from me. I only want to help. I'm the one who found you in the alley, remember?"

She didn't believe him and she didn't fear him. The hell she'd been through had burned all the fear from her. She wanted to die She had nothing to lose, so she feared nothing now. No, she *hated* him. Never had an emotion burned so pure and clean inside her.

He pulled a chair up to the side of her bed and sat down. She spit at him, but he only calmly wiped it away and continued to speak. "I found you in the alley and brought you to my home here in Milzyr and called a doctor for you. See? I mean you no harm."

That's what she'd thought about Ivan too. But all men meant harm. Anything else that came out of their greasy mouths was a lie.

"My name is Byron. What's your name?"

No response.

He pushed a hand through his hair. "All right. I'll leave you alone. Give you some time. Maybe when you're ready, you can tell me your name. I can notify your family that you're safe. You must have someone in the world who cares for you. Let me know when you're ready to send word."

Nothing. She only stared at him as though she could kill him with her eyes. How she wished she could.

He got up, giving her a last concerned glance, and left the room. *Finally.* Her anxiety eased.

Time passed. Her wounds healed. The months spent in the bedroom of Byron's home renewed her body, but not her mind. She barely suffered the doctor's hands on her for the next four months while her broken limbs repaired themselves. Sometimes, when she simply couldn't help herself, couldn't stand one more moment of his touch, she fought him.

Her silence continued, although Byron visited her daily. He came and read to her, tried to entice her into playing strategia with him, brought meals to her and coaxed her to eat. He never unlocked the door, fearing, she supposed, she would escape into the night . . . which she would. He never allowed anything in the room that he deemed useful in a suicide attempt either. Every day she prayed the doctor would forget his bag of sharp instruments, if just for a few minutes, or that Byron would allow her to sleep on sheets that she could use to hang herself. *Something.*

She'd wished for death the way she'd once wished for love.

Early on, he sent a woman named Roxana in to help her bathe, take her measurements, and be her companion. Lilya never spoke to her either. And though she could bear a woman's gentle touch more than a man's, she hated it. Roxana, a sturdy dark-haired older woman, seemed unaffected by her rejection of her. The woman spoke to her in low tones of the recent news from the city, the goings-on at Belai Palace, and of Roxana's family that seemed to constantly vex her. Lilya watched her with fascination. She seemed like such a happy woman.

Every day Byron asked her name and every day she refused to answer. He never gave up on her and she hated him for it.

One night when she was almost completely well, she discovered a knife had been left behind from her dinner. Her fingers closed around the cold, smooth silver handle and she examined the sharp blade with fascination.

Finally. Relief was only a cut away.

This knife could remove all her pain. A sharp slice and all the memories that gave her nightmares would vanish. Her blood on the floor and her worthless self would disappear just like that. Her blight on the world gone. No one would be able to treat her like she was disposable again. No one would be able to hurt her.

She set the tip of the knife to the base of her wrist and watched numbly as it bit deep into her skin. Fire raced along her flesh as she dragged it upward, her blood welling hot on her skin and dripping down to plop onto the thick carpet.

The door burst open and Byron was there, ripping the knife from her fingers and pulling her toward him. She screeched. The first sound she'd made in months. The sound was of pure agony and despair. Rage that he'd taken her opportunity to die away from her. She pushed at him, fighting him, blood smearing his face and clothes. But his arms were like steel and she was far too tiny to break free. He pulled her against him and wouldn't let her go. He grabbed her wrist and forearm and bore down with his huge hands, pressing her wound closed and swearing the whole time.

"I knew it the moment I realized the knife was in here," he yelled into her face. "What are you doing to yourself? *Why do this?*" he raged on and on at her, holding on to her wound until the bleeding had slowed. Then he lunged for one of the curtain ties, binding it around her wrist and forearm and tying it tight. "I won't let you! I've put too much work into keeping you alive."

Sobbing, totally bereft, she looked up from her bandaged arm with a sense of loss and into his face. His eyes were glistening with tears. He blinked and they rolled down his rough cheeks.

This big, strong man? Crying? For her?

"Why?" She wasn't sure what she was asking. Why was he crying for her or why had he bothered to keep her alive? Maybe she was asking both those questions.

He just looked at her quizzically, as if he couldn't understand her befuddlement.

She slumped back against the bed. "You should have let me die in the alley." Her voice came out rusty, whispering, rasping, and halting from disuse. Her throat hurt from the act of speaking and the words felt strange around her tongue.

He leaned in toward her, cupping her face in his bloody hands. "No. Don't ever say that. *No.*"

Realization struck her. This man actually cared if she lived. All he'd done for her since the day he'd found her hadn't been able to sink through the confused, grief-stricken fog of her mind, but now she saw it. This man wanted her well-being more than she did. He wanted her healthy, strong . . . safe.

"Why?" she whispered again. Bafflement ruled her mind.

"Because you matter." He crushed her to him and held on tight.

All the emotion that had been caught inside her like a dammed river let loose. Deep, racking sobs broke free and rushed forth. Tears streamed down her face. Her body convulsed with deep

grief, like sludge dredged up from the depths of her. It was a cathartic experience, clearing her out and emptying her until she
sagged with exhaustion and all her tears were gone. Her head
hurt and her throat and eyes burned, yet she felt better than she
had in a very long time.

Byron held her through it all.

Finally she lifted her head, wiped her cheeks and said, "My
name is Lilya."

That was the threshold. From that moment on, her mind began
to heal as well as her body. Slowly, she clawed her way back to a
place where she could hate men a little less, thanks to Byron, and
love herself a little more.

Six months passed. She lived in Byron's home and slowly
forged a friendship with him. They played strategia, read books,
and ate meals together. After she was fully healed and ready to
face life again, they attended concerts together and went for
carriage rides. He bought her dresses and took her out to dinner.
Thus, slowly, she returned to the world.

She remained shy with him, as she did with all people, especially
men, for a long time. But eventually she regained herself, every inch.
She regained her confidence, her self-esteem, and her will to live.

The next part was something she omitted from the story she
told Alek.

Although she could not say she'd fallen in love with Byron,
since love was so far out of her reach as to be impossible, she
came to care for him a great deal. When the memory of her ordeal
had faded a little and her mind had readjusted itself as healthily
as it could, she had wanted Byron to make love to her. She wondered if his touch could erase the taint of what had been done to
her somehow. Like his caring hands had some magickal quality

she could benefit from—to dissolve the past. Perhaps it would rewrite history for her, leave her with another, better memory. However, Byron resisted her every attempt in that direction.

Then one day she woke to find he'd left the house. Not only that, he'd left the house *to her*, the deed signed over to her name. He'd left her a bank account as well. It was a good thing, of course, but heartbreaking because he'd been gone.

She omitted that last part too.

Six

Alek studied Lilya as she spoke. It was as though she'd left the room, but her body was still in the chair. Her gaze was unfocused, far away, as if she gazed into the past. He felt like he'd gone there with her.

"I lived in the house for another six months before I grew too lonely to stay. I didn't discover that Byron was Byron Andropov, heir to a huge elusian crystal fortune, until two years after he'd left."

Her eyes focused, found his, then her gaze dropped into her lap. She was back in her body. "That's it. That's my history with Byron. It's not trifling. In fact, even though I only knew him for around twelve months, Byron is the most important person in my life. He says I owe him nothing, but I know I owe him everything."

The room fell silent. The fire in the hearth snapped and popped, but was the only sound. During the time Lilya had been speaking, twilight had enveloped the sky beyond the huge windows of the library. He'd been so engrossed in the tale he hadn't even noticed the time passing.

Alek sat considering both of them. Byron, for never having shared this story with him. What had kept him from telling Alek something that had had such a huge impact on his life? Byron had spent that year in Milzyr, unreachable to most everyone. He'd told Alek it had been business he'd been doing there, on behalf of his ailing father. He'd lied, rather than share this story with him. To Alek, that said a lot about how important this woman was to him.

And, Lilya. Now he saw her through different eyes. Her situation was far more layered and complex than he'd ever imagined. Instead of a courtesan sitting in that chair, he saw a woman who had been to hell and come back from it.

"And Ivan." Alek broke the silence. "What ever happened to him and his men?" His fists clenched. "I hope Ivan died with a knife through his throat in a back alley. All his thugs too."

Lilya met his eyes. "Ivan is Ivan Lazarson. Ah, I see by the look on your face you know who he is. He wasn't so powerful, not back then. His rise in the crime world was still to come. I would like to see him punished, but for someone like me, he's untouchable."

"Not to someone like me." Byron's words came out hard and low.

Lilya dropped her gaze into her lap. "I'm sorry. This is the first you've heard of Ivan being Ivan Lazarson, isn't it?"

"He was only a faceless bastard to me before, anonymous and untraceable. Now—"

"*No!*" Lilya's eyes flashed as she looked at Byron. "You will do nothing against him. He had the Imperial Guard paid to look

the other way before the revolution and now he's got the Milzyrian Protectors doing the same. It's too dangerous. Promise me."
She paused, staring at him when he made no response. "*Promise
me, Byron.*"

He raised his gaze to hers, a muscle twitching in his jaw.
"That's a promise I cannot make, Lilya, but if you want me to
stay away from him, I will."

Her brow knit, but the answer seemed to satisfy her. Alek
knew him better than she did. He could hear the words he knew
Byron had added to his last sentence in his mind.

For now.

Alek pushed a hand through his hair. "But I don't understand
why you chose to take up work as a *courtesan* after what you've
been through. It seems to me that you would push away all men
and, especially, sex. You didn't *need* to do it since you had the
house and money from Byron."

Lilya pulled back the wrist cuff of her dress to Alek, showing
him the scar from where she'd tried to take her life. "Ivan destroyed any possibility of my maintaining a loving relationship
with a man, so marriage was completely out. Thanks to Byron
giving me financial stability, I could have stayed in that house and
shut myself away from the world and all men. Or I could have
chosen a new path for myself, one that allowed me to reenter the
world on my own terms. Choosing my current profession was my
way of taking control, Alek. I choose my clients. I control *every
aspect* of my relationships with them. I'm financially independent
without having to be married, something I don't want and doubt
I could manage, anyway. I'm happy with the choice I made and
would make it again."

"I guess after all you've been through, it just seems strange."

"You can never understand the decisions another makes un-less you've walked in their shoes. My choice of career has empow-ered me by allowing me control where men are concerned."

He studied her, thinking that wasn't necessarily the healthiest way for her to deal with her trauma. Yet, it wasn't his place to point that out. He might very well be guilty of unhealthy dealing himself. After all, how many times had Byron accused him of burying himself in his studies to avoid the past?

Instead he said, "I truly am sorry for the insult I offered earlier."

Lilya smiled. She was beautiful, captivating, and had a charm that drew men easily to her. Some people had a spark inside them that attracted people. Ivan had not doused it in Lilya and that was something like a miracle. "It's not the first time I've endured them."

"If I had known, I never would have—"

"I know. Your apology is accepted. Anyway, all that happened a long time ago."

Yes, he liked to say the same thing. Brush it under the carpet. Not talk about it. Ignoring some things made them easier to deal with.

Byron cleared his throat. Alek looked over and saw emotion on his face. Not much could make Byron Andropov show his feelings. "Is your curiosity satisfied?"

"More than."

"Good." He cleared his throat again. Alek knew Byron well enough to know he was attempting to mask his reaction to Lilya's story. "It's late and it's been a long day of traveling. I think we should all go to sleep. Would you show Lilya to one of the guest bedrooms, Alek?" Byron stood.

Ah, Alek understood. Byron needed to be alone. "I'd be happy to."

Alek fell into step with Lilya as they went up to the second floor of the house. He'd had enough schooling to see the emotional and psychological underpinnings of her desire to become a courtesan since it gave her control of men, instead of the other way around. Unhealthy though that might be. He wondered if there weren't other things in play too, perhaps ways she might be using her obvious beauty and charm to punish her clients. He wouldn't doubt it—or blame her, really—if that were the case.

He led her to the nicest of all the guest rooms, one not far away from Byron's. Byron may profess to have invited Lilya here for Alek's sake, but he wasn't blind or stupid. Lilya and Byron had a chemistry that snapped like a current of elusian crystal. Every move they made, every gesture, every word they shared seemed like foreplay. He sensed there was much unfinished and unsaid between them and her time here would consummate their relationship.

She looked into the room, noted the huge soft bed, the fireplace, and heavy carved-wood furnishings. "It's beautiful."

"I can start a fire for you, if you wish."

She shook her head and smiled at him. "I can do it myself. I see there's kindling there and flint."

"I'll just bring up your bag, then."

"Thank you."

He turned to leave, but she caught his arm. Her touch was light, nice. Her hand on him made him think about things he hadn't in a long time. He eased away from her, a flare of something long forgotten igniting inside him.

She withdrew her hand. "I hear you're a scholar of history."

"I'm getting a degree specialization in the Purion Era right now."

"Do you intend to teach?"

"I intend to write books."

"Ah." She pressed her lips together and looked down at the polished black toes of her expensive pair of boots. It seemed like she wanted to say something else.

"What is it, Lilya?"

She raised her gaze to him, her cheeks a charming shade of pink. "I never went to school. Or, at least, I stopped going to school once my father died. He was a good man who thought education was very important, but he was also a poor man who couldn't make provisions for a daughter with no other family once he'd died."

"He was right to value education."

"You say you don't intend to teach, but I wondered, if while I'm here, maybe you could impart to me some of what you know. If it's too much of an imposition, just forget I asked."

His eyebrows rose and he wondered for a moment if she was sincere, or if she was only trying to lure him in, using something she knew he loved in order to grow closer to him. But judging from the blush on her cheeks and the embarrassed way she wouldn't meet his eyes, he came to the conclusion her request was genuine. Either that or she was a wonderful actress. "It's not an imposition. What topic would you most like to learn about?"

She shrugged and met his eyes for the barest of moments. "You're better suited to selecting one. Your choice. I have only a rudimentary grasp of the history of Rylisk."

He nodded, his mind already whirling with possibilities. "We can start tomorrow morning after breakfast."

"Thank you." She smiled, leaned in, and kissed him on his

cheek. He went very still at the feel of her soft mouth on his skin and the barest waft of her scent that surrounded him for a moment.

He was still standing there like an imbecile after she'd backed into her room and closed the door.

That night, after the fire was doused and the lights were out, Lilya found herself unable to sleep. She tossed and turned in the huge four-poster bed. Even though the mattress was comfortable and the blankets stroked her skin like the soft wing of a bird, she couldn't find rest.

Sitting up, she surveyed the room by the waning silver light of the moon coming in through the large windows. It cast shadows along the thick area rugs, the sofa, and the chairs. The hearth showed the muted red coals of a fire that wished to be.

The fire inside of her didn't wish to be—it burned. Ever since Byron had shown up at the temple, she'd been in turns uncomfortable, frightened, bliss-filled, and desirous. That man seemed to sow nothing but emotional chaos in his wake. She'd been happy to see him again, yet a part of her wished for the bland reality she'd been living since he'd left.

Thoughts thus occupied, sleep was only a distant aspiration. She rose, found her night wrap, and headed downstairs for a drink of water.

"Lilya?"

She froze at the bottom of the stairs and searched the darkness for Byron. She spotted him at a window to her left and walked to him. "You scared me. What are you doing staring out the window in the middle of the night?"

"I couldn't sleep." She studied his profile in the silver light of the moon, stony and a little rough. No, he wasn't pretty, but she thought he was beautiful.

Clearly, she was doomed.

With a sigh, she settled in beside him and stared out the window at the sweep of lawn that surrounded his home. "Usually when I can't sleep there's a reason for it." She had a reason tonight, but she wasn't about to share it with him.

He moved a little, seemingly restless. He remained silent for a moment longer than it took for her to wonder if something was really wrong. "Bad dreams. Why are you awake?"

"I often have trouble sleeping when I'm away from home. I was going to try and find the kitchen for a glass of water."

"I'll show you where it is."

She followed him down a corridor and into a large kitchen, larger than the one at the Temple of Dreams. Their footsteps echoed. He lit two lamps, sought a glass for her, and filled it with water from the water pipes running through his home. Not many could afford pipes or had a large enough water supply to draw from.

"Don't you get lonely in this big house all by yourself?" She accepted the glass of water and sank into a nearby chair. It was chilly in the huge room and she shivered.

"Now that my family is gone, yes, sometimes, but I'm used to it being big and empty. You're used to a bustling house with lots of people in it at all times."

"It helps me feel less lonesome. I hate feeling lonely." She sipped her water. "I guess I felt so alone after my father died that I developed a serious aversion to it. It's one of the reasons I didn't stay in the house you so graciously provided for me. After what happened, I could have easily become a recluse there."

"I'm glad you didn't. The world benefits from your presence." He paused. "Alek is already warming to you."

In the low light of the room, she studied him. "You're a strange man, Byron, wanting what you want from me. I don't understand it." She finished the rest of her water and stood, pulling her wrap more firmly around her against the chill. "I've never met anyone like you."

"I'm unique, am I? I'll take that as a compliment."

"Indeed, you're matchless in your inscrutability."

His brows rose. "Am I now?"

Hiding a smile, she walked over to set the glass on the counter, coming deliberately close to him. She was pleased when he didn't back away. His body felt nice, warming her through her clothes. They had nice rapport. There were few men she shared this kind of energy with and, with this particular man, she wanted to explore it further. And not because she could control it, or use it, or because she wanted him to pay her.

She just wanted him because he was *Byron*.

He turned toward her and cupped her face in his hands. Lowering his head, he tasted her lips and her knees went weak. His mouth dragged across hers slowly as he rocked her back against the counter. It seemed like she'd been waiting forever for this.

"Lilya, I want you," he whispered. "Having you here, so close to me, and not touching you, it's torture."

"I want you too, Byron, you know that." Her hands found his waist and the hem of the shirt he slept in. His skin beneath felt warm under her palms, the muscles of his back tight as he moved. He brushed the shoulder of her night wrap, pulling it down and off. It slithered to the floor at her feet. She didn't even feel the cold, not when she was in his arms.

"I've wanted this for a long time," he murmured against her lips.

"So have I." Her nipples had gone hard and pressed through the thin fabric of her nightgown. "I've chosen all my partners, but I'm not sure I've wanted to be with a man as much as I want to be with you right now." Her voice trembled from the force of that desire.

He stilled in the semidark, one hand at the nape of her neck, and stared down at her as if he couldn't believe what she'd just said. For a moment he looked like he would say something, but instead he lowered his mouth and kissed her again, this time slanting his mouth hungrily over hers and slipping his tongue deep into her mouth.

She gripped his upper arms, appreciating the bunch and flex of them as he made minute movements. Anticipation thrilled through her body, raced through her veins, and set her heart to thumping out a crazy rhythm she hadn't felt in years.

He broke the kiss softly and murmured against her lips, "Then come to my bedroom and let's do this right."

Her answer came without hesitation. "Yes." She forced herself not to whimper and add a *please*. The depth of her desire for this man frightened her, yet she was far too immersed in her need to put a stop to this. Desire overrode good sense and she didn't care.

He took her by the hand, a hand that felt warm and strong in hers, and led her up the stairs to his bedroom. Anticipation of being intimate with him raced through her blood in a way she'd never experienced. Six years ago he'd been all she'd wanted and had never been able to have.

And now, he was hers, if perhaps only just for a night.

A low fire burned in the enormous stone hearth that dominated one wall. To her right stood a divan, two chairs, and a low table. At the other end of the room was a huge four-poster bed, the size of which only the very wealthy possessed, covered with pillows at the top, soft sheets, and a thick comforter, all mussed from his body. For a crazy moment she resisted the urge to dive across the room, into the bed, and roll in the scent of him that undoubtedly lingered in the blanket folds. Soon she would have the real thing— his bare body up against hers.

They'd left her wrap on the floor of the kitchen. He lifted her nightgown over her head, tossing it to the couch. Then he stood back and took in her nude body, bathed by the gentle glow of the fire that burned in the great stone hearth.

"You are more beautiful than I ever imagined." His voice was low, gruff, filled with an intense arousal that heated her blood.

She stepped toward him, intending to make him every bit as nude as she was, but he lifted her suddenly into his arms, making her squeal with surprise. He walked her over to the bed and tossed her down onto the mattress. The softness of the bed enveloped her, making her laugh for the sheer joy of being with him. She rolled in the comforter, burying her face in his pillow and inhaling the scent that clung to it—leather, a little wood smoke, and a hint of his spicy aftershave. *Heaven.*

Byron made a low, hungry sound in the back of his throat. "You look good in my bed, Lilya. I may decide to keep you there for the next three weeks."

She rolled onto her back and looked at him. "I have no problem with that." The words came out a little breathless. "Come here."

Seven

He pulled his shirt over his head and Lilya's breath caught. Like Alek, Byron was not as weak-limbed as one might presume since he was rich and, therefore, relatively idle. She would have to ask both of them about that soon. She'd always known that Byron had strength; it was apparent under his clothes. His chest and upper arms were pleasingly muscled as if he engaged in some kind of hard exercise on a regular basis.

It was rare she had such men in her bed, but she enjoyed it. It made her feel protected in a way that she supposed harkened back to the primal days of their species. Woman, wanting the protection of a man's strong arms. Byron was the first and only man ever to make her feel that way . . . truly protected.

This was the first time in years she'd had a liaison with a man that wasn't carefully planned out, but this was Byron. She felt free to let herself go with him. She trusted him.

Byron lowered himself onto the mattress, coming over her, his gaze completely caught with hers. "You're going to break my heart, Lilya," he murmured a moment before his mouth came down on hers.

She wanted to reply, to protest that eventuality, but his mouth dropped to her breast and she became suddenly incapable of speech. His hot tongue skated over her nipple, making it hard, sending shocks of pleasure through her. All the nerves burst to life and she arched her back, moaning, while he sucked it into his mouth.

Her fingers found his hair and tangled through it, mussing the thick tendrils, before she dropped her hands to his shoulders and slid them down his back. She loved the heat of his body, the smooth iron silk of his warm skin covering hard muscle. Touching his body was a sensual treat.

Her hands smoothed downward, finding the waistband of his cotton sleep pants and pushing them down. Her fingers found and wrapped around his cock, and a low groan vibrated up from his throat. He was thick and long against her palm, utterly fascinating. She stroked him and he moved against her, murmuring her name. Then he moved down her body, out of her reach.

His hands slid over her breasts and her abdomen, finding her thighs and parting them. He ran his mouth over the sensitive place where her inner thigh met her sex and brushed his lips against it, giving it a kiss. He remained that way for several long moments, making her want to squirm with anticipation. Right when the word *please* had risen in her throat, his tongue found her clit and licked. She shuddered with pleasure, her fists finding and clenching in the sheets and blankets.

Making a hungry sound in the back of his throat, he pinned

her thighs to the bed and closed his mouth over her achy, swollen clit, gently sucking the aroused area between his lips. The thought of Byron's sensual mouth on her was even more exciting than the actual act. The sight of his dark head moving between her thighs nearly undid her.

Her back arched, and her head fell back against the pillow. Body tightening, she cried out. He'd taken her to the very edge of a climax, where only teasing, delicious pleasure existed. Her mind emptied of all but his mouth on her and the ecstasy slowly building to a shattering crescendo.

He dropped his mouth down a degree and found her sex, spearing his tongue inside her and thrusting in just the way she wanted his cock. Men rarely did this to her and never with such sure hands and mouth. Instead she was usually one the taking the lead and giving all the pleasure. It made sense, she guessed, since it was her services the men had paid for. This was different, something that even in all her experience she'd never had for herself.

He licked over her as though he'd waited forever to do this, like he loved it. Lilya clung to the bedclothes and hung on, dangling deliciously on the precipice of a powerful climax. He sucked her clit into his mouth again, tonguing it, while two of his thick fingers found her entrance and pushed inside. He found a sensitive place deep within her and dragged his fingertips over it.

"Byron." His name came out a low, pleasure-laced gasp a moment before delicious, explosive pleasure burst over her body, sweet as the ripest berry, stealing her thoughts and nearly her ability to breathe. She hung on as it washed through her body, making her tingle and moan, making her toes curl and her sex convulse around his thrusting fingers.

Then he was there, above her, his dark gaze intense. The head of his cock found the entrance of her sex and she welcomed him, tilting her hips up and guiding him inside her. He rocked in and out, easing himself deep within her inch by inch, stretching her inner muscles until he'd seated himself root-deep inside her.

Her arms came around him and she buried her nose where his throat met his shoulder, inhaling the scent of him. His hand smoothed down her back, cupped her rear, and he began to move inside her, first with long, slow strokes, coming nearly completely out of her with every outward thrust and then filling her again. She could feel every inch of him deep inside her, every vein, and every ridge of his shaft. Then his rhythm grew faster and she met him stroke for stroke, their bodies fitting together perfectly. They moved like one being, sharing pleasure.

Taking her hands in his, he stretched them over her body, pinning them to the mattress as he moved deep inside her. His mouth found hers. He murmured her name against her lips in a way that made emotion burst through her chest like she'd bitten into the sweetest piece of cake.

Heaven.

Tears pricked her eyes. His lips brushed hers and then slanted over her mouth, his tongue finding hers in the deepest part of her mouth and then his physical possession of her was complete.

They came together, their limbs and mouths tangled and enmeshed. A second climax exploded through her body, making her sob. He murmured her name, gave a hoarse shout, and spent himself deep inside her.

When it was over, he clung to her like he didn't want to let her go—or maybe that was wishful thinking on her part. Tears silently squeezed out of the corners of her eyes. She didn't want him to leave her body and hung on to him as though drowning. She'd never known she'd been drowning until now, until this man had made love to her.

And this had been making love, even if they weren't actually in love. There was no other term for it. This hadn't been fucking or even merely having sex. This had been no careful act, where she'd taken the lead, coaxing some shy man to touch her. This had been powerful, explosive, an even give-and-take of pleasure.

Slowly, his cock went flaccid inside her. He rolled to the side and pulled her toward him, kissing her lips gently. "Why are you crying?" he whispered.

She wiped a stray tear away and laughed. "I don't know. It's stupid." Her emotions were a painful mess inside her chest and she couldn't seem to parse them all out. "That was beautiful."

He kissed her again and sighed against her lips. "We fit well together, you and I. In almost every way, even in bed."

She cupped his cheek. "I always thought we did."

"Mind what I said. I might just keep you here in my bedroom for the next three weeks."

She smiled and ran her fingers down his cheek. He needed to shave and his skin prickled her palm. "That won't help Alek."

"Fuck Alek. I want you for myself."

The vehemence with which he said those words made heat flare inside her. She snuggled into his chest and enjoyed the feel of his bare body against hers. She hadn't been this content in a very long time and she intended to enjoy it for as long as it lasted.

Alek entered the kitchen, found a pot, and filled it to make coffee. As soon as the heated cooking counter had been made available for sale, Byron had had one installed. It was very nice. Alek didn't even have one in his kitchen yet.

The Tinkers' Guild had been releasing many useful inventions since the fall of the royal family and the populace watched them all with interest. Alek already saw that the new devices were creating a rift between the haves and have-nots, however—not unlike the rule of the Edaeii family. It would be fascinating to watch how materialism widened that gap in the coming years and the effect it would have on their society.

He set the pot onto the heating implement and his shoe caught in something on the floor. He looked down to find a filmy woman's night wrap under his boot. He knelt to pick it up, frowning as to why it would be there, when realization dawned. A whole possible nighttime scenario played itself out in his mind.

Of course. And why not?

They hadn't come out and said it yesterday, when Lilya had been telling him her story, but her feelings had been clear enough in her voice and eyes when she looked at Byron. Alek knew Byron well enough to know that he never would have taken advantage of a woman who'd gone through something like what Lilya had endured. That meant the emotions between them had been simmering for six years. It was about time they give physical voice to them.

Just as the water was growing hot, Byron and Lilya entered the room, both laughing. They saw him and immediately sobered, but Alek caught the bright look of happiness in Byron's eyes before his smile faded.

"Good morning." Alek walked over and handed Lilya her robe. "I found this on the floor."

"Oh, thank you." She took it and glanced at Byron, coloring

a little. It was a wonder that a courtesan could color when caught having a nighttime liaison with a man. That probably meant Alek didn't know as much about courtesans as he'd thought. Or, at least, about this one. Lilya was captivating to him, like a riddle to solve. Irresistible to the mind of a scholar.

"I made some water for coffee." Alek motioned toward the cooking counter.

"I just came in for a piece of fruit." Lilya walked over and took an apple from a bowl on the table. "I thought I'd go outside for a walk. It's an unusually beautiful morning and this late in the autumn there won't be very many more of them."

"Do you wish a history lesson in about an hour?" Alek asked her.

She nodded. "Yes, thank you. In the library?"

Alek nodded.

"Gentlemen." She smiled, bowed her head at little, and left the room.

Byron walked toward the steaming pot of water. "I'll take some coffee." Fixing his mug and one for Alek, he retreated to the table to sit down. "History lesson?"

Alek sank down across from him. "Last night she explained she'd been forced to leave school at a young age and desires that I instruct her on some of the topics I know so much about while she's staying here. I wonder if it's just a ploy to get closer to me, since that's what you're paying her for."

Byron frowned. "She's very intelligent and has a mind keen to learn. I wouldn't be so quick to assume *everything* is about you, Alek."

Alek twisted his lips a little ruefully. "Point taken."

"Anyway, I already told you, I'm not paying her a cent to be here. She's a guest. I tried to offer her payment, but she insisted I give the amount as a donation to Angel House instead." His lips twisted in a smile as he took a sip of coffee. "After she doubled the price."

"Why didn't you ever tell me about her?"

Byron sipped his coffee and didn't reply for a long moment. "I don't know. I think part of me wanted her to remain mine. Telling you about her would have meant I had to share some part of her."

"You love her."

He gazed out the window to the kitchen gardens, overgrown with a tangle of dead weeds this late in the season. "Everyone loves her, Alek. Yes, I love her, but I know I can never have her. She's been through too much and she's been too damaged. You heard her say it herself; she's not able to commit to any man. Not anymore."

"That's a dark thing to assume."

"You weren't with her those twelve months. She acts fine, looks fine, seems normal in every outward way, but she's hurt badly inside. She sustained wounds that no poultice or medicine can ever heal."

"Time heals. I know the truth of that. And perhaps she was never as damaged as you presume."

"No." He shook his head. "I will take what I can from her and love her enough to accept that I can't wish for more."

"Maybe, but a man would have to be blind not to see the way she looks at you."

"She cares about me. I know that, but her feelings stop short of love."

Alek wasn't sure. He looked out the kitchen window to the

path beyond, where movement had caught his eye. Lilya, bundled up in her heavy cloak, and munching her apple, walked the paths of the ill-kept herb garden. Byron really needed to hire help. "I think you're wrong to think she's incapable of love."

Byron looked over at him and grinned. "I hope you're right."

"So, here's the million-gold-coins question, my friend; why introduce her to me if you care about her so much? Why bring her here in her capacity as a courte—?"

"*Stop*. How many times do I need to repeat this? She's not here in that capacity. I told you; she's here visiting. But I do hope she'll have an impact on you. Should a physical relationship develop between you, so be it. If not, that's all right. Either way, I feel sure I'll have what I want by the end of her stay."

Alek shook his head. "You're insane."

He shrugged. "Maybe. She thinks I am."

Alek looked out the window at Lilya. It had been a very long time since he'd been with a woman, but Lilya had a beauty and a charisma he found enchanting. Of course, Byron had known he would. Lilya stirred things inside him that had long been dormant. Byron had known that would happen too. "So, you love her, but you'll be all right with me sleeping with her?"

"Yes." The answer came easily and sure.

"I don't understand you, Byron. Not even after all these years."

"I may be a little in love with Lilya, but I know better than to think I can keep her."

Eight

◆

"She's gone, sir."

"What do you mean, *she's gone?*"

Daniel, a messenger who, at this moment, really wished he wasn't, stood his ground and tried to make his voice steady. This job wasn't worth the two coppers he was being paid, not when he had to face the biggest crime lord in all of Milzyr. "The Temple of Dreams delivered a message to Edgar Romanoff saying that she'd gone out of town with an old friend for three weeks."

The man in front of Daniel had his back to him. He bowed his head, his long, dark hair shot through with silver hung in his face. His hands clenched. *"An old friend."* His voice was deceptively soft. Soft meant dangerous from Ivan Lazarson.

Daniel fought the urge to take a step back, out of the opulently decorated room he now stood in. "A man, sir. When Romanoff questioned the other courtesans, they told him he was a huge man, wealthy, dark hair, and blue eyes, a little bit ugly."

"I know who it is." He roared the sentence suddenly, rounding on Daniel, who couldn't help taking a stumbling step backward. Ivan Lazarson wasn't a muscular man, but power wasn't always wielded by biceps and fists. Not when knives were second nature. Ivan had a sharp, shiny one sheathed at his belt. Daniel's eyes fixed on it. "It's the only person for whom Lilya would ever leave the Temple of Dreams. *Byron Andropov.*"

Daniel wanted to ask why he cared, why he'd been paying Edgar Romanoff all these years to keep an eye on this woman. But one didn't ask Ivan questions if one wanted to stay unmaimed.

Ivan paced the room, rubbing his hand over his chin and frowning. The man looked worried, upset. For a moment the scariness of Ivan Lazarson evaporated and he looked like a man instead of a monster, a man with a heavy concern.

Then Ivan whirled toward him with insanity edging into his icy eyes and the momentary patina of harmlessness faded to threat. He pointed at Daniel. "Get me a horse and pack him for a day's journey."

Lilya spent most of the afternoon in the library with Alek, soaking in everything he had to teach her about basic Ryliskian history. With vibrant words that painted vivid mental images, Alek brought the past to life for her. Instead of staid, dry figures from history, he created characters. Instead of reciting dates and events, he told her stories.

They paused for a lunch of sandwiches, lemon biscuits, and tea, and then went back to work at her urging. Alek made learning enjoyable and her mind thirsted for what he had to teach her like a desert thirsted for water.

The end of the afternoon, she closed the book they'd been reading from. "I'm sure that you're a wonderful writer, but you really should consider teaching. Your enthusiasm for the subject shines through when you speak and makes the material much more interesting than it's got any right to be."

"Teaching?" He shook his head and his lips twisted in a rueful smile. "I'm not good with people."

"You're good with me."

His hair was mussed from the constant habit he had of running his hand through it. She itched to fix it for him, but she knew the contact would not be welcomed. It was far too intimate and that *was* something he seemed to have a problem with.

He glanced up at her. "You're one person, not a classroom full."

"How did you become so fascinated with history, anyway?"

"It's always been an interest of mine." He closed his book and pushed it away. "Since I was in school as a young boy. I went to the university, thinking I'd become a doctor and follow in my father's footsteps, and met a woman named . . ." He trailed off, his face losing its charming half smile. "I met a woman. She was a history major." He paused and storm clouds seemed to move into his eyes. "In order to get a foot in the door with her, I told her I was having trouble in my history class and needed tutoring. Then she did for me what you're saying I'm doing for you—she made history come alive."

Lilya connected the dots. Perhaps this woman was the reason Byron had wanted her to come to his house for these three weeks. Did the mystery woman have some kind of hold over Alek that was crippling him emotionally? Perhaps holding on to history the way he did wasn't just because he had a love for the subject, maybe it was his way of holding on to her.

"I see." She studied his face, which was completely shuttered, making her believe her theory might be correct. Clearly, he didn't want to talk about her. That meant the woman was a painful subject and Lilya knew all about burying those.

He piled the books, not looking into her eyes. "If you had continued on with your education, what path would you have chosen?"

The question was like a sucker punch to her solar plexus. Her breath whooshed out of her and she lowered her eyes. No one had ever asked her that and it brought up memories long secreted away. "Art. I would have pursued . . . art."

It was amazing how much the loss still weighed on her. The room her father, Oren, had given her in their small home, the smell of the paint, and the feel of fresh paper under her hands. It had been hard for Oren to find money for the supplies, but he'd believed so much in her and had wanted to see her happy. It wasn't the loss of the art itself that bothered her; the art was more a symbol of a time when she'd been safe and loved.

Then fever had come to their home and taken it all away.

"Art? The study of it or the actual—"

"Painting." She raised her eyes to him. "That's what I loved most to do as a child. I feel certain that if I been allowed to finish my schooling, I would be an artist today. My father always said I had a natural aptitude for it. A gift. It's been a long time since I put paint to canvas, however."

"Not much money in that."

"No, but some things mean more than money."

His eyes clouded for a moment. "Yes, you're right. They do."

She studied him as he gathered books, papers, and pens. For the first time since she'd met him, he seemed unguarded and a little lost. Again she suspected the woman was the cause.

After she'd finished her afternoon with Alek, avoiding the subject of magick and the mystery woman—it was too early to approach either of them—she headed up to her room. She hadn't seen Byron since the morning and she was sad about that. She couldn't remember the last time she'd felt *sad* at the absence of anyone, especially a man.

Another testament to how different Byron was—no rules seemed to apply to him. Where he was concerned she was lost, whirling around in the air with nothing to hold on to. She couldn't plan for him or control him. She definitely didn't have the strength to deny him.

Suddenly cold, she stared at the fireless hearth and hugged herself. The last time she'd had these types of feelings for a man, he'd beaten her and thrown her like a scrap to a bunch of men who'd literally tried to tear her limb from limb.

Her rational mind knew that Byron would never do anything to hurt her. She trusted him. Yet what had happened to her still bruised the back of her mind, even if it was irrational. That emotional bruise linked deep caring for a man with her utter destruction. No matter how she tried to untangle that knot, it wouldn't come free.

Someone knocked on her door. She called for the person to enter and Byron walked in with an armful of kindling. Something light fluttered through her chest. Ah, the man who made such trouble in her mind.

Smiling, she walked toward him, still hugging her chest against the late autumn chill. "You really should hire a few people to come and do this work for you."

He set the kindling down in the metal basket near the hearth, then stood and brushed off his hands. "But then I would have no excuse to visit your room."

"You don't need an excuse, Byron, and think of the good work you'd be providing people who need it. And now, after the revolution, people *do* need it."

He opened his mouth, and then closed it. "I can't argue with that logic."

She smiled sweetly. "I never imagined you could."

His expression went soft and he motioned to her. "Come here."

She went to him and let him envelope her in his strong arms. Closing her eyes and inhaling the scent of him, she buried her nose near his throat. Longing sang through her, an emotion that placed itself somewhere on the scale between wistfulness and hopefulness. It made tears touch her eyes and something in her chest give a little squeeze. Her arms came around him and she held on like she would never let go.

She wanted him in her bed for the night, but her urge had little to do with sexual fulfillment and a lot to do with wanting him near her in the closest way possible. The feel of his bare skin. The scent of him. The comfort of his arms. The tenor of his voice in her ears.

If she couldn't have him in her life forever, she could take tonight.

The quality and intensity of her emotions made her pull her arms away and back up a few steps. She couldn't raise her eyes to his, afraid he might see the naked need she felt for him reflected there. This was becoming unmanageable. Frightening. Her desire for him made her feel out of control.

"Lilya? Are you all right?"

Suddenly she felt like she was suffocating. "I'm fine. I think I need a little air, though. A walk maybe."

"Let me come with you."

"*No.*" She paused, drawing a breath. "I mean, I think I need to be alone." Before he could say anything else, she hurried out the door.

When she'd agreed to come here, she'd known she had feelings for Byron, but she hadn't known they'd run this deep. Lilya had always believed, and had told Evangeline and Anatol as much, that a courtesan couldn't be a courtesan if she were in love. Had coming here changed everything as she'd feared it had at the transport station? Would she ever be able to go back to her old life at the Temple of Dreams and have sex with men she didn't love?

Because she was seriously beginning to fear that what she felt for Byron was, indeed, that. *Love.*

Scary, chaotic, reckless love that made a woman blind and vulnerable to a man.

She was practically running by the time she got to the front door, her steps echoing into the foyer. She heard Alek call her name, but she ignored him, closing the door behind her and making her way to the late autumn–dead garden and the stone bench she'd found that morning. Sinking down onto it, she tipped her face to the sky. Away from the city there was less pollution to cloud the skies, and the moon and stars seemed to shine more brightly here.

Someone sat down beside her and she sighed, not wanting

company. She looked over and saw Alek's profile in the evening light. He held her pelisse on his lap. Immediately she shivered, realizing she'd forgotten it and hadn't even felt the cold of the evening in the tangle of her emotions.

He eased it around her shoulders and she snuggled into it gratefully. "Thank you."

"I saw you rush out of the house." He flipped up the collar of his coat against the chill in the air and then stuck his hands in his pockets. "Figured you might want your pelisse. There's a kiss of winter in tonight's air. Snow will fall soon."

"I just needed to be alone for a while."

"Do you want me to leave?"

She let out a slow breath. "No." Maybe it was better if she wasn't alone with her thoughts. They were darker than the skies tonight. Anyway, it was Byron's presence she was running from, not Alek's.

They sat in silence for a long time. Then, finally, Alek asked, "If you were in Milzyr tonight, what would you be doing?"

"It's Lansday evening, right? I'd be at a concert with Edgar. He loves them. We go every week." She glanced at him. "Don't look so surprised. It's not all about the sex, Alek. My clients are lonely men. They want me more for companionship than anything else, friendship, conversation, not only for carnal pleasure."

"I *am* surprised."

"Most are."

"Byron tells me all men fall in love with you."

She snorted, looking down at the stone pathway that wound through the garden. "Byron is overly impressed with me."

"Or maybe he's just talking about himself." Alek murmured it while looking up at the moon.

"In love with me?" Lilya jerked at his comment, her bemused smile fading. "Impossible."

Alek's attention locked on her. "Why do you say that?"

She shrugged, a lump growing in the back of her throat. "He can have any woman in the province. All he needs to do is crook a finger. He would pick an educated, cultured woman. He wouldn't pick a courtesan."

"He spent ten months nursing one back to health."

She tipped her head a little at him and tried to smile. "I wasn't a courtesan back then." *No, you were just trash, thrown away.*

Alek made a low sound of disagreement. "I guess maybe I know Byron a little better than you do. By the way, you may be lacking a formal education, but you are *not* lacking intelligence."

Eager to change the subject, she said, "He said you've been friends since childhood."

"We've gone through school, numerous girlfriends, and the loss of our families together. He's more than just a friend."

They lapsed into a companionable silence. There was a note of wistfulness sometimes in Alek that she recognized both in herself and in the men she took as clients, loneliness. Yet Alek's particular brand of loneliness wasn't like that of the clients she took on; he wasn't quite as . . . hopeless. He didn't have any social awkwardness that prevented him from meeting women. No shyness or lack of confidence. Relationships were something he apparently avoided by choice.

Maybe his loneliness was a choice too; she didn't know him well enough to make a judgment on that issue.

She liked Alek, but her feelings were nothing compared to what she felt for Byron. Could she be intimate with Alek now, after the full impact of what she felt for Byron had hit her? Would it be enough to see Alek as a client? Would it be enough to merely like him, to feel compassion for him, maybe see a little of herself in him?

Or was her life as a courtesan over now? It was an important question.

She moved her hand to cover his. At her touch, he looked over at her in surprise. She smiled. "You know, you might be an important man at that university, but you don't know everything."

"I don't?"

She tilted her head to the sky. "You're right that I never had a formal education, but I do know a bit about the stars. Astronomy has always been a fascinating topic of reading for me."

"Really? You're right. I don't know much about astronomy."

"And I've never seen the stars quite as bright as they are this evening." She stood and held out her hand to him. "Care to walk with me? I'll point out the constellations."

He studied her for a long moment, as if weighing his decision, then stood and took her hand. "I think Byron might be right."

They began to walk. "About what?"

"All men falling in love with you."

She laughed. "It's just an illusion, Alek, nothing more."

He stopped and turned toward her. Pushing her hair away from her face, he murmured, "I'm glad Byron brought you here."

She held his gaze for a long moment and then, just to see if she could, she went up on her tiptoes and kissed him. There were no sparks like there were with Byron, but she didn't want to draw away from Alek either. The press of his lips on hers was nice, inviting. She wanted more.

He made a low sound in the back of his throat and dragged her up against his chest. His hand skated up her back to cup her nape and he slanted his mouth hungrily over hers. His tongue pushed into her mouth and tangled with hers hotly. He didn't just kiss her; he possessed her mouth.

Shock rippled through her. This kiss was so unlike mild-mannered Alek, the one she thought she'd been dealing with. This was not a scholar's kiss, or a gentleman's. This kiss was . . . savage.

Her eyes opened wide, but still she felt no need to pull away from him. His tongue skated possessively along hers, sending little ripples of passion through her body. He might not touch her heart the way Byron did, but he definitely made her body react.

Alek Chaikoveii was full of surprises, it seemed.

This kiss made her wonder what she'd started. His erection poked through his clothing, stabbing her in the lower stomach. She wondered for a moment if he'd push her back to the stone bench, raise her skirts, and take her right here and now.

The only question was—would she let him?

Her mind whirled in chaos at the possibility, but her body had melted into a low thrum of pleasurable anticipation. Her nipples had gone hard and tight and her sex had grown warm. The thought of him lifting her skirts, sliding his cock inside her . . . excited her.

Her question regarding her future appeared to be answered. Perhaps there was still time to rescue herself from the dangerous clutches of love.

His hand slid over her back, cupping her buttocks. He pressed his cock into her belly and then buried his face in her neck, kissing and nibbling at her skin until her knees went weak and goose-flesh had erupted all over her body. Her veins felt as though they were filling with warm butter. Soon she would be a helpless mess of need.

A frustrated growl rose in his throat and he gently pushed

away from her. He turned his back to her, rubbing his hands over his face. Then, without looking at her, he cleared his throat and said, "I apologize. You took me by surprise. I'm attracted to you and it's been a long—"

She touched his shoulder. "Alek. It's fine."

He turned to face her. Shadows masked his face, leaving her unable to read his expression. "No. It's not. First I was rude to you, now I'm kissing you like I expect something from you."

"It's all right, really." She swallowed hard, also trying to bring herself back from that surprising moment of lust. She laughed. "That was quite a kiss."

"It wasn't a nice kiss."

"No, it definitely wasn't."

"You deserve—"

"Do you really think women like nice kisses? Not all of the time." She held a hand out to him and smiled. "Now what was I saying about the constellations?"

Nine

❖

When she returned to her room, she saw that Byron had started a fire for her. It burned low, lighting the room and casting flickering shadows. A small part of her had hoped that Byron might have decided to stay until she returned, but her bed was cold and empty. She ran her hand along the top of the comforter and over the pillow.

It was probably better that way.

She undressed and slipped into her nightgown, slid her feet between the chilly starched linens and rested her head on the pillow. The path she'd abruptly found herself headed down was not a good one. A cliff loomed in her future unless she could somehow alter her path.

A soft knock sounded on her door. She rose onto her elbows in the bed, figuring it was Byron. A knot formed in her stomach at another thought that had been rolling around in the back of her mind, something she didn't want to face—how could she keep sleeping with Byron if he didn't feel the same way about her?

She called to the person on the other side of the door to come in and Byron entered the room. He walked to the bed, sat, and, without a word, bent to kiss her softly on the lips.

Something in her melted.

She should have asked him to leave. She should have maybe even told him she couldn't go through with the three-week commitment and left for the steam transport that very minute. Unfortunately, she found herself incapable of doing any of those things.

So when he pressed her back against the pillows, she went with only a sigh.

Her fingers tangled in his hair, her body heating from his aggressiveness. He fumbled with her nightgown, pulling it over her head and dropping it to the floor. His mouth closed over her breast, licking and sucking each nipple until a ragged moan escaped her throat.

She pushed his shirt up, her hands smoothing over the hard flesh of his chest and stomach. Touching him chased all her concerns away and left her with only need. He helped her pull his shirt over his head and she threw it to the floor. Good riddance. She wanted nothing between them, not even fabric. The only sounds in the room were their labored breathing, the sounds of material being discarded and their sighs.

Standing at the side of the bed, he yanked her to him, leaning over and covering her body with his. He kneed her thighs apart and settled between them. The bed brought her sex up to the perfect height to meet his pelvis. The rough material of his pants rubbed against her sensitized flesh, making her shudder with need. Her mind clouded with lust, she rubbed against him, begging him soundlessly.

He undid the button and zipper of his pants, grabbed her wrists and pinned them to the mattress. The head of his cock found her slick entrance and he pushed slowly inside. Her back arched and a moan of primal need ripped through her throat. He thrust forward—inch by devastatingly thick inch—stretching her muscles and filling her until all she could do was pant and moan. She spread her thighs as far as she could, welcoming him inside her.

When she opened her eyes, it was to find his gaze intent, feral, focused on her face. Leveraging his body on hers, he began to slide in and out of her. His long, wide length touched every part of her. He started with slow strokes that became progressively harder and faster. Pleasure poured into her, through her, so quickly and powerfully it dragged low, animallike sounds of need from her throat.

He dropped a hand to thumb her clitoris, pressing and rotating, as he thrust. A climax burst over her, making her cry out and grab on to him, the muscles of her sex pulsing and rippling, her body shuddering from the force of it.

On the tail end of her orgasm, he pulled out of her, urged her to the center of the mattress and onto her stomach. Understanding what he wanted, she moved onto her hands and knees and tilted her hips, offering herself to him. He paused, just looking at her. Then he groaned, covered her body with his, and guided his cock back inside her, thrusting in hilt-deep.

She gasped at the abrupt fullness, grasping fistfuls of the blankets, while he moved inside her. Harder, faster. Pounding. An exquisite pleasure that bordered the sweet, fine edge of pain burst over her with every inward thrust. She ceased being able to form rational thoughts, her whole world became Byron's body against hers, inside her. Pleasure became her ruling force.

Her second climax made her see stars, bursting over her like the boom from an explosive charge. Her hands fisted the comforter and she nearly lost the ability to stay on her knees, her muscles going soft as butter. Behind her, Byron groaned her name, shouted, and his seed burst inside her.

When it was over, they collapsed in a tangle, breathing hard. The blankets and sheets a mess around their legs, Byron pulled her against him, running his hands through her hair and kissing her.

"Let me stay with you tonight," he murmured against her lips. "I want you to sleep in my arms."

She shivered and kissed him softly. Pleasure that had nothing to do with making love rushed through her. "Of course."

He pulled her close and she laid her head on his chest, hearing the steady, comforting thump of his heart. "I'm sorry I was so rough. I couldn't help myself."

She wanted to laugh. That was the second time that night a man had apologized for being too aggressive. She lifted her head. "Sorry for giving me two incredible orgasms in a row when I don't often get even one."

He blinked. "What?"

"Did you think that the gentle, ineffectual men I take as my client-lovers are explosive in bed?"

"I just assumed."

She smiled. "They are not very good with women. That extends to the bedroom too. Once in while, when they're listening to me about the proper way to please a woman, they are able to give me an orgasm. But not"—she stopped, her smile fading and swallowing hard as she remembered—"it's never anything like *that*, Byron, how it is between you and me. They can't make me go animallike in my lust, or yell out during sex. They don't give me orgasms that steal my thoughts or make my knees go weak. Afterward, my body doesn't tingle the way it does now."

He brushed the hair away from her temple. "Now you're just stroking my ego."

"It's true."

"And the women you've been with?"

"Are better at it, for obvious reasons." She smiled. "Does the thought excite you? It excites most men, two women together."

His eyes went dark. "Of course it does. I am a man, after all."

Yes, yes, he was. Smiling, she snuggled back down against his chest.

"And two men?" His voice rumbled through his chest and vibrated into her. "As a courtesan, you've been with two men at once I can only presume."

"Yes." She rubbed her hand over his chest. "But only twice."

"Did you enjoy it?"

She shrugged. "It was nice both times, but nothing like what you and I just did. It takes the right combination of personalities for something like that to be truly successful."

"You need to be comfortable with them, you mean."

She raised her head to look at him for a moment. "Oh, I'm always comfortable with the men that come to my bed. They don't make it past my selection process otherwise. But I can't always tell by interviewing them how they will be in bed."

"Of course."

She lowered her head again, snuggling against him. The fire crackled and snapped. "I mean something else. Sexual compatibility. I never know when I first meet them if their brand of lovemaking will excite me or not. With a three-person scenario, all parties must suit each other. It's a difficult balance to achieve." She paused, smiling. "*Your* brand of lovemaking excites me, but don't let it go to your head."

"Which one? Both of them are swelling at the moment." He rolled her over onto her back and pretended to attack her. She gave a squeal of delighted surprise and attacked him right back.

Through the doorway Byron watched Alek and Lilya studying in the library. They appeared not to notice he was there at all. Talking, laughing about things that sounded like they had nothing to do with history, it was clear they were hitting it off.

This was exactly what Byron had wanted.

Her presence had sparked interest from Alek he hadn't seen in many years—at least interest in things other than his studies. It was a sign that in Lilya's company he was beginning to pull himself back from the grief-laced haze he'd been in for so long. Perhaps he was entering the world of the living once again.

Byron had been sure Lilya would have that effect on his friend. She was just the sort of woman Alek liked—smart, quick of wit, and not afraid to challenge a man in his way of thinking.

Yes, this is what he'd intended.

Yet, there were other ramifications of her presence in his home that he'd never anticipated—highly disturbing ones.

The night before he'd followed Lilya out of her bedroom, even though she'd said she'd needed to be alone. He'd been worried about her. He'd watched her race out of the house and had seen Alek go after her with her pelisse.

After that, he should've let it go and not spied. Yet, he had. He'd glimpsed Lilya and Alek through a window as they'd sat on a stone bench in the garden. He'd also seen them kissing . . . and it hadn't been just a peck. It had been a lush, heated kiss involving lips, tongue, teeth, and hands on each other's bodies. He'd seen sex in that kiss. Naked, undisguised lust. The level of desire coming from Alek had surprised him. Apparently his friend was suppressing far more than he'd ever imagined.

It had made him feel more possessive of Lilya than he ever could have anticipated. Rage . . . no, *jealousy* had reared in him. He'd had to literally hold himself back from rushing out to the garden, pulling them apart, throwing Lilya over his shoulder like some caveman, and marching her up to his bed and tying her there.

His bed. *His* Lilya.

That primal part of him emerging in such a way had taken him off guard. And it wasn't rational. Lilya wasn't *his*; she was a *courtesan*, for the sake of all of Joshui's angels. More important, this was why he'd brought her here in the first place.

Ostensibly, anyway.

Perhaps there was a part of him that had hoped Lilya would draw Alek out of his self-imposed punishment without sleeping with him. After that kiss, Byron was certain that would not happen. That kiss had possessed the promise of sex. It was only a question of time.

He'd managed to talk himself back into a place of calm rationality, but it still hadn't stopped him from entering her room once she was in bed and falling upon her like some kind of animal. He'd wanted to claim her, mark her, make her his.

But, of course, she would never be his. She wasn't made for that. He needed to tamp down this irrational reaction, accept it, and let things unfold as they would between Lilya and Alek.

It was his own damn fault. All of it.

* * *

Ivan checked into a bed-and-breakfast in the town of Ulstrat near Byron Andropov's home. His motions sharp in every way, he tossed his gloves onto the table near the quaint brass bed and threw the curtains open to stare down at the street below. Almost every establishment in this place bore the name of Andropov. It was enough to make him vomit.

His fists tightened on the fabric of the curtains until his hands ached. He hated that she was in that man's house. Her clients, the men she fucked at the Temple of Dreams, they meant nothing to Lilya and so they meant nothing to Ivan.

Byron Andropov was different.

Ivan knew about every single person who'd occupied Lilya's bed since the time he'd been in love with her, and although Ivan didn't want her—not anymore—the man who took her from the alley was not welcome to have her.

Ivan had cataloged every move Lilya had made from the moment he'd seen her on the street corner surrounded by flowers up until this very moment. She had been the only woman he had ever loved and she'd turned out to be a betrayer and a whore. When he'd caught her in the hallway with one of his employees, he'd been angry enough to kill her.

She'd protested the act, had sworn up and down that she'd been innocent, but he knew better. There was *no way* one of his men would *ever* have touched *his* woman. All of them had been handpicked by him and none of them had been crazy, suicidal, or stupid. They had all known that Lilya was special, the woman he'd intended to make his wife and bear his children. Touching her had meant death.

No.

A far more likely scenario was that Lilya had tempted the man into the situation and he hadn't been able to resist her. He'd paid for his lust with his life. That had been the easy part. Dealing with Lilya had been far more complicated.

After she'd received the beating she'd deserved, he'd decided that if she wanted to act like a whore . . . she could. Knowing he would never touch her again, he'd tossed her to his men and simply turned away.

It had been harsh, but she'd reaped exactly what she'd sown. She was lucky he'd allowed her to live.

He'd never forgiven her, but he hadn't been able to get his mind off her either. His heart was too soft where she was concerned. He'd even felt *guilty* for delivering the punishment she'd deserved. After a couple of days the remorse had been too great. He'd tracked down the men who'd taken her and killed every last one of them. Then, fully expecting to find her dead, he'd gone to retrieve Lilya from the alley where they'd dumped her.

Except he hadn't arrived first.

He'd stepped into the mouth of the alley just in time to see Byron Andropov scooping her up off the pavement.

His woman, no matter that she was soiled beyond forgiveness.

Even then he'd recognized Andropov as a powerful man. Lacking the ability to confront Andropov for possession of Lilya, he'd followed them, watched them for the long months she'd been in Byron's care. Ivan had seen her slowly come back from the dead in Byron's presence. One day in the park he'd seen her look at Byron with something far too close to love for his liking.

Ivan hated Byron.

He would have had him killed during Lilya's recuperation, but some part of him had still felt guilty about her condition. Stupid. Weak. But he'd felt that way anyway. Then Byron had left the city with no warning and Ivan had lost his chance.

That had been all right. Byron was gone, and as long as he didn't come back, he could keep his life. Lilya entered the Temple of Dreams—no big surprise to Ivan since she was a whore in her heart—and that had been that. He'd watched her from afar, controlling the clients she took. If she seemed interested in a man he didn't approve of, he would "dissuade" him. None of them could be too big, too virile, too much like Byron.

Then he'd received word that Byron had come back. Not only that, he'd taken Lilya out of the city, away from Ivan's control. And all the hatred had come flooding back along with a healthy dollop of murderous rage. *No one* took Lilya away from him.

She had been just fine where she'd been. A courtesan close enough to him that he'd possessed a measure of influence over her life. Now all that was gone and with Byron in the picture he wasn't sure he'd ever get it back. He didn't like change.

This was unacceptable.

He stepped away from the window and looked in the mirror that hung on the wall to his right. Smoothing his dark goatee with a well-manicured hand and dragging his fingers through his long silver-streaked black hair, he studied his reflection. Cool gray eyes—the eyes of one of the most powerful men in Milzyr—gazed at him. He wanted Lilya back where she'd been for the last five and a half years. Ivan always got what he wanted.

And he wanted Byron dead, once and for all.

Ten

The carriage lurched to a stop in front of a large area in the center of Ulstrat that was thronged with stalls of late-autumn fruits and vegetable, stacks of clothing and shoes, and other sundry trinkets for purchase.

"This is where you've taken me?" Lilya stared out the window of the carriage. "To the market?"

The driver opened the door and the scent of roasting chestnuts reached her nose. She inhaled and closed her eyes, drinking in the moment. She hadn't been to a market in years.

"I gave Mara the day off. I thought we could do the shopping ourselves." Byron offered her a hand, helping her out of the carriage. Alek followed.

"I think it's a lovely idea." She glanced around her. "This must be one of the last village markets of the season."

"It is *the* last day of the outdoor market. It moves indoors next week, but will be reduced in its offerings." Byron came up beside her.

She glanced at him. "We can find the ingredients for dinner tonight."

"Yes, but you'll have to prepare it. Alek and I both lack that particular skill."

"I would love to. Cooking is a hobby of mine."

He lingered near her, looking out over the stalls of vendors who had already recognized him and begun calling to him using his first name. It was a testament to his friendliness with the people of Ulstrat. The heat of his body radiated out and warmed her. The scent of him teased her nostrils and reminded her of the night before, how he'd brought her to a shattering climax over and over again. Just having him near her was a heady experience.

Dangerous. So dangerous.

Yet she knew she was in deep now, too far gone to ever come back. She wasn't sure what the future held. . . .

But she was pretty sure it included heartbreak.

Alek moved to her other side and handed her the basket. "I really don't want to hold this."

She laughed and pulled it from his fingers. He was grouchy about the fact that they'd pulled him from his study that morning. Alek rarely seemed happy away from his books.

"I'll take it," said Byron, slipping the basket from her fingers and giving Alek a cutting look. "I'm very secure in my masculinity."

Ignoring Byron's barb, she linked her arm through Alek's. "What do you like to eat, Alek?" The old saying was true, often the way to a man's heart was through his stomach and Alek's heart was buried deep . . . though she suspected the man's libido rested *very* close to the surface.

Maybe the way to a man's heart was through his libido?

He shrugged, his gaze roaming listlessly over the vendors.

"Don't ask him," Byron growled. "I'm the one with the insatiable appetite."

She gave him a sidelong look. That was for certain.

Alek shot him an annoyed look.

"Well, let's see what we've got." Lilya walked into the market. "The ingredients will be limited, considering how late it is in the season. Still, I'm sure we can find enough things to prepare a delicious meal."

She headed down an aisle. A man caught her eye and called her over to a table filled with warm wraps for the cold season. Perusing, she picked up and rubbed her fingers over the soft, heavy fabrics, inspecting their quality. She lingered on a peach-and-cream wrap made of wool, admiring the intricacies of its woven pattern. Just as she stepped away from the vendor, Byron laid it over her shoulders.

She looked up at him in surprise.

"I thought it would look pretty on you." He leaned in and kissed her quickly. Just that little peck made her body heat.

"Thank you."

Alek had wandered down the aisle, seemingly unconnected to the world around him. She motioned at him, pulling the wrap more firmly over her shoulders. "Is he always like this?" she asked Byron.

"Since . . . what happened, yes. The only thing that seems to soothe his soul is his studies."

"Why won't you tell me what happened?"

"It's not my place. Just as I never thought it was my place to tell your story."

She pressed her lips together, studying Alek's broad shoulders as the man drew farther and farther away from them. "He mentioned a woman in his past but did not name her. I feel strongly that whatever forced him away from the world has something to do with her."

Byron's gaze lingered on her. "Women always seem involved in a man's heartbreak."

She grinned. "Not if they prefer men."

"Ah, yes, but neither Alek nor I do."

"Well," she said, securing the wrap around her shoulders. "I can assure you that men are usually at the heart of a woman's soul-deep wounding as well. You answered my question, of course. Alek is mourning a woman. I just don't know if she left him or died."

"Again, it's not my story to tell. When Alek is ready maybe he'll share it with you."

"I think it's wonderful the way you respect his privacy."

"I love Alek."

She glanced at him. "He's a lucky man to have a friend like you."

Byron laughed. "Most days I think he would call me a pain in the ass."

They wandered the aisles, inspecting the vegetables, meats, and cheeses. Occasionally she added something to the basket, an evening meal taking shape in her mind.

As she finished haggling with a turnip merchant, Alek slipped a pendant in the shape of a butterfly around her neck. She stopped, surprised, and fingered the piece. "Thank you, Alek."

Byron stood a short distance away, his eyes suddenly stormy.

Alek pointedly caught Byron's gaze and said to her, "It reminded me of you."

She blinked, saying nothing. The degree of testosterone in the air had suddenly ratcheted upward. Apparently the men were feeling a bit of rivalry for her affections. She wasn't really surprised it had happened—just by the rate of speed at which it had occurred.

Yes, Alek Chaikoveii definitely *was* full of surprises.

In the middle of that competitive moment, some other unexpected sensation made the hair on the back of her neck rise. She went still, uneasy for a reason she couldn't identify. Somewhere near her, she felt the pressure of someone's gaze. Turning in a slow circle, she sought to identify the person watching her with such intenseness.

"Lilya? What's wrong?" Alek glanced around the crowd.

The malevolent sensation eased. She stilled, gathering her thoughts. That had been so odd. "I don't know. It felt like someone was staring at us, someone who meant us harm."

Alek took her arm and drew her against him. "How could you sense such a thing?"

"It's a throwback to my time on the streets. When you live that way, you learn to develop your intuition. It kept me alive."

Byron had come up to protectively flank her opposite side. "I'm well known in Ulstrat. It's not out of the realm of possibility that someone may not like my family as much as everyone else."

She glanced at the basket, filled with fresh meat, vegetables, and a few dried spices. "We have what we need. Maybe we should return to the house." She looked up into the heavily clouded sky. "The air has a hint of snow in it anyway."

"Good idea." Byron twined an arm around her waist and they made their way back to the carriage.

By the time they'd reached the house and Lilya was happily

cooking in the warm kitchen and a roaring fire had been lit in the hearth, fat white snowflakes had begun to fall outside, quickly covering the tangled, dead garden beyond the window.

While morsels of sautéed fish simmered in a pan behind her, she took a moment to look out the window and enjoy the scene. She wished she could be here in the spring to take that garden in hand, and the thought made wistfulness wash over her.

Of course she wouldn't be here in the spring; she'd be back in Milzyr and her time with Byron would be long over. There was a garden behind her house, but the thought of working it alone sent a pang through her.

"It smells delicious in here."

She turned to find Alek behind her. The fish! Hurrying back to her slowly simmering fillets, she tended them and turned the heat down a smidge.

Setting her fork on the counter, she glanced at him and touched the pendant he'd bought for her. "Thank you for this." Honestly, she really didn't think he'd bought it for her. It had been a way to compete with Byron more than anything else.

"A beautiful piece of jewelry for a beautiful woman. Are you feeling better?"

"Better? Oh, you mean from sensing that unpleasantness at the market." She shrugged. "Likely it was my own imagination."

"Or, like you said, your intuition. I never discount such things."

"Really? I would think that as a scholar you would trust logic more than some unprovable perception."

"I don't discount any possibilities. Life's far too strange to be sure of anything."

Smiling, she took a fortifying sip of her wine and lifted her glass. "Here's to that."

"Even three years after the revolution, those wealthier than others need to watch their step. There's a lot of animosity out there."

She set her glass on the counter and poked the fish again. "Byron seems well loved in Ulstrat, but I can see how he might still have to be careful. Blood ran hot during the revolution and with good reason. The Edaeii pillaged Rylisk for centuries, creating a gap between the lower and higher classes, impoverishing people. I know firsthand of that. The taxes the Edaeii levied on my father wiped out his shipping business and took everything we had."

"Ironically, I feel the inventions the Tinkers' Guild is releasing could do the same."

"What do you mean?"

He shrugged and walked close to her. "The rich can afford them and the poor cannot. It breeds hostility. Unfairness. Widens the gap the revolution was meant to close."

She pressed her lips together. Somewhere along the line she'd gone from being a have-not to a have, and the lines became harder to see when one sat on the privileged side of them. "You're right, but the possibility never occurred to me."

"It's occurred to Gregorio Vikhin. We'll see what he has to say about it."

"If anyone can affect change in Rylisk, it's Gregorio." Indeed, he'd been the father of the revolution. She pulled the pan of fish off the cooking surface and checked the vegetables. "Dinner is ready."

"Fantastic. I'm starving."

She smiled, but her smile faded when she saw the look on his face. The hunger in his eyes seemed to have nothing to do with food.

He moved toward her, twining a hand around her waist and bringing his head close to hers. She stiffened as his lips pressed to hers, wondering what he would do, but this kiss lacked the desperate heat of the one in the garden and she relaxed.

Threading her fingers through the hair at his nape, she tilted her head a little for a better angle and kissed him back with interest.

Byron's voice came from the corridor and they broke the kiss and backed away from each other almost guiltily.

Silly. They had nothing to feel guilty about.

Alek took the bowl of vegetables and she slid the fish onto a platter to serve . . . her hands shaking.

Ivan stood outside the Andropov family estate, snowflakes catching in his eyelashes, melting on his cheeks, and dropping onto the wool of his long coat. The place was immense and rich-looking—*of course*. Nothing Andropov owned was ever second best.

Thick, gray stone walls marked the edges of the property, matching the gray stone of the house. In the warmer months Ivan felt certain the grass and gardens were lush and green, not the dead tangle they were now.

Lights flickered from inside the mansion, marking the places in the huge structure where Byron, Lilya, and that other man were likely spending most of their time. It looked cozy—nice.

Lilya didn't deserve *nice*.

He'd followed them to the market that morning and had seen there was not just one man in the house with Lilya, but two. The other man was of an age with Byron, good-looking. Ivan doubted he was low-born. Not judging by the way he dressed or carried himself.

More than likely his companion was Alek Chaikoveii, Andropov's closest friend. He hadn't brought any of his men with him to do legwork for him, but that was no matter. If one had enough money, one could find out anything. He would have the man's identity verified by tomorrow.

Maybe there was more than just one man for him to kill.

Eleven

"So what are we studying today?" Lilya tried not to smile as she flipped open the book they'd been working from and peered over the rim of the reading glasses she'd found in Byron's room.

Alek looked up from the book he was reading, stared, and then burst out laughing.

"What's wrong?" The picture of innocence, she looked up at him through the glasses that made everything look a little hazy. "Why are you laughing?" Unable to hold it in, she laughed herself, and then she snorted. *Loud*. Her hand flew to her mouth. She paused, arrested with surprise for a moment, and then burst into fresh laughter.

Alek laughed harder.

They both dissolved into helpless mirth that fed off each other's reactions. It was the kind of laugh that comes from a small thing and ends up inexplicably big, feeding an emotional delight that washes away stress. The kind of cathartic laughter that's difficult to stop. It felt really, really good and she realized she'd needed it as much as Alek.

The glasses teetered on the tip of her nose. They fell off and she caught them before they could hit the table and break.

Finally, they both calmed. He picked up the glasses. "These are way too big for you. Byron's got a huge head. You looked like an owl."

She smiled. She'd been trying to get a laugh out of him and she'd succeeded with interest. It was a good sign that such a simple, silly thing had drawn amusement from him. "I can't see out of them either. I was trying to look more like you is all."

He set the glasses aside. "What a pity. Don't do that. I think you're pretty."

"Thank you." She tapped the book. "Seriously, now, what are we studying?"

"Let's see." He looked down at the book and began to thumb through pages.

Just then Byron walked into the room. "I'm headed into town for a few things."

"Byron, why don't you hire someone to do that?" asked Alek, not looking up from the book. "You'd be providing jobs for people who could use the work."

Lilya lightly hit Alek's upper arm. "That's exactly what I told him!"

"I'd rather do things myself and maintain my privacy. I'll be back later." He leaned over and kissed Lilya's cheek, which made her flush with pleasure. "I gave Mara the night off again. Since you cooked last night, I'm cooking dinner tonight."

Alek groaned.

Byron laughed as he left the room. "I'm not *that* bad."

"Yes, you are," Alek called.

The front door slammed a moment later.

Lilya watched Alek, who was still thumbing through the book, and chewed the edge of her thumbnail. "Is he really that bad?"

Alek looked up at her. "I hope you brought indigestion medicine with you."

She winced. "He just doesn't know it?"

"No and I humor him . . . mostly." He shrugged and looked down at the book again. "He tries."

"Do you think the reason he doesn't hire servants is really because he values his privacy so much?"

"It's that, but it's also a measure of his manliness."

She nodded. "I suspected as much. He thinks a man should do everything for himself. Typical of a man like Byron, though not typical of a wealthy person."

"True." Alek nodded. Then stabbed the book with his finger. "Here we are, the rise of the Edaeii family and the decline of magick. It's a fascinating period of Ryliskian history. We can take a look at this."

She crowded nearer to him and looked down at the book. He was very close to her. Every day he seemed to grow closer. Now his arm was right next to hers. It was nice. Alek had a beautiful body; that was clear enough from the way it moved beneath his clothes.

She looked up at him, remembering what she'd been meaning to ask. "Alek, speaking of behaviors not typical of wealthy men, why aren't you and Byron skinny and weak-looking?"

He looked up at her, blinking behind his glasses. "Excuse me?"

"You and Byron both come from wealthy families. It's not as

if you have to do physical labor to survive. And neither of you, as far as I know, were ever in the guard or trained as soldiers. Byron is doing a lot of work around this house, which could explain his build, but *you* I am especially perplexed by, since you spend all your time with books. So, by all expectations, you both shouldn't be as"—she eyed his upper arms— "*robust* as you are."

He gave a short laugh and took off his glasses, setting them aside to rub the bridge of his nose. "Your honesty can be very astringent sometimes, Lilya."

"I'm giving you a compliment."

"I'm glad you think we're robust and I'm very glad you don't think we're . . . what did you say . . . 'skinny and weak-looking'? The reason we're in shape is crossball. Byron and I play it almost every week. And you probably haven't seen it yet, but Byron has a room here in the house with equipment that helps us to stay in shape so we can compete physically. There's a crossball team here in Ulstrat that we both play for. In fact, the Andropov family built the stadium."

She nodded. "That makes sense. Nature is rarely so kind as to bestow bodies like yours for free. I figured there had to be a reason behind your builds."

His lips twisted. "Yet we're still the idle rich, playing games with our massive amounts of free time."

"Crossball is entirely respectable. It's a game played across all the social spectrums. I would even go so far as to say it brings the low- and high-born together."

"I would say that as well." He looked down at the book, and then slammed it shut. "Come on, I'll show you the sport room."

The room was on the same floor as the library, but the house was so huge she'd never noticed it before. The vast space was filled with machines, the likes of which she'd only ever seen in the Tinkers' Guild. The machines were set up with pulleys and ropes, all with weights attached. She wandered around, running her fingers over the metal. Some had places to sit, others didn't. A close examination let her see that each of the machines helped to work a different part of the anatomy.

She turned to him. "This one exercises the upper body?"

Alek nodded. "Very good. You can tell that just by looking at it?"

Turning back to the contraption, she murmured, "I've never seen such a wonderful thing before."

"Byron designed and constructed all of them."

She glanced at him, surprised.

"Yes." He grinned. "He's not just the *idle rich*, he's got a sharp mind."

"How did he think to do such a thing?"

"He never told you? Long ago he went to the university to study medicine. He never did become a doctor, but he was enrolled in the program for some time. While there, we began to play crossball, but we couldn't compete against some of the other players who came from harder-working backgrounds. They were bigger and stronger than us. One day Byron read a treatise on rehabilitating the injured, written by an enterprising physician who had his patients working with weights. Byron thought that might be a solution for us in regard to playing crossball."

She smiled and glanced at him while she wandered the room. "Hmmm, yes. I see his mind was very much on his studies."

Alek laughed. "That's why he left the university. He never felt the fire for study the way I do. I think he only went because his father wanted him to explore paths other than the family mining business. Byron wanted to move, do things, and invent things. So he created these. They work very well."

"Has he ever considered submitting his designs to the Tinkers' Guild?"

Alek frowned. "I don't know if he's ever considered it seriously. He's got more money than god already."

She walked to another machine and tugged a pulley. It was far too much weight for her to handle. "There are reasons to do things other than money. These could benefit people. He could submit his designs, have the tinkers create the equipment, and donate the money to charity."

"Perhaps. You should present the idea to him." He walked over and motioned to the contraption. "Would you like to try it?"

"Try it? Me?" She glanced at him and shook her head. "I'm not exactly dressed for it, and these weights are far too heavy for me."

"They're adjustable. Go on, sit down." He motioned to the padded seat.

She sank onto it, feeling a little ridiculous with her skirts billowing around her legs, and took the handles at the ends of the pulleys into her hands. Behind her, Alek did something with the weights. She could hear them clanking together.

"There, that's only three stone. You should be able to lift that."

She extended her arms down and the weight behind her came up. Surprised and pleased, she beamed up at him. "This is fun."

"If you're working with these machines, you start out at a low weight—perhaps three stone—and work your way up. Little by little your muscles grow stronger."

She slowly pulled down and let the weight draw the rope back over and over, enjoying the motion and feeling the muscles of her back working. "How much weight can you and Byron pull?"

"We're both at two hundred sixty stone at the moment."

The pulleys slipped out of her hands and the weight slammed down on the others with a clank. "That's more than twice what I weigh!"

Alek grinned. "We're very serious about crossball."

"Maybe I can watch you play sometime."

"We have a game coming up soon, so I'm sure you'll be able to." He peered at the pulley ropes. "They're tangled. Let me fix it." He leaned in near her, so close she could feel his body heat and inhale the scent that was wholly Alek—a mixture of his aftershave and a touch of tobacco, which he enjoyed in the evenings after dinner.

She reached up and slid her hand around his neck. He immediately stilled. Leaning in, she closed her eyes and inhaled deeply. He smelled so good, almost as good as Byron.

When she opened her eyes, she found him looking at her intently. His eyes were dark and full of want. This was probably the way his eyes had looked that night in the garden, when he'd kissed her so savagely. Barely banked lust shone on his face, from need long repressed.

He kissed her, bringing his mouth close to hers and barely brushing his lips over hers. It was soft, just a tasting, more like the kiss in the kitchen than the one in the garden. His breath felt hot against her lips and she felt him shiver against her.

His arms came around her and he pulled her off the machine, laying her on the carpeted floor. Propped on one elbow beside her, he stared down into her face for a long moment. His expression seemed tormented—as if he wanted to resist her, but couldn't. It was flattering, yet perplexing. Was it the mysterious woman in his past that caused so much emotional tumult in him?

Lilya wished this woman would butt out because she wanted Alek to kiss her.

Finally he lost whatever internal battle he fought and lowered his head to hers. This time his mouth came down harder on hers, hungrier. His lips slipped over hers, searching, becoming more demanding.

She responded, her hands coming up to twine through his hair and cup his face. His body came down over her, his thigh easing between her legs with a rustle of the fabric of her skirts. His mouth, hot and demanding, slanted across her lips and forced them open so he could slip his tongue within.

Her hands slid over his upper arms, across his back. She loved the sensation of the hard curves of his body under her hands and the warmth of his skin. Yet she sensed resistance in him. He'd sealed his mouth to hers, but he held his body away as if he endeavored to maintain control. He wasn't succeeding. She also sensed he was only a breath away from giving in to what he wanted to take from her.

This war that raged so violently within him perplexed her. What was it that held him back? What internal dialogue took place in his head that kept him from giving in to the primal urges that all men possessed? Lilya felt that if she was to help him, she needed to force him past that barrier.

Why she wanted to help him remained a mystery. It was Byron, she supposed. He'd asked and that was enough.

She moved under Alek, wrapping her arms more firmly around him as he sought to part her lips and slip between them. His tongue brushed hers hungrily and he made a low sound in the back of his throat that made her body warm. Soon all concerns of Alek's resistance and her desire to help him were washed away in a flood of rising need.

All of a sudden, he pushed up and away from her in one powerful move. He stood and whirled away, giving her his back. Breathing hard, Lilya pushed up on her elbows. "Alek?"

He didn't answer her.

She pushed to her feet and walked to him. Reaching out, she almost placed her hand on his shoulder, but stopped herself at the last moment. "Alek, what's wrong? Please talk to me."

He turned and walked past her, toward the door. "Byron should be back soon. It will be time for dinner."

Then he was gone.

Dinner was as bad as Alek had said it would be.

Lilya swallowed a bite of something that resembled shepherd's pie, but tasted nothing like it. There were vegetables, she was fairly certain. Maybe bits of meat? "Mmm, good."

"Don't lie, Lilya," said Alek with a good-natured smile. He seemed to be back to his old self after the incident in the sport room.

"I'm not lying. It's . . . very interesting." She coughed. "Texturewise."

Byron gave her an arch look. "Do you know what it is?"

She looked down at her fork as if it might tell her. "Uhm."

"It's beef stew." He grimaced at his own plate. "It's not very good, is it? Alek's right, cooking is not my strong point. I should have let someone else make dinner."

Lilya set her fork beside her plate. "Cooking may not be your strongest skill, but Alek showed me today that you're very good at inventing things."

"He showed you the sport room? Well, apparently need really is the mother of invention." He shrugged. "I needed something like those machines, so I created them."

"Don't be so modest."

He pushed his food around the plate. "I'd rather be a good cook."

"I'd be happy to teach you. Cooking is a simple pleasure of mine. Once I arrived at the Temple of Dreams and was able to prepare meals in the kitchen, I found a certain freedom there." She smiled. "Loving to eat was a big part of it. I hadn't had that kind of access to food since, well . . . ever. I gained ten pounds the first year I was there and never lost it. Yet I gladly traded a portion of my figure for a constantly stocked larder. It was quite a change for me."

"And a lovely ten pounds they are too," Alek interjected. He seemed jovial tonight. Such a contrast to the torment she'd glimpsed in him earlier. It had to be an act.

Byron took a bite and grimaced, forcing himself to chew and swallow. "Yes, I would love to learn how to cook." He glanced at Alek. "But I don't know how much time you'll have to teach me."

A secretive look had just passed between the men. "What's going on?"

Alek stood. "We have something to show you. A present."

"A present?" She couldn't keep the pleasure off her face or from her voice. Men often gave her things, mostly jewelry boxes, colorful baubles, or flowers. However, instinctively she knew that

Alek and Byron would be offering her something much more meaningful. She couldn't wait to see what it might be.

She followed Byron and Alek out of the room. They traveled up to the second floor, where her room was located. Just down from her door, they led her into another chamber, one that was situated on the far corner of the house. The walls of the room were painted white and two large windows on the corner walls overlooked the grounds. As in all the rooms of such a huge, unheated house, a fireplace dominated one wall. A white sheet covered the hardwood floor and near the largest of the windows sat a blank canvas. On the table near the easel stood a table filled with paints and brushes.

Standing inside the doorway, she took in the scene. When it all registered, she pressed her hands to her mouth, swallowing hard against an abrupt rush of emotion. In a flash she was ten again, walking into the kitchen of her father's house to find a tattered, half-broken secondhand easel, sheets of expensive paper, partially used paints, and a few cheap tufty brushes that must have taken her father a year to save enough money to buy.

A rush of grief that had long since been buried bubbled to the surface and she had to turn her head away and close her eyes for a moment to prevent herself from completely giving in to it. She could feel the pressure of the men's gazes on her. Sweet Joshui, she missed her father so much. The pain of his loss never went away; she'd only learned to push it down and away so she could function.

"Lilya? We can take it away if that's your wish. We never meant to upset you." Byron's voice sounded confused and concerned. "Are you all right?"

She didn't move or respond for another few moments, trying to gain a handle on her sudden, explosive rush of emotion. When she felt certain she wasn't about to completely break down in embarrassing sobbing tears, she opened her eyes and flew into Byron's arms.

He enveloped her tightly and she held on to him, burying her face in the curve of his neck. "Don't you *dare* take it away." Her voice came out hoarse from the tears she was forcing back. She hated to cry. "I love it."

She held on to him for a moment longer, then launched herself into Alek's arms. He seemed surprised by her gesture and it took him a moment to return her hug, but when he did, it was fierce. "Thank you," she managed to push out.

He kissed her temple. "We didn't know it would mean so much to you."

Taking a deep breath and clearing her throat, she backed away from them. "Seeing that easel and those paints brought back a memory, that's all. The memory reminded me of a loss. It's been a long time since someone has gifted me with my heart's desire."

Byron walked to the easel. "When Alek told me about what you said you would've done with your life had things not gone in the other direction, I knew we had to create this space for you. The light is very good in here and you have this wonderful view of the grounds for inspiration. I hope it's adequate."

"It's more than adequate. It's incredible. Thank you both so very much."

Byron stepped toward her, the look on his face serious and his blue eyes intent on her face. Somehow she'd managed not to let any tears fall. "You can consider this your space not just for the remainder of your visit"—he paused—"but for the rest of your life. I will always keep it for you. You are welcome to come here and use it anytime you wish."

The smile left her face and her words left too. She had no idea how to respond to his gesture. "Are you certain you want that? What if you marry one day, Byron? Your wife may not want a courtesan coming for visits."

Byron marrying. The thought of it sent a pang through her.

"I will never marry and you will always be welcome here."

She pressed her lips together, studying him fiercely. It was what she wanted to hear, of course, but life had taught her that she rarely got what she wanted. Things changed. Byron might very well meet a woman in the future and fall in love. That would break her heart to watch.

No, she would never return her after these three weeks were up. She wouldn't be able to bear it.

Byron took Alek's arm and led him out. "We'll give you some privacy to get started."

After they'd gone, Lilya stepped up to the blank canvas and stared at it, cold fear making a fist in her stomach. What sort of new mark should she make on that pristine piece of paper? It felt more important than simply a challenge of creativity. It felt like a fresh start.

Twelve

Alek looked up when Lilya slid in next to him at the table in the library that was now strewn with books and papers. Over the last few days, he'd been more focused on finding interesting tidbits from history to teach Lilya than he had been on his own studies. It was the first time in a long while that he'd been distracted from his work.

To complete his degree, he needed to write what amounted to an entire book on the ramifications of the Meteo-Orusian War of 1230, yet that endeavor had been tossed aside in his quest to please her. Her comment that he made history amusing to learn had clearly gone straight to his ego. More important, he was worried about disappointing her. A disconcerting reaction indeed.

She smiled at him, her face freshly scrubbed and rosy from her bath. "Morning."

The scent of her soap wafted toward him and he had to stop

himself from inhaling deeply. He wondered if she'd spent her night in Byron's bed, and he found himself unaccountably annoyed by the possibility. He had no claim over her. No right to be annoyed.

"Morning. Have you eaten?"

"Yes. A sweet biscuit with butter and a cup of coffee. Byron may not be able to bake, but his cook certainly can. I'm well fed and ready to learn." She picked up the book they'd been working from.

All suspicion that she was just acting interested in history to get closer to him had disappeared a long time ago. Lilya would need to be a consummate actress to be feigning her enthusiasm for the subject. She had a bright and eager mind. It was a true shame that her younger years had gone the way they had. Even poor, with a mind like hers, the university would likely have welcomed her with open arms. She could have been anything.

She pressed her lips together as she opened the book and found the place where they'd left off the day before. His gaze lingered on the curve of her cheek and her mouth. He enjoyed kissing her very much.

Of course, Byron had the privilege whenever he wished.

The house was large and the walls were thick, yet he was certain that she and Byron were intimate most every night. And the way they looked at each other—when they thought the other wasn't looking—had not gone unnoticed by him. For a woman that Byron proclaimed could never fall in love, she certainly looked headed that direction. Although the couple times he'd said as much to Byron, he'd shut him down.

Byron thought he knew Lilya so well; but Alek wasn't so certain. Perhaps Lilya wasn't as emotionally broken as he presumed.

Perhaps it was wrong that Alek felt a little jealous over the way they looked at each other, but it was only because he remembered feeling that way once. In an ocean of women he'd found one that matched him . . . and then he'd lost her. The ache of that loss was an ever-present thing inside his chest. The only thing that ever eased it was immersing himself in his studies. They reminded him of her. They provided him with an escape, a numbing balm for his aching soul.

"Alek? Are you all right?" A hand touched his shoulder.

He blinked and saw Lilya frowning at him.

"You went somewhere far away just then. I said your name three times and received no response."

He cleared his throat and looked down at the text of the book she'd opened. Suddenly he didn't feel like making history amusing for Lilya. Right now he wanted to be alone, immerse himself in the history books of Rylisk and transport himself to another time when his life had been lighter. Yet, he'd promised her. "I'm fine. Let's get started. We'll begin with this treatise on the Edaeii family tree. Do you want to begin?"

She stopped frowning at him and focused on the page, moving a little closer to him. So close their bodies touched. He gritted his teeth, but not because he minded the contact. On the contrary. There was one other activity that could take his mind off painful memories, one he only barely held himself back from initiating with Lilya on a daily basis.

She began, "In the middle part of the third reign of Queen Astrid and King Nicholas . . ."

Alek knew the words by heart, so he allowed her voice to fade away in his mind and he studied her instead. She was one of the loveliest women he'd ever seen. For her, probably more curse than blessing, considering the trouble she'd had in her life. But there was much more to this woman than a pretty face. He was coming to see that and appreciate it. Every new thing he learned about her made him want to learn more.

In a way, perhaps his love of study had transferred to her. She was a mystery he definitely wanted to explore.

He hated it when Byron was right. Alek was growing more and more enamored of this woman and not just purely in a physical way. Although, right now, as he watched her full lips form the words she read from the book, his mind was on all the physical ways he wanted her.

It had been a long time since he'd been with a woman. Years and years. Too long, perhaps. Maybe men weren't meant to go so long without satisfying their urges.

His gaze strayed over the milky skin of her slender neck to the bodice of her gown. She never dressed to show off her breasts. He knew librarians who wore a lower décolleté on their gowns. Her fashion was stylish but conservative. Maybe she understood that less could be more, that the slight hint of the curves of her breasts at the top of her garments made a man wonder what she'd look like completely bare. Her breasts weren't large, but they were more than enough to cup in his hand and lick. He wondered what her nipples looked like. Were they as pale a color as her skin, or were they rosy red?

How would her sex feel? Hot and slick? Tight and welcoming? Would she moan if he slid inside her? Could he make her come, and, if he could, what would she sound like?

He wondered what would happen if he touched her. Would she let him or slap him away? Judging from the way she'd reacted to his kisses so far, he suspected she would welcome his advances.

But would she truly want him? Or would she just be doing the job that Byron had brought her here to do?

In that moment, with his cock straining against the zipper of his pants, he wasn't sure he even cared. He just wanted her. He wanted to quit fighting the attraction he had to her and let go. He wanted answers to all those questions, like the scholar he was.

He wanted to study her in every way, but most of all right now, he wanted to study her in a very, very carnal way.

He dropped his hand to her thigh to gauge her reaction.

Glancing at him, her words stumbled, but she kept reading. A light blush tinged her cheeks and her voice sounded a little tighter than it had a moment before. Taking those signs as unease, he nearly drew his hand away.

But he couldn't make himself.

Instead, he took things even further. He bunched her skirts up, drawing them higher until his palm touched flesh. Her skin was warm and smooth. It made a light shudder of want go through him. He'd forgotten how a woman felt, so soft and nice.

She left off reading and swallowed hard. "Alek?" she queried in a trembling voice, looking down at the book.

He leaned in close to her neck and inhaled the scent of her skin. He closed his eyes, letting it waft through his senses. His cock was hard as steel. He murmured near her ear, "If you want me to stop, tell me, and I will. Otherwise, keep reading."

She did nothing for a moment. Then, licking her lips, she continued, "The Trivac War of 1692 was a turning point for the growing dominion of the Emperor of Haynes. . . ."

She'd basically said she wanted him to touch her, yet her voice still trembled. It fascinated him. She was a courtesan, but nervous about this encounter. Why?

Then it dawned on him. *Of course*. It was because he was controlling things. Because this hadn't been previously agreed upon and discussed. She hadn't planned it out. It was spontaneous and he'd put himself in charge.

And he wasn't Byron.

He slid his hand between her thighs. Her voice caught, but she spread her legs to give him better access. That was good; she trusted him. Otherwise she'd be shutting him out now that it was becoming clear just how far he meant to take this. He'd decided to stop fighting himself—he wanted *all* of her *right now*.

The silk of her panties brushed his fingertips and the heat of her sex warmed his skin when he slid them over her delicate folds through the panel of material covering her cunt. He found her clit through the thin fabric and stroked it softly, pressing and rotating, feeling it swell beneath his touch. Ah, he remembered this, how a woman became aroused. Her breath grew a degree heavier and her voice a tad huskier.

It was hard for him to resist simply moving her chair away from the table, ripping this little piece of almost-nothing off her body, spreading her thighs, and burying his aching cock deep inside her. That's what he really wanted to do, but he felt she needed this—a sort of tempting, a preparation.

He wanted her to desire him, beg for him. He wanted her to yearn for him the way she yearned for Byron.

Pressing and rotating the swollen nub, he teased her through her panties. Her words fumbled more and more and her cheeks were flushed. He could feel the silk covering her growing warmer and damper. She moved her thighs apart in a welcoming gesture.

Her chest swelled with increasingly labored breathing and he couldn't resist anymore. Moving his hand from between her thighs, he undid the buttons of her bodice, revealing little by little the delectable mounds of her breasts. When he'd reached her abdomen, he dipped his hand within and drew her breasts out one by one. Her nipples were the pink of a perfect rose and were tight and hard. He rubbed his thumbs over them each, wishing he could taste them.

He realized she'd completely stopped reading and had closed her eyes. Her lips were parted and her breathing came faster.

Leaning in, he nibbled the skin beneath her earlobe and was rewarded with a rush of gooseflesh. "Keep reading," he whispered.

After a moment, her recitation of the political effects of the Trivac War on the Edaeii family began again, if in a slow, stuttering, completely aroused and distracted fashion. Never had history been so erotic to him.

Abandoning her beautiful breasts for now, he found the waistband of her panties and slid his hand down, finding the sweet, naked flesh of her cunt. She shuddered and tipped her pelvis up, practically begging for him to touch her. He found her clit again and stroked it until her breath caught and she moaned. Then he found her entrance and pressed two fingers deep inside her, up to his second knuckles.

Now it was his turn to shudder with pleasure. She was everything he thought she'd be—tight, hot, and wet from wanting him.

"Alek . . . Alek, please. I can't read anymore. I need—"

He did too. He drew away from her, stood up, and pulled her from the chair. Dragging her up against his chest, his mouth found hers. He kissed her hard—lips, tongues, and teeth all at work, as though he intended to devour her.

His tongue forced its way into her hot mouth at the same time his body pressed her backward, looking for somewhere, anywhere to brace her.

Alek pressed her against the wall, his cock pushing into her stomach. Her body felt on fire from the need he'd catapulted her into. She'd not expected his hands on her this morning, or for his hands do such diabolical things to her body once there. He had known exactly how to touch her to drive her straight to carnal want. From his touch, her sex felt achy with the need to be filled.

He turned her face-first against the wall, making her gasp with surprise. Then he bunched her skirts up to her waist. She closed her eyes, her hands near her face and fisting against the wall. His bare hand moved over the curve of her rear, delving between her thighs for just a moment to feel how hot and wet she'd become.

Yes, she wanted this.

His hand slid around to her bare abdomen and plunged down her panties from the front, between her thighs. His palm covered her sex, the warmth of his skin teasing her. She cried out, her hands splaying in front of her to help brace her.

"Tell me to stop." His voice was rough against her ear, filled with barely leashed lust. "Tell me to stop and I'll back away right now."

"Don't you dare stop," she breathed.

His rumble of approval made the fine hair along her body rise. He found her clit and stroked it, making it go large and swollen against his fingertips—pushing her to the edge of a climax. Her breath went ragged and her teeth sank into her lower lip as she fought a whimper of need rising in her throat.

He found the entrance to her sex and pressed a finger deep inside, then two. She moaned and closed her eyes. Slowly, he thrust them in and out, making her soak his hand.

"What about Byron? I thought you had feelings for him." His voice was a low, rough murmur near her ear.

Her breath arrested painfully in her throat. "I don't know what I feel for him."

"You *do* know. You love him."

She shook her head. This wasn't something she wanted to talk about now. It was far too painful and confusing. "He brought me here for you, remember?"

"Yes, he brought you here for me, but this isn't about obligation right now, is it? Am I just a job to you?"

She swallowed hard. "This is me, as a woman, responding to you as a man. I want you, Alek. *Please*."

His reply was a rip of fabric as he rent the side hem of her flimsy silk panties. He worked his hand between her thighs, thrusting his fingers in and out of her, until her knees went weak and her mind faded into a haze of pure sexual need. He stroked her clit over and over until she nearly came against his hand.

Fingers sure, he worked up to her bared breasts. His hands were not gentle as he massaged them, rolling and pinching the nipples until she existed somewhere between the sweetest pain and the sharpest pleasure.

"I'm going to fuck you right now, Lilya," he murmured. "Up against this wall."

His coarse words made her prime for him. She spread her legs and tipped up her rear, waiting for him. The sound of his zipper and the gentle whoosh of fabric down skin met her ears, then he was there, pushing the head of his cock deep inside her.

He didn't shove inside; he was too large for that. Little by little, he worked his way in, stretching her muscles to accommodate him.

Breathing hard, she braced herself against the wall as he began to move in long, hard strokes, filling her completely, and making her cry out. His hand found her breasts and played, then dropped once again between her thighs, where he pressed and rotated her clit until an orgasm burst over her as if forced out of her.

It was a freight train. Sweet, powerful ecstasy washed over her, stealing her ability to do anything but hold on against it. Tears filled her eyes. She yelled as it overtook her body and she hung on desperately to the wall so she didn't collapse.

"I want to see your face," Alek said, withdrawing his cock from her once the waves of her climax had passed. He turned her to face him. "You've got the most beautiful eyes." His voice was gentler now, less filled with that sudden, mysterious anger that she'd known wasn't directed at her, but at something beyond both their reaches.

He smoothed his hand over her face and pressed his lips gently to hers as he guided her leg over his hip and pushed inside her again. This time he took her slower, staring into her eyes and kissing her.

A strong man, he held her up against the wall with ease as his cock slid in and out of her. His body rubbed her postclimax-sensitive clit in this position, driving her into another orgasm. Closing her eyes, she moaned as pleasure washed through her a second time. The muscles of her sex gently spasmed, milking his thrusting cock until his head fell back on a groan and he spilled himself inside her.

They clung together for a moment, both breathing heavily. It happened so fast and had been so powerful that Lilya could barely comprehend the event. Surprise seemed to freeze her words in her throat.

"I'm sorry," Alek whispered. "I didn't mean for this happen, not like this. Not up against a wall."

"No. Stop apologizing." She finally found her voice. Cupping his face in her hands, she looked into his eyes. "It's all right. I'm fine." Her body still tingled from their encounter. "I'm just a little stunned. I wasn't expecting this."

She hadn't been sure he would ever break through the emotional barrier that had been holding him from her. Once broken, the flood of desire had been alarming.

He pulled her away from the wall and she followed him to the divan. "It was too rough. Especially for—"

"Stop it." She pushed him down onto the divan and came over him, straddling him. Putting his hands on her still bare breasts, she kissed him, nipping his lower lip. "It wasn't too rough. It was incredible," she whispered.

He cupped the nape of her neck and his kiss intensified, his tongue plunging between her lips and tangling with hers deep in her mouth. His kiss was ferocious; it made her breathless. His hands moved over her breasts and his hot tongue found one nipple, then the other. Need rose once again in her and his cock grew hard, pressing against the swollen, aroused flesh of her sex.

His mouth still on her breast, she shifted and pressed the crown of his cock inside her. Slowly, she sank down on the long length until she whimpered from feeling so filled.

He groaned deep, his hands catching in her hair and forcing her mouth to his as she began to ride him. Moving up and down on his cock, he slipped in and out of her in long, deep strokes while they panted into each other's half-open mouths. The bunch of her skirts pouffed like a cloud of silk around them.

Straining, connected, they moved like one animal beneath her heavy dress, faster and faster, both plunging toward yet another powerful orgasm. When she came she threw her head back and cried out, the muscles of her sex pulsing and rippling around his length. He yelled out her name and burst inside her once again.

Then they collapsed together on the divan, books and papers on the table forgotten.

After it was over, they lay tangled together, breathing heavy. Alek hooked her hair behind her ear. "That was . . ." He trailed off and swallowed hard.

She gave a small laugh. "From that first kiss I knew you weren't the tame scholar you seem to be."

He kissed her. "It was you; you made me crazy with lust. Just watching you this morning—"

"Watching me read from a book about history?" She laughed.

His fingers stroked over her bare breast, making the nipple go hard. "Just watching *you*. I could have been watching you scrub pots and had the same reaction."

Her hand moved over his chest, wishing his shirt was off so she could feel his skin. "You seemed so hungry." She paused, not sure she should broach the subject. "How long as it been since you were with a woman?"

He stilled for a moment, even his breath seeming to stop in his throat.

Her hand rested on his chest. Had asking him that question been a mistake?

Finally he answered. "It's been four years."

"Four years." She knew there was something here but she didn't want to push him. If he wished to tell her, he would do so in his own time. "Well, I'm happy to be the one who broke the drought."

And this, of course, was what Byron had brought her here to do. He must have known that Alek would eventually relent in the presence of an accessible woman.

He kissed the top of her head. "I am too."

The room had a chill to it, so eventually she redid the buttons of her bodice and Alek built up the fire in the hearth. Then she snuggled down beside him on the divan. For a long time they talked softly and listened to the crackling fire, until they both dozed off.

Byron walked into the library and found Alek and Lilya entwined and asleep on the divan. A pang of regret clenched his chest, looking at them, knowing what they'd done.

Lilya's skirts were wrinkled as if they'd been clutched in Alek's hands. Her hair was coming down from the pins she'd put it up in, the loose tendrils curling around her still-flushed face. The buttons of Alek's pants were not done up correctly, nor were the buttons of Lilya's bodice.

Gaze lingering while his heart broke a little, he took a step back and sat down in a nearby chair, pushing a hand through his hair. *Be careful what you wish for, Byron.* This was what he'd hoped would happen between them, yet now that it had occurred—and much quicker than he would have ever presumed—a heaviness had settled into his chest.

He'd known this to be the danger by bringing her here. He'd

known that his feelings for Lilya might cause chaos with his goal of helping Alek.

Fists clenching, he stared at the sleeping face of his friend. He hated that Alek had touched her even though it was irrational and unfair.

Shaking his head, he stood. *No.* He had *no* right to feel that way. *This* was why he'd bought her here. For Alek, not for himself.

He stood staring at them. *What a lie.*

After one last long look at the both of them, he left the room, only narrowly preventing himself from punching the wall on his way out.

Thirteen

Lilya entered Byron's room after lightly knocking on his door. He sat at a desk near his bed, riffling through a stack of papers and wearing his reading glasses. He set the glasses aside when she entered.

She crossed the room toward him and sat on the edge of his desk, the corner nearest him, and drew a breath. "You need to know what happened between me and Alek this afternoon when you were out of the house."

He sat back in his chair with a squeak of the fine leather. "I know what happened."

She drew a careful breath. "I figured you might have guessed."

"I came back from town to find you tangled like lovers on the library divan, fast asleep. The picture was quite clear."

Her cheeks heated at the slightly aggressive tone of his voice. "It's what you brought me here for."

He reached out and pulled her into his lap. His hand went to her nape and he forced her to look at him. His gaze was hard, his pupils dark, and his gaze intense. "I thought so too, but I may have been wrong."

"What do you mean?" Her heart thudded in her chest.

His hand wrapped around her waist. "When I found you with him I was jealous, Lilya. No matter how irrational that sounds. No matter how unfair to you or Alek. I can't control my emotions where you're concerned."

She had to stop herself from smiling. Something in her chest let loose, a free, light emotion—*hope?* "You were . . . jealous?" she prompted for more information.

His gaze had focused on her mouth. "As in, I want you for myself."

"I want to be yours, Byron." The words slipped out of her softly and without warning. Truth, complete and total.

He pulled her head toward him and kissed her. Her hands rested on either side of his face as his lips skated over hers so slowly and tenderly it made emotion ball up in the back of her throat. A sensation she could only name as yearning made her close her eyes and send out a wish for this man, yet as much as she wanted to think he loved her—she couldn't believe that was true.

Not her.

It wasn't possible for a man like Byron to find that much value in a woman like her. He might want her for a sexual relationship, but nothing more. Surely not.

And she wanted more from him. She wanted everything.

*   *   *

"Add a dash of kerr." Lilya peered over the pot of gently bubbling chicken and vegetables as Byron sprinkled a pinch of the spice into the dish and stirred. "That will give the meat just a little sweetness."

"I've had that spice in my kitchen for the last three months and didn't know how to use it."

"Now you do." She gave him a tight smile.

After that exchange in his bedroom, she wasn't sure how to act around him. She wasn't sure what he expected from her now—and what she could expect from him. The comment he'd made had changed the rules and fed the spark of the fantasy that burned in her heart—that perhaps Byron wanted her. Not just sexually and not just for these three weeks—but forever. Yet, as much as she yearned for it to be true—how could it be?

She looked back into the pot. "All right, let that simmer awhile to combine all the flavors. Let's check the bread."

He walked over to the baking cavern in the wall and pulled the platform out of the fiery innards of the device.

Byron was so wealthy that he could afford all methods of cooking and baking. He had the old-fashioned tools, like the cavern, that was fueled by fire and was good for baking and cooking some things. He also possessed all the more modern devices.

The sad thing was that he didn't know how to use any of it properly. She'd spent much of the day instructing him in which methods were best for which foods. Now he had an entire note-book filled with scribbles from her instructions.

To help him remember, since, obviously, she wouldn't be here forever.

She glanced at the loaf of bread with a heavy heart and tried to smile. "Do you see how it's got that nice golden color on top? I think it's done. You can pull it out."

"It smells delicious."

"It will be very good at the dinner table with the chicken stew. Warm bread with fresh butter. There's little better than that."

He shot her a grin that made her heart skip a beat. "I don't know. I could think of a few things."

Her cheeks warmed. And he could have it anytime he asked. She hated that weakness in her when it came to this man, but she couldn't help it. He crooked a finger and she did whatever he wanted.

Alek walked into the kitchen. "Is it ready yet? My stomach is about to gnaw through itself, it smells so good."

She smiled. "Is the table set?"

"Yes."

"Then let's eat."

They carried the still bubbling pot of chicken stew to the table, poured glasses of wine, and sliced the bread. The mahogany dining table was large enough to seat thirty, but they occupied only the end, nearest one of the fireplaces, making the immense room feel intimate and cozy. Outside the large window, fat snowflakes fell.

It was a cold and snowy night, and it looked as though it would get worse before it got better. A good night for fresh-baked bread, chicken stew, and good company—even if that company was a little uncomfortable for Lilya this evening.

She considered each of the men as they tucked into their meals, making sounds of appreciation as they sampled the dish. She'd slept with both of them, her skin had slid bare against theirs. Both of them had kissed her, touched her, whispered sweet and dirty things into her ear. Each of them had made her cry out in ecstasy, made her lose herself completely to the act of joining physically with them.

Never in all her dreams would she have been able to guess that this was going to be the outcome of this trip. With Byron, yes, perhaps she could have predicted it.

But Alek.

She studied him. He'd bent his reddish gold head reverently over his bowl, his full lips sampling the dish. She could never have predicted she would find the same pleasure in his arms. With Alek she'd fully expected to be able to retain herself, as she did with her clients, giving him her body—but not her mind, emotions, or self-control. Not lose herself. With her clients, she was always able to feel a little removed from the experience of sex . . . but not with Alek. In his arms she'd completely lost control. Worse, she wanted to do it again.

And, of course, she'd presumed Byron would make her lose herself. And he had.

In spades.

Sitting here at the table with both of them was a surreal experience after so many years of removed, calculated couplings with men. Byron and Alek had both made her lose control and that was a frightening, wonderful thing. For her, a breakthrough of sorts.

One she suspected might change her life forever.

Alek groaned and closed his eyes. The sound was almost a sexual one and it went right to the female heart of her. "This is delicious."

"I've never tasted anything like it." Byron swallowed down another mouthful.

She ducked her head and took a taste. It was good. "Well, no, you wouldn't have. It's a peasant dish from the time of the reign of the Edaeii. That is, when the peasants could manage to find meat to include in the stew. More often it was only made with vegetables harvested from their own gardens."

"Delicious, and it was simple to make too." Byron tore off a hunk of bread and slathered it with butter. Both these men ate a lot. She supposed they had to in order to fuel their muscular bodies.

She shrugged a shoulder. "I don't find cooking difficult, not when you have access to all the ingredients you need and a wonderful kitchen to prepare them in."

"Will you teach me to make something else tomorrow?" Byron bit into the bread.

She glanced at Alek. "That depends on whether or not my history teacher will let me have some time off from my studies."

Byron set down his knife with a clatter. "I'm sure Alek will agree." His smile at Alek seemed a little colder than usual. Her heart thudded. Was it jealousy? Did Byron fear another encounter between her and Alek?

Alek returned Byron's smile, but it didn't reach his eyes. Tension suddenly filled the room.

Lilya set her spoon down, suddenly not very hungry anymore.

"I would do just about anything for another meal like this, Byron, but you're forgetting what tomorrow is." Alek waited, expectantly.

Realization overcame Byron's expression. "The crossball game. That's right." He glanced out the window. The wind had picked up. "I'm not sure it will still be scheduled. That snowstorm is looking more like a blizzard with every passing moment."

Alek turned his attention back to his meal. "I guess we'll see tomorrow."

"I hope it's not canceled. I would love to see it." Lilya forced a smile and took another bite of her stew. She didn't want to be the cause of conflict between them.

The men relaxed and began to talk of the sport, their teammates, and the impending game. The tension in the room eased a bit, but not her confusion. If Alek came to her again, wanting her in the night, she would want Alek too . . . but how would Byron feel about that? Could his jealousy be great enough to make him wish for her to *not* be with Alek anymore?

Her jaw locked in frustration and a rush of anger quickly followed. Byron was unreadable. And why should she bow to his wishes if he only wanted her for sex? Her feelings for Byron might run deep, but she was no bought-and-paid courtesan. Not here. They had no contract and she possessed free will.

And there was the matter of why she'd been brought here— that impossible thing that Byron thought she could do for Alek with merely her presence.

When the meal was almost finished, she brought up the subject they'd been dancing around since she'd arrived. She put her spoon down, her bowl scraped clean of the simple, filling meal. "I want you both to tell me about your magick."

Making a disgusted sound, Alek pushed away from the table. "This is a nice evening, why talk about that?"

"Because, Alek, I am told that you possess a very unique and valuable gift. You seem like an intelligent and giving person. Why selfishly keep this gift from the world? Why not encourage it? Train it? Use it? You've got nothing to fear from the Edaeii anymore. Gregorio Vikhin and Anatol Nicolison are trying to construct a safe haven for the magicked population. You could be helping them."

There. She'd gone straight to the heart of the matter. Even Byron appeared surprised by her directness. Astringent honesty indeed.

Alek looked as though she'd punched him. For a moment he studied her, his handsome face pinched. Then he pushed farther away from the table, stood, and walked to the window to watch the snow whirl against the pane of glass. "You and Byron give my ability far too much credit. It can't help anyone; I know that firsthand."

"Alek—" Byron's voice held a warning.

Without turning around, Alek raised his hand to stop the flow of Byron's words. "No. I don't want to hear it again. You've said everything already and I agree with none of it."

Byron stood, his chair scraping on the floor of the dining room. "It's all true, Alek." His voice was loud, low, and sure. "No one could have helped her. *No one.*"

"What happened?" Lilya was sick of dancing around this woman, this ghost.

Alek's shoulders tightened.

After a moment, Lilya pushed away from the table and went to Alek at the window. From behind she put her arms around his large frame. All his muscles were rigid and she feared for a moment that he might push her away, but his body seemed to relax at her touch. "Please tell me, Alek," she murmured, putting her head against his shoulder blade. "I shared my story with you. Trust me enough to share yours with me."

She didn't want him to tell her to simply ease her curiosity; she wanted him to tell her so he could lighten his heart a little. So she could help him, if she could, heal some of the pain of this obviously devastating part of his past.

In that moment she realized she didn't want to help Alek for Byron; she wanted to help Alek because she cared about him.

He remained motionless for long enough to convince her that he wasn't going to tell her about the mysterious woman who had so broken his heart. Clearly, he did not feel safe enough or trust her enough do so. It made her heart sink since her trust in him grew greater every day.

Then he turned and embraced her, holding on as if the lack of her touch would kill him. His head rested on top of hers. "Her name was Evianna. . . ."

Fourteen

. . . With a smile on his face at her eagerness, Alek watched Evianna cross the green grass of the Aljorian Plain, mud clinging to her boots. . . .

They'd traveled all day from the university to make it to the Ruins of Ay. The light was failing and they probably should have waited until the morning to do their exploration, but nothing could have kept her from the ruins today. His stomach growled from a lack of food, he was road-weary, but there was nothing he could deny her, so there they were.

"Evianna, wait for me," he called at her rapidly retreating form. He broke into a run, his pack heavy on his back, and he wondered how she managed to keep up her quick pace in the rain-slick grass.

She turned to face him, hopping backward for a moment as she tried to keep her walking speed. A smile illuminated her pale oval face and rain had plastered her blond hair to her head. "I've been waiting five years to get here. I can't wait a moment more," she called. "You'll just have to try and keep up."

Her foot slipped in the grass as she turned. She caught herself, laughing, and kept hurrying toward the jagged mass of ancient, broken buildings that rose in the distance. She cut a beautiful sight, wearing, under a long coat, men's breeches, shirt, and boots. Her long, pale hair was caught up at the nape of her neck.

Evianna's specialty of study was the origin of ancient cultures. When she graduated she would seek work like this, traveling on the coin of the royals to distant ruins to dig through the rubble of long-destroyed civilizations, salvaging what she could and studying it. The university and the royals had granted her the ability to come to Ay as a part of her final project and she'd selected him as her research partner, not only because he was her lover, but because he had the most knowledge of Ay than anyone besides herself; Ay before the Kaulish had sacked and burned the city so many centuries before.

Evianna loved fieldwork more than he did and she would be doing much more of it in the future. That would mean she would be away from him for long periods of time, but hopefully she would always be coming back to him. Reaching into his pocket, he fingered the small box that contained the ring he meant to give her this evening.

They reached the ruins and he followed her inside, his boots crunching on burned and crumbled bits of the structures rising around him. Standing there, looking at the husks of these old dwellings, he could pick out the now partially blocked thoroughfares of what had once been the most prosperous streets of Rylisk.

Inhaling the dry scent of crumbled rock, he stood and took it all in. For a moment his deep knowledge of Ay and his imagination took him back in time. Instead of burned-out ruins, he saw a bustling, vibrant city filled with people. He could smell the horses in the wide roads, hear the chatter of passersby and the jingle and creak of wagons loaded down with items for trade, smell bread baking, and hear the echoing laughter of children.

After a moment it was gone and the city was dead again. The weight of the loss of this place crashed down on him. That's why he didn't like fieldwork. Instead of being invigorated by the possibility of answering old mysteries while sifting through the ruins, he always felt the sorrowful loss of a civilization. It had been so since his father and mother had died. Evianna said he was too emotional—and maybe he was.

She certainly didn't share his sentiment where the ruins were concerned. Evianna had entered one of the roofless structures, slung her pack down to the rubble, and was currently digging into it for her tools.

He walked over and stood beside her, wondering when would be the right time to ask her to marry him. He knew he was definitely in the right place for it. If he asked her here, tonight, it would be a story to tell their children. He wasn't nervous about her answer. She loved him every bit as much as he loved her.

They were made for each other. Everyone thought so, even Byron.

"I need to hurry to get anything of value done today." She glanced up at the sinking sun. "The royals didn't give me enough time to truly do justice to this place."

No, not even close. Just a week. He glanced around him. "Five years and a team of a hundred probably wouldn't be enough for this place."

Her breath hissed between her teeth in frustration. "You're right, but how do I get that boneheaded, inbred Edaeii family to see that? They give no importance to history, research, or science. They're even suppressing new inventions that could change our way of life for the better." Aggravation made her movements sharp. "All they care about is the glory of their line and their precious J'Edaeii."

"I have no doubt that one day you will convince them of their ignorance."

She stood and looked at him with that bright, determined light in her eyes that he loved so much. "I will. *I will*, Alek. That's why this trip is so important. I need to find something here that will impress them enough to let me come back with more resources, more men, and more time."

He grinned. "Then go. Don't let the bookworm stop you."

Her mouth broke into a smile. "Like I said, try to keep up with me!" Then she turned and rushed off, digging tools in hand.

Watching her leave, he gripped the box in his pocket. It was for later, then. Maybe at sunset. "Just be careful!" he yelled after her.

"I will," she called back, sounding distant.

She was already far away. Frowning, he dropped his pack next to hers, took out his own digging tools, and followed her. He knew she was a capable woman, but he still felt an urge to protect her. Plus, it would be getting dark soon.

He ghosted after her, helping her determine what parts of the city were the most likely to contain something of curiosity. Finally Evianna decided on a location and they settled in to dig while they still had light. In what Alek believed had been an ancient kind of cook shop, they uncovered a half-broken clay pot and a stone tool that had been used to spoon up food. Still, Evianna was not satisfied.

Standing, she shielded her eyes against the brilliant sunset on the horizon, searching for what she hoped was more fertile ground for exploration. The lowering sun had painted the sky in shades of rose, lavender, gold, and blue.

Alek clutched the box in his hand, thinking this was the moment he'd been waiting for. "Evianna . . ." He pulled the box from his pocket. "I have something very important I want to ask you—"

"There!" She pointed at the skyline. "Do you see that? Is that what I think it is?"

He slid the box back into his pocket and squinted at the horizon. She'd pointed out a flat place on high ground, away from the city. A cliff sheared away on one side of the plateau. A long stone tablelike structure sat silhouetted in the middle. He squinted. "It looks like a ground of human sacrifice."

She looked at him, beaming. "Yes." She gathered her tools and made for it.

"Wait!" He ran after her. "Evianna, wait. It's getting late and that area is far away. By the time we get up there, it will be too dark to see anything. Plus, we'll have to pick our way back down in the dark. It's not safe. We should explore it in the morning."

"Haven't you seen this place, Alek?" she yelled without slowing her pace or turning around. "It's huge! We'll have other places to explore tomorrow and if we don't at least make it up there to take a preliminary peek, I won't be able to sleep all night."

Giving in, as he always did with her, he followed. They found a crumbling set of stairs. After centuries of erosion they were no more than slight, broken jutting stones leading toward the sky. Only the toe of his boot fit on each one, forcing them to search the rock face for handholds as they progressed.

By the time they reached the ground of sacrifice, almost no light illuminated the world and they had no torches with them. Dirt marked them both from head to toe and Alek was certain they'd never get back down before morning—not in the dark. Sighing, he glanced around. A ground of sacrifice, no matter how ancient, wasn't his idea of a cozy place to sleep. At least it was going to be a warm night.

Then Evianna turned and smiled at him. "I love you, Alek." All the world lit up clear as day. The hardship was worth it if she was happy. "Do you forgive me?"

"I'd forgive you anything."

Once it became too dark to explore, she would calm down. They could build a fire and maybe then he could finally ask her to marry him.

Evianna looked up into the sky, where a full moon shone at the edge of the world, struggling to make its way to its apex. "At least we'll have her to light our way when she rises."

Uncertain, he glanced into the sky.

They explored the stone sacrificing table, though time had long since scoured away all the brown stains of the dead. The wind whipped wildly at this elevation and the bones of the destroyed city stabbed into the air below them. Now that the light of the sun was gone, the ghosts were out. Alek imagined the souls of all who had died here—it was thought to be nearly seven hundred thousand who'd lost their lives when the Kaulish had come knocking. Their hollow voices seemed to press in on him, making the hair rise on the back of his neck.

Especially here, on the ground of sacrifice, where the Ay had slit the throats of their own people to appease their gods and bring luck in manufacturing, harvesting, and fertility.

But those sacrificed had had no luck. Not in the end. They'd only had slit throats.

"Oh, sweet and blessed Joshui," Evianna breathed. She'd gone to stand at the edge of the cliff shearing away from the sacrifice stone. "Alek, come see this."

He walked over to see the cliff was not a cliff at all. It was the edge of an enormous pit. The lip they stood on was high, probably around ten stories. It was too far down and the light was too bad to see anything of consequence, but a shiver ran up his spine. He knew in his gut that if they went down there and dug . . . they would find the decaying bones of the sacrificed.

"A death pit," she whispered.

Alek's breath whooped out of him as though he'd been hit in the stomach. The implications of this were enormous. "What we thought was wrong. They never burned the bodies as we presumed. After they killed them, they threw them in here."

"Or maybe they put their victims in this pit wounded and made them die in there. I read a treatise once by an historian who thought so."

"No." He shook his head, examining the pit. "The sides aren't that steep. The victims could've climbed out."

"It's been a long time. The walls of the pit might have been steeper back then, or there could have been guards to keep them in, or perhaps the victims were too wounded to climb out."

He stared down, rubbing his chin. "Maybe. I guess we'll have to dig to find out. We could tell more if we found some skeletons buried in the dirt." Dead men, if viewed with an educated eye, told many tales.

"Yes." She blew out a breath of amazement. "We need more time. More men. More *coin*." She looked at him, amazement on her face. "We've found it! Surely this pit will be enough to convince the Edaeii family to give me what I need to do a proper dig!"

He hated the idea of disturbing the dead. Absently, he rubbed his chin. That's where he and Evianna differed, his sentiment coming into play. He knew if he gave voice to his misgivings, he would be met with levelheaded logic he could not argue against.

And it was true that perhaps they'd found evidence here to debunk all the current research about the way the Ay had sacrificed. Amazingly, they'd found it by merely stumbling around in the twilight.

He turned back to the city, suddenly feeling as invigorated as Evianna for digging in this place. What else would they uncover here?

It happened so fast that even to this day, telling Lilya the story, he still couldn't be sure what had happened. It was almost as though some unseen hand had pushed Evianna, though his rational mind rejected that idea. Perhaps she'd taken a step forward, toward the pit. Either way, her boot had slipped in the mud at the lip of the sacrificial pit and she'd fallen, screaming, over the side.

He'd turned and reached for her at the last moment, his fingertips only barely brushing the fabric of her overcoat but unable to grab her.

She hit the ground and rolled down the steep incline, coming to a rest at the bottom, on top of the decayed bones of the fallen.

There she lay, perfectly still and silent. He could only just make out the lump of her body in the murky light.

Just like that.

Alek stood for a single heartbeat in complete shock, trying and failing to process what had just happened. Then he jumped over the side and made his way down into the pit as quickly as he could without missing a step and tumbling down. If he was wounded he couldn't help Evianna, and he *would* help her.

She was fine.

His heart thudded dully in his chest as he chanted an overlain mantra in his head. *She's fine. She's fine. Just a little scrape or two, that's all.*

But she hadn't been fine.

Back in the dining room with his arms tight around Lilya, he squeezed his eyes shut, caught in the memory.

He reached Evianna to find her leg bent at angle that no leg should ever be forced into, the white of her bone bright white in the rising full moon's light. He knelt beside her and tipped her chin toward him. Half her head, her hair, and most of her face was sticky with quickly cooling blood. A huge gash marked her forehead.

He felt for a pulse and got nothing. Her skull had been split by the rock she'd hit.

Shock and fury ripped through him as he sat there in the mud with the body of the woman he loved cradled in his lap. The desire to make her well, to heal her, had been so great and so powerful, it had ripped his magick from him like the hand of Joshui reaching into his chest and squeezing his heart.

Light erupted from him, focused on Evianna. It enveloped her, illuminated her from the inside out, showing him the bones of her body, the break in her leg and the vicious, heartbreaking crack in her skull.

He tipped his head back and bellowed from the exertion of power. It bowed his spine and split his head. The roar of primal rage and the will it took to heal her ripped through his throat and filled every crevice of that forgotten city.

The magick was fading, the light going dim and then dark, leaving him weakened to the point of near unconsciousness. He slumped over her dead body. Evianna hadn't moved, hadn't been affected by that rush of magick in any way.

She was dead and she was never coming back.

Too exhausted for tears or even grief, fatigue and blackness took him. When he woke and found her cold and lifeless beside him in the morning light, that's when the grief had come . . . and it had never left.

He'd buried the ring box in the mud of the pit that day, after he'd hauled her body out. Then he'd gone home, buried his head in his studies, and buried his magick somewhere very hard to access. . . .

The room was quiet when Alek finished his story. Lilya had hidden her face in his shirt, absorbing every syllable of his story through the words rumbling through his chest. Tears burned in her eyes. She couldn't say she was sorry—that was far too mild. She couldn't say anything meaningful at all.

"My magick couldn't save her, so what good is it?" His voice sounded empty.

She pressed her lips together. Evianna had likely been dead before she'd hit the bottom of the pit, but Alek knew that. Alek also must know that what Byron had said was correct—it had been far too late for Alek's magick to help. He couldn't bring people back from the dead. No magick could do that.

Alek must have some knowledge of the limits of his power, but perhaps not much. He probably didn't know if he could merely heal a scratch or bring someone back from the brink of death. She presumed from the way he'd told the story that the incident with Evianna had been one of the rare times he'd focused and used his power. That wasn't surprising since showing off his skills while the Edaeii had been in power would have earned him a one-way passage into Belai.

She couldn't stop imagining what hauling her body out of that pit must have been like. He'd been all alone, grieving. She raised her head and looked at him. "Alek, I don't have any words that come even close to expressing my sorrow."

"I had to bury her up there." His eyes were distant. "I got her out of the pit, but there had been no way for me to get her down the cliff and through the ruins. Her family had been devastated that I couldn't bring her home."

"I think she would have approved of being buried there." Byron had come nearer to them while Alek had been telling the story. Now he was only an arm's span away. "She loved that place."

Alek glanced at him and smiled. "I think so too."

Byron gazed out the window at the falling snow. "She was an amazing woman. Strong, self-sufficient, independent, intelligent. Evianna never let anyone tell her she couldn't do something."

"Do you think she would have said yes?" Alek asked.

Byron laughed and Alek shifted, his body relaxing. "Do you even have to ask? She was completely in love with you."

"I think she would have said yes too."

They all went quiet. After a moment, Lilya stepped away from them and began to clear away the dishes. Alek needed time alone with Byron. They were, after all, best friends.

"I saw dessert in the kitchen," Alek commented, turning toward her.

She looked up at Alek and blinked. "Dessert?"

"Didn't you make some kind of sugary, chocolaty thing with Byron this afternoon?"

"Cake." She stood with a plate cradled in her hands. The tension in the room seemed to have eased. Perhaps talking about Evianna's death had been a good thing for Alek. "Chocolate cake. Do you want some?"

"You're asking me if I *want* chocolate cake?" Alek gave her a slight smile, but sadness still lingered in his eyes.

"I'll get it." Byron walked to the kitchen. "Mara just bought new coffee too. I'll make some hot water for it. I can do at least that much in the kitchen on my own."

She and Alek finished clearing the table. While they worked, Alek told her more about Evianna. How they'd met, what her parents had been like. Evianna Grusov had been born to a noble house that had originally made their money in the mining of precious gems. Heir to a vast fortune, Evianna hadn't been required to do anything in life besides make a good marriage, yet her mind had been keen to explore the world. She'd caused her doting parents heartache with her headstrong and unconventional ways.

Eventually they'd allowed her to follow her passion—education—and had sent her to the university even though it had been against their wishes. She'd flourished there, fast carving a reputation for herself as a female with an exceptional mind.

Byron served up the cake and the three of them talked more about Evianna as they settled in to eat it. With every anecdote that Alek shared, his shoulders hunched less and his voice and body relaxed more. By the time only crumbs remained on their plates, they were all laughing at happier memories the two men had of her.

After the dessert dishes had been cleared, they went into a smaller sitting room at the back of the house since it was a very cold night and the fire warmed that room more efficiently than the library. A large, thick throw rug covered the stone floor and a fire burned bright and hot in the hearth.

Byron had finally given in to the rational reasons she and Alek had given for the hiring of people to do work in the house, but they were like phantoms and Lilya hardly ever caught sight of them. They ghosted here and there, lighting fires, clearing snow from the front steps, and completing other tasks that Byron had been doing himself. Someone had built this fire to a roaring, pleasant inferno while they'd been enjoying their cake.

Around the fireplace sat an overstuffed, comfortable-looking couch and two wingback chairs. Alek took a chair and she curled up on the couch with her feet up. Byron took the opposite end.

A contented smile playing around her mouth. She watched snowflakes fall against the velvet black of the sky beyond the window of the room while an easy silence descended over them. The evening had begun a little tense between the three of them because of the edge of rivalry the men seemed to have where she was concerned, but they'd found a good rhythm during dinner, all enjoying each other's company. She was glad they had—she liked these men, both of them, more than she could remember liking anyone in a very long time. She hated being the cause of discord between them, no matter how transitory it might be.

The snow came down harder and the wind gusted. It was looking bad outside and getting worse, but here it was safe, warm, and comfortable. She snuggled back against the soft cushions of the couch and sighed in contentment.

"Do you remember the blizzard during our freshman year of university?" Alek asked Byron.

He nodded. "We were snowed in at our dorm for three days."

Alek laughed. "We lived on stale crackers, old candy, and melted snow."

"And you're laughing about it?" Lilya asked.

Byron put his hand on her calf. "It wasn't that bad. We had friends there. It turned into a big party."

"Still, stale crackers and old candy. Yuck." Though Joshui knew she'd lived on less for longer periods of time. She wouldn't mention that fact since the evening was turning out to be so nice.

Byron rubbed the tension out of the muscles of her calf. "Well, we did have a little brandy too."

"And whiskey."

"Oh, yes, the whiskey."

"We played strategia the whole time," Alek added. "Marko cheated, remember? Tried to steal a whole pile of coin from you before we caught on."

Byron made an angry sound in the back of his throat that made all the hair on Lilya's nape raise. "I remember."

"Remember Tamryn and how he used to . . ."

Byron and Alek took a stroll down memory lane and she rested her head on the cushion behind her, happy to walk along with them. Their younger years had been far more carefree than hers had been, and a small part of her was envious of that fact.

Her adolescent and teen years had been spent finding safe places to sleep, locating food, and avoiding the hands of men who wanted to use her ill. She'd been remarkably successful at the latter, up until she'd walked right into Ivan's clutches. She couldn't help but feel a pinch of jealousy that these men had gone to school, had friends, families to come home to on the weekends, and had never had to worry about food, medical care, avoiding harm, or finding shelter in the winter the way she had.

Mostly she tried not to think of those years of her life. They were a painful haze of survival in her mind, cut through with jagged tears of grief over her father's death.

She could remember one winter in particular as being bad. She'd learned during her first winter that scrambling up high and living on roofs provided her the most protection. She'd found the warmth-radiating chimneys of cook shops were the best places to make wayward shelters, and had stolen bedding from people's clotheslines to create makeshift walls and a roof that insulated the heat. If she managed to find the right chimney, out of the line of sight from people on the ground, she could go the whole winter in relative comfort—well, at least what had passed as "comfort" for her back then. Her standards had been low.

One winter she'd been ousted from her spot in the dead of night by a homeless boy who'd also discovered the secret world of rooftops. He'd been bigger than she and had kicked her out of her little hovel, down to the ground. When she'd fought him, she'd received a fat lip. She'd been lucky to keep her life.

Worse than losing her warm place had been the loss of her father's scratched, broken pocket watch. It had been the only thing she'd had to remember him by. The night had been bitter cold and she'd curled up at the base of a wall in an alley and cried for the first time since he'd died. Losing the watch had been like losing him all over again.

She'd almost given up that night. Despair had sapped all her energy.

But the will to live was strong, and she'd known her father would have wanted her to make it through. Finally, she'd risen on numb legs, knowing that if she didn't find shelter she'd get frost-bite, and trudged off to find some kind of place to curl up until morning. She'd survived that night, survived to build another hovel from scratch—rebuild, as it was. She'd never see her father's watch again, though.

The conversation had lulled them all into a comfortable space. Byron shifted his head to watch her, his eyes intense with the arousal she'd come to know so well. She returned his gaze, hungry for him, wanting to spend time with him, wanting to touch him.

How she wished she didn't feel that way. She would much rather have her customary reserve and control. Being with him made her feel like she was in a free fall, nothing to hold on to and only pain to cushion the impact.

Feeling the pull of another set of eyes, she looked over at Alek and found a confusing mirror of her emotions. She was coming to care for Alek too, in a slower and softer way. Her feelings for the scholar weren't as intense and explosive—although the sex cer-tainly was—but what she felt for him was becoming richer, more nuanced . . . *deeper* with every passing day. She found she trusted Alek, which was not an easy emotion for her to achieve with men.

Confused, she looked at the fire so she didn't have to face the truth of her feelings in both their faces—she was not only falling for Byron . . . but for Alek too.

Silence fell over the room as Byron and Alek finished their conversation and Lilya slipped into growing disquiet. The logs snapped in the hearth and the wind howled outside, buffeting snow against the thick windowpane.

She was just about to excuse herself and go to her room when Byron reached out and touched her. Her breathing quickened as he caught her ankle in his hand. He slipped one shoe off and then the other, and began to massage her foot. Her stomach clenched and then unraveled into slow warmth at the sensation of his hands on her. He moved up to her calf with his big, sure hands, massaging out all the tension until her muscles went soft and pliable. The entire time he touched her, his gaze, filled with erotic promise, held hers.

Fifteen

Alek watched from the other side of the sitting room, his pupils growing darker. Lilya wasn't sure if it was lust or anger that clouded his chocolate brown eyes. Was it that edge of competitiveness he possessed or was it desire? Either way, she felt something unidentifiable building in the room, like a storm gathering.

Her eyes widened as Byron moved up farther, dragging his hand over her knee and up to her thigh. Her breathing quickened and a haze settled over her mind as it did whenever he touched her. His motions were hidden by the layers of her skirt, but it was clear to all in the room where he was headed.

"Byron, what are you doing?" Her voice came out a tremulous whisper, an inquiry.

A glance at Alek showed her that his hands had clenched on the armrests of the chair. His gaze had narrowed to an intense focus on Byron and his hands on her. She now identified the look on his face as lust, not anger—though the two emotions seemed so often paired in him.

Byron moved up, his fingertips brushing the silk of her panties and delving between her upper thighs, rasping over her sex, which was becoming warmer and wetter with every passing second. Her breathing had deepened and her hardened nipples rasped against the material of her bodice with every tiny movement she made.

She had no defenses against Byron. He touched her, she responded. What he wanted from her, he got. It took away everything she'd thought she'd needed—control. Yet here Byron was, for all intents she could perceive, ready to make love to her with Alek as an audience . . . and she would let him. She would give up control to him and love it because she trusted him.

His thumb found her clit through her panties, pressing and rotating. Licking her lips, she closed her eyes, trying to fight the power he had over her and failing. Her clit grew under his finger, growing more and more deliciously sensitive.

Then Alek was there, unbuttoning the bodice of her gown and freeing her breasts to the gentle, warm air of the room. His face looked as tormented as hers as he lowered his head to her nipple and sucked it into his mouth, making a low moan rip from her throat. Her head fell back against the cushions and she closed her eyes, her fingers tangling in Alek's hair. The sensation of both of them touching her at the same time was better than Joshui's heaven.

Byron pulled her panties over her hips and down her legs, while Alek worked to pull her gown over her head and throw it aside. Soon she was bare between them, their clothing rasping over her skin and making her shiver.

Alek slanted his mouth across hers, delving his tongue between her lips as his hand roamed her breasts restlessly, brushing her nipples and sending little jolts of pleasure through her.

The question *"Why?"* was poised on her lips, but the sexual haze she was under prevented her from uttering it. Why were they doing this when each of them seemed jealous and competitive where she was concerned? Yet here they were, both of them touching her.

Wordlessly, Byron pulled her down onto the thick carpet in front of the fire and forced her thighs apart, dipping his head between them. All questions and wonderings left her brain and her body took over. Her breath came in fast pants as his lips closed over her clit, licking and sucking the sensitive, swollen bit of flesh. Pleasure radiated out in sweet waves over the rest of her body, making her shudder in sexual bliss.

Alek came down over her and laved and sucked each of her nipples to hard little peaks and soon Lilya was lost in a haze of ecstasy. Having both of them touching her was nearly more than she could handle. Her fingers caught in Alek's hair, the pressure of her impending climax building inside her. Her back arched and she moaned, lost to their hands and mouths, her hands skating over the bunching muscles of Alek's upper arms and shoulders.

Alek raised his head, his eyes dark with desire. "Are you going to come, sweet Lilya?"

Her back arched and her head fell back on a moan. The ecstasy of having them both touch her at once overwhelmed her.

Byron thrust two fingers inside her, stretching her inner muscles as his mouth sealed over her clit, tongue working. He knew just how to drive her over the edge. Her climax burst over her, sending waves of ecstasy through her body. Lilya bucked and moaned as she came. Alek was there to inhale the sounds of her pleasure into his mouth.

Once the sweet waves of her orgasm had passed, her fingers caught on Alek's shirt, tugging it off. She wanted both of them naked. Alek unbuttoned his shirt and she rose up onto her knees, running her hands over his chest, into his hair and kissing him. Byron came to her side and she switched to him, her fingers finding and undoing his pants.

"Please," she whispered against Byron's lips. "You've both made me insane with need."

Soon their clothes were a forgotten heap and their bodies moved skin against skin, Lilya in the middle. She felt incoherent, drunk on lust. Moving between them, she kissed them each in turn, her fingers finding and stroking their cocks as their hands moved restlessly over her body, across her breasts, stomach, and between her thighs.

Leaning down, she took Alek's cock between her lips, taking him deep into her mouth and stroking him with her tongue the way she knew men liked to be stroked. He groaned, his hands tangling in her hair and his back arching.

After giving Alek several minutes of pleasure, she moved to Byron and did the same, made him groan her name, his voice rumbling through him and into her. Back and forth, she moved between them, giving them each strokes with her mouth and tongue, while caressing the other with her hand.

Soon both men were harder than iron and practically growling with need. Byron forced her up, slanting his mouth over hers and kissing her deeply, murmuring how much he wanted her between hungry stabs of his tongue.

"So, take me. I'm yours," she murmured. How true it was.

He forced her down on all fours, her rear toward him. Knowing what he wanted, she slanted her hips up to give him better access.

He took in the sight of her, making a low, needful sound in his throat. "Is that not the prettiest thing you've ever seen in your life, Alek?"

"It is, and if you don't take what she's offering soon, my friend, I will."

Byron's fingers raked over her swollen, needful sex, making her moan, then delved deep inside her. All she could do was hold on as he thrust, her fingers digging into the carpet, while he took her that way for several minutes.

Alek moved to her front and she slid him into her mouth, working him with her tongue, while Byron replaced fingers with cock, pushing the crown deep within her. She was wet and very willing and he worked it back and forth easily until he was seated base-deep. She gasped around Alek's cock at the sensation of being so spread and possessed.

Soon Byron began to thrust and all their movements fumbled. It took all three of them a moment to find a rhythm—Byron deep inside her sex and Alek within her mouth. Then they began to move together, each one part of a whole. Every inward thrust that Byron made carried her forward into a mouth stroke on Alek. Together they found a cadence of pleasure that allowed all of them to give and receive, Lilya as the centerpiece.

Alek's cock jerked in her mouth and a hot rush poured down her throat while he groaned out her name. Once he'd moved to the side, Byron eased her to the carpet onto her back, spread her thighs, and entered her once again. His gaze fastened on hers with such intensity it made her breath catch as he pushed inside her root-deep. Closing her eyes as her body adjusted once more to accommodate his girth, her teeth sank into her lower lip. Alek watched them with dark eyes from his resting place near the fire.

Reaching up, Byron caught her hands and pressed them to either side of her head as he moved slowly in and out of her. In this position and at this deliberate pace, she imagined she could feel every bump and vein of his cock as he thrust. Every movement he made drove her closer to her climax. Her breathing quickened and her body tensed.

"Come for me, Lilya," Byron murmured. "I want to hear you climax again. I want to feel your body as you come undone."

Her body tensed and ecstasy rolled over her. Her body convulsed in pleasure, her inner muscles milking his thrusting cock. A hoarse moan ripped from her throat and she arched her back, toes curling, as it rolled through her. Her orgasm triggered his. Bodies straining together, they came at the same time, each of them sighing the other's name.

When it was over, the men settled in on either side of her, cuddling against her, their hands moving restlessly over her body as though neither of them could get enough of the feel of her skin. They touched her breasts, delved between her thighs, sometimes both at the same time, one stroking inside her and the other caressing her climax-sensitive clit.

All at once another orgasm stuttered to brilliant, startling life, making her buck and moan out her pleasure between them on the floor.

Completely spent and exhausted, she eventually fell asleep cradled in their arms, waking up only once, briefly, when Byron carried her up the stairs and put her into his bed.and then curled up beside her.

Lilya woke between two very large, naked men. She blinked, orienting herself, then remembered what they'd done together the evening before. Her body still tingled from it.

She shifted, noting that Alek's arm was thrown over her waist and his leg was inserted between her calves.

In his sleep, Byron reached out and dragged her close, nuzzling her hair with his nose. She smiled happily, allowing herself a moment to imagine how it would be to wake up like this beside him every day.

Or, better yet, waking up with *both* of them like this every morning. It was a nice fantasy.

Alek cuddled closer to her back, his pelvis finding and cupping her rear. He mumbled something in his sleep and brushed his lips against her nape, making her shiver. His body was warm and strong. He made her feel safe.

A smile curving her mouth, she settled in against Byron and let sleep take her once more.

Sixteen

Lilya trailed her fingers in her hot, scented bathwater, closed her eyes, and sighed. Running heated water from a spigot right into the bathtub was a luxury she never passed up. The Temple of Dreams still didn't have pipes, nor did the home Byron had given her. She'd soon have the wonders installed in there, though. Joshui bless the Tinkers' Guild.

The water eased away the pleasant ache in her body left over from the night before. It had not been the first time she'd been with two men at the same time, but it had never been like that, so intense . . . never when she'd been so emotionally invested. It had made the experience exceptionally pleasurable.

This morning it frightened her to the center of all she was. These men were changing her, changing her life. She'd spent so long clawing her way back from her attack to create the life she had now that it was scary to see it transforming into something else. It was a loss of control she did not enjoy.

During the night the winter storm had intensified, drifting snow up against all the doors outside and making it impossible for carriages or even horses to travel the streets. The crossball game had been rescheduled and they were stuck in the house for the day, something Lilya hardly minded despite her edge of uneasiness. Not with these two men.

Her head told her she should run screaming from both of them, blizzard or no blizzard, before she got hurt. Yet her heart wouldn't let her budge.

Her eyes opened when she heard the door open. Byron entered the room and crossed to her, his face grim. She watched him move, appreciating his body under his clothes. He pulled a chair up next to the bathtub and sank down into it. He searched her eyes.

"What's wrong, Byron?"

He let out a slow breath. "Are you all right? I never planned for that last night. It just happened."

She looked away, down into the bathwater. He meant the actual sexual act, she was certain. He could not guess the turmoil of her emotions the morning after. "Of course. You saw clearly that I was fine with it." She glanced at his face and offered a smile. "It was exquisite. A little unexpected, I'll admit."

"It was unexpected for me too." He looked away from her, running a hand over his face. "I care deeply for you and I would never want to put you in situation in which were uncomfortable or that brought bad memories or feelings."

Oh.

She caught his gaze. "Byron, I was fragile for a time, long ago, when you first met me. I'm not fragile like that anymore. I'm not a doll you have to fear might break. Believe me, if I'm not comfortable with something, I'll tell you."

He nodded. "Good. And I know you're strong."

She dropped her gaze to the water again and played in the soap bubbles with her fingertips. "I'll admit I am a little confused, however. After you found me and Alek on the divan and deduced that we'd made love, you seemed jealous. You seemed as if you didn't want him touching me anymore, then last night . . ."

He rubbed a hand over his face. "I did feel that way, Lilya." He met her eyes. "I still do."

"Then why share me?"

"Because I care for you both. I see clearly that Alek is falling for you just as I predicted he would. I also see caring on your face when you look at him. I brought this situation on us all and I have no right to impose my will on it. It's out of my control and it's my own fault." He pressed his lips together, apparently deep in thought. "Despite the feelings of possessiveness I have where you are concerned, what happened last evening felt right."

She narrowed her eyes at him and wagered a guess that had been lurking in the back of her mind. "That wasn't the first time you and Alek have shared a woman, was it?"

"No. We've been doing it since we were teenagers. We lost our virginity that way, with one of the maids in his house." He chuckled. "We've shared many women, even—" He broke off.

"Evianna?"

He nodded. "Threesomes aren't uncommon in Milzyrian universities. We shared her in the beginning, but early on it became clear that Alek and Evianna shared feelings that went beyond adventuresome sex. A deeper relationship was blooming. The fun was over and I bowed out."

"I wondered. You both seemed to know what you were doing." She grinned. "The chorography, I mean."

"I never intended for it to happen, but it feels natural with him. I saw you, I wanted you, you seemed to want me back, so I took you. I knew that Alek wouldn't object."

She nodded and met his eyes. "And neither did I, all right? Not on any level." She wouldn't talk about the confusing tangle of emotion that clogged her chest.

"Sharing you seemed less painful than knowing you might be with Alek alone. It was somewhat selfish of me."

She made a frustrated sound and studied the soap bubbles fiercely. "You say those things and you confuse me again. I do care for Alek and am coming to care for him more every day. You brought me here to enter into some kind of relationship with him and then you—"

He reached out, gently cupped her chin, and guided her gaze to his. "You are free to do as you want with him. I have no hold over you, and I would never wish to put one on you. You control your body and the decisions you make."

She pressed her lips together, her eyes pricking with tears. The woman she'd been before Byron had reentered her life would have welcomed those words, but the woman who feared she was in love with Byron wanted a different set of sentences. She wanted him to say. *I love you. You are mine and no one else's.*

Sweet Joshui, she was a stupid, naive woman. She would never hear that from him and she needed to get used to it.

She dragged in an uneven breath and moved her chin, breaking his hold on her. "We'll see what happens between Alek and I."

"Whatever happens, I will accept."

His gaze drifted to her breasts, just barely covered by the top of the soapy water. She smiled at how dark his eyes had gone and raised an eyebrow. "Want to come in here with me?"

"I want to be wherever you are."

Her smile faded and her heart squeezed. He sounded so honest when he said that. She reached out, caught his hand, and yanked. Of course, he was too big for her to truly pull into the bath, but he came anyway, clothes and all. They laughed, water splashing over the rim of the bathtub and sloshing onto the floor around it.

His wet clothes rasped her bare skin as he sat up and caught her face between his hands, kissing her. "I'm glad to have you here, Lilya."

She smiled against his lips. Yes, and having to leave was going to slice her through, she could feel it already. This man had a power over her she couldn't deny. One minute it made her want to hold him close and never let go. The next minute she wanted to run as fast as she could away from him.

The latter reaction was the healthiest and most intelligent. Apparently she neither cared about her health nor was she all that smart.

The snow reflected the cold winter sunlight into her painting room and lit up her work area. It had been a long time since she'd put paint to canvas and even when she'd been younger, she'd had very little formal instruction. It had taken her two days to work up enough nerve to dip her brush into the paint, a day more to actually set it against the canvas.

She'd feared she wouldn't be able to do it anymore—not

the way she used to. So much had happened since she'd last opened herself up to paint, and back then, when she'd been a child, she'd been poor . . . but she'd also felt safe and loved. It had provided her a freedom she'd taken for granted.

After she stared at the blank canvas in challenge for a moment, she closed her eyes and imagined the scene in her head that she wanted to paint, cementing that image solidly in her mind. Then she opened her eyes and began to stroke her brush across the canvas, according to the picture she held in her mind's eye. Slowly, it began to take form.

Her father had always marveled at her ability to do this. He called it raw talent. For her, it had always simply been an escape. After her father had died and she'd been on the streets, she hadn't had paint, brushes, or canvas, but she'd had her imagination. She'd become good at closing her eyes and imagining herself far away from her harsh reality and, sometimes, depending on how much her stomach hurt, even her hunger.

She stepped away from her work, tipped her head to the side, and frowned. She'd chosen an alley of Milzyr to paint. Joshui knew enough of them were emblazoned in her mind's eye. This one was shown in the dead of winter, from one of the nights she remembered vividly. It had been one of the times she hadn't been sure she'd make it through. Somehow, though, she'd always managed to find shelter.

Someone knocked on the door and then opened it. She leapt in front of the canvas to block her work with her body, not totally certain it was good enough for outside appraisal just yet.

"I thought I'd find you here." Byron strolled toward her. "You've been up here since this morning. Aren't you hungry?"

At the word *hungry,* her stomach growled. She'd been so

immersed in her work, she hadn't even known she'd skipped lunch. "I am a little, I guess." She paused, repositioned herself in front of the canvas. "I've been working."

"Don't want me to see, right?"

"I'm not sure."

"I'm really curious, Lilya, but if you want me to leave, I will."

She chewed her lower lip. "No. I don't want you to leave." Hesitating only a moment, she stepped to the side. She trusted Byron not to criticize her work or belittle her in any way.

His face went blank as he walked toward it, taking in the scene. "Lilya, I had no idea that you were at this level. This is an extremely detailed painting. The angles, the shadows." He glanced at her. "Who taught you to paint this way?"

"No one. I've always been able to do this. When I was a child I used to draw on the front stoop of our house using charcoal. I don't know how I do it. I just see the scene in my mind and re-create it on paper."

He studied it. "It's beautiful and I'm incredibly impressed." His praise made her flush. "It's a little depressing though. Is this is a scene you remember from after your father's death? A Milzyr alley in winter?"

"Yes." She came to stand beside him. "But I don't find it depressing. I was just remembering back to how fortunate I was, actually."

He glanced at her. "Fortunate? I don't follow."

She shrugged a shoulder. "It's wasn't easy, living the way I did, but I was so much luckier than some of the others I knew. I always managed to find somewhere warm on cold nights." She paused, remembering back. "I found this little alcove on the top of a dressmaker's shop. She had an apartment above her store with a fireplace she used constantly. I set up a little nook there, near the warm pipe and shielded it from the wind with wood and old blankets I found."

"That's not luck. It's intelligence."

"Either way, I never lost any of my toes to frostbite. I was never caught and mistreated by a man." She stopped, swallowed hard. "At least, not then. I made it through. I survived. So when I look at that scene there, I don't see anything depressing."

He pulled her to him and kissed the top of her head. "You have a perspective not many others would have. I love you for that." Her heart rate sped up. He reached out and touched her nose. "You have paint all over you. You're going to need a bath again."

She turned into his arms and went up on her tippy-toes to kiss him. "Maybe you can help me with that."

His arms came around her waist. "What an irresistible suggestion."

She closed her eyes and sighed. Contentment washed through her like a warm breeze. Alone on the streets of Milzyr she may have been able to imagine herself away from time to time, but she'd never imagined being this happy. *Never.* If only it could last.

Lilya slipped down the hallway, headed to her room, and passed Alek's door. It was ajar, almost as if he was waiting for someone. She paused, considering it. Firelight flickered out into the cold corridor, licking at the paintings on the walls and bathing the accent tables and vases in its warm light.

Frowning, she tightened the tie of her wrap around her a little better and peered into his room. Alek sat propped on his large four-poster bed with his eyes closed. The firelight licked over the muscled plane of his chest and down the strong build of his arms. The house was frigid tonight, despite the fact many of the hearths burned bright, but she'd noticed that the colder temperatures didn't seem to bother him much.

Her mind traveled back to the story he'd told about Evianna. Her heart broke for this man. She could see why he'd given up his magick after the traumatic experience he'd had with it, yet couldn't he see what an asset his ability was? She could think of at least five people in Milzyr who she knew personally could benefit from his skill.

It was selfish of him to hold it back from the world, no matter how devastating the reason. On that point, she completely agreed with Byron. Now they just needed to make Alek see it.

Silently, she entered his room. He appeared to be sleeping. His glasses had been laid carefully on the bedside table and a history book lay facedown on the mattress beside him. Once at his bedside, she reached out and laid her hand on his chest, just above his heart. His skin warmed her palm.

His eyes popped open, startling her. Before she could back away, he grabbed her wrist and tumbled her to the bed, rolling her to her back. Dragging her beneath him and covering her body with his, he murmured, "Good evening." The history book fell to the floor with a loud thump.

The pressure of his body on hers made her crave more of it, hopefully the kind where both of them had their clothes off. Fighting to get her breath back, she smiled up at him. "Good evening."

"To what do I owe the pleasure of your presence in my room?"

"I was just on my way to bed and I noticed your door was open."

His smile went a little mischievous. "Ah. Thank Joshui I forgot to close it, then."

"I'm happy you did too." Her voice sounded a little breathless already and he hadn't even touched her yet. His presence seemed to have that effect on her.

He raised an eyebrow. "Now that you're here, what shall we do?" Mock innocence tinged his tone.

"I can think of a couple things."

"So can I." He lowered his mouth to hers and kissed her gently. It was change of pace from the Alek she'd come to expect. His lips slipped over hers, sipping her, until her insides felt warm and her knees were the consistency of melted butter.

She twined her fingers in the short hair at the base of his neck, her other hand sliding down over the muscles of his arm, admiring its strength.

His eased his hand from its resting place on her hip, down over the curve of her rear to the back of her thigh. Her wrap slipped open and his fingers found bare skin. He made a purring sound in the back of his throat and his kiss deepened into something hungrier. His tongue pushed into her mouth and stroked up against hers, sending shivers down her spine.

Making quick work of her wrap and nightgown, he soon had her bare beneath him. She pushed up against him, pushing the waistband of his soft cotton pants down until she could wrap her hands around his cock. He made a groan of pleasure as she stroked him from crown to base. Wanting to hear more of that, she dropped her head and took him into her mouth.

Alek went still for a moment, then let out a long, low groan. His head fell back against the mattress and his fingers found and twined in her hair. She worked him in and out of her mouth, her tongue exploring him to find all the secret places that made him react with pleasure. She liked taking men this way, especially ones that enjoyed being in control, like Alek. It was amusing the way a woman could render a powerful man helpless with only a few swipes of her tongue.

Finally, he rolled her to her back and covered her body with his. After staring into her eyes for a long moment, he dropped to worship one breast with his mouth, then the other, sucking each nipple into hard reddened little peaks. After transforming her into a panting mess with his lips on her breasts, he moved down, kissing her abdomen and the insides of her thighs before settling his wicked mouth on her sex.

Her back arched at the sensation of his hot tongue exploring her folds, he found her clit and lapped at it, making her moan out his name. His fingers found her entrance and slipped inside, thrusting in and out while he gently sucked on her aroused clit. The edge of a climax teased her, but he withheld it, skillfully letting it ebb away and build back up, making her crazy with need.

"Alek," she breathed, pushing up at him. "I need you." She went on all fours, her rear to him and her hips tilted up. She knew what she looked like, her cunt wet from his mouth and swollen with arousal. "Please."

He ran his hand down the arch of her spine, over her rear, and between her thighs. He speared one finger inside her, then two. Her breath hissed out of her. "You are so beautiful, Lilya," he murmured. "What do you want me to do to you?"

"I want you fuck me, Alek," she moaned. He continued to thrust in and out of her and she rested her head on her forearms, her breath coming fast. "Please."

He eased up behind her and set the head of his cock to her

entrance. Slowly, he pressed the smooth crown into her, inch by inch. Her head snapped up and she let out a low, guttural groan of pleasure as he hilted inside her.

Rising up onto her knees, she braced her hands on his hips behind her and rocked on him, driving his cock deep inside her. His hands roamed her breasts, teasing her nipples as he thrust into her. Together they found an easy, slow, rolling rhythm that worked for the position, their bodies moving like one.

He nipped at her ear and slid a hand down between her spread thighs to stroke her clit. He knew just how to touch her to bring her to the edge of a climax and suspend her there in a haze of heavy pleasure. "Are you going to come, Lilya?" he asked in a low, silky voice near her ear.

"Yes," she breathed.

He continued to stroke into her until she shattered. Crying out, she went down on all fours as the orgasm washed through her. He grabbed her hips and took her hard and fast in long, deep thrusts. Their bodies smacked together, every inward stroke jarring her. Her climax stuttered to a halt, then reignited, exploding over her and making her cry out anew.

Behind her Alek called her name and she felt his cock jump deep inside her.

He pulled out of her and rolled to the side, taking her with him. "Ah, sweet Joshui," he breathed.

She snuggled against him, her head nestled in the curve of his neck. Running her hand over the curves and valleys of his chest, she dropped a kiss to his warm skin.

He rolled her over and dragged her beneath his body, his mouth down close to hers. "Stay with me tonight. I want to wake up beside you."

She smiled. "I want that too."

His hand slipped over her breast and abdomen to between her thighs, where she was still very slick from the remnants of their lovemaking. He found her clit and petted it softly. She sighed, closing her eyes. "I love to make you come."

Her eyes fluttered open and she licked her lips, her body already flaring hot for him again. "You do it very well."

"Spread your legs for me."

She complied and he slipped his hand down to her nether hole, gathering moisture as he went. He didn't ask, because Alek wasn't the asking type. He just slid the tip of his finger inside.

She started in surprised. "Alek . . ."

"Shhh . . . relax." He eased in another inch.

All the nerves exploded to life, pleasure of a sort she didn't often feel radiating through her. She sighed and closed her eyes, giving in to it.

He eased in a little more, then added a second. She gasped as her body adjusted to accommodate him and the pleasure grew hotter and brighter. "Alek," she said again, but this time it came out on a low moan.

Readjusting his position, he used his other hand to stimulate her clit. Soon she was lost in a haze of ecstasy. Strange, intense pleasure tingled through her body, made her wiggle on the bed beneath him. When she finally came, she did it bucking and stifling her cries with the blanket stuffed into her mouth.

When it was all over, she rested against him, feeling completely satisfied and a little dazed. "My . . . *goodness*" was all she could say.

Alek chuckled and kissed her forehead. "And the night is young," he whispered.

Seventeen

"Would you like to come in to the university with me today?" Byron asked, entering the dining room the next day.

She set her coffee cup on the table and gazed out the window at all the snow. "Can we? That storm was pretty bad."

"To my knowledge, the transports are running. Alek already went this morning. He had classes. I know where to find him; we can take him a meal at midday."

"Why do you need to go in?"

"I took these three weeks off from the initiative, but I do have a couple pressing things I need to clear up if I can."

"All right, just let me get my coat."

They dressed for the frigid temperatures and took the transport into the city. Once there, they boarded a hired carriage that took them to the university. It was a series of buildings on a large plot of land that in the spring and summer was ripe with fruit trees and green grass. Now it was covered with a thick coating of snow.

The university had always been a bright spot in the normally very classist society during the reign of the Edaeii family. Any child showing enough intellectual promise could be allowed in, even if they couldn't afford to attend on their own, but the spots reserved for such students were extremely limited. Only the very brightest of lower class families ever made it. Gregorio Vikhin had been one of them, as had his sister. Mostly the population of students attending were like Alek and Byron, extremely wealthy.

Post-revolution the university showed a much more diverse body of students. Most of the noble houses in Rylisk had suffered death and destruction at the hands of the mob. Alek and Byron's families had only survived due to their generosity to their respective communities. That meant most of the student population was now of the lower class variety. Whoever could pay the tuition—a much lowered one—or who made it in via the lottery attended these days. Bloodline notwithstanding.

They exited the carriage onto a freshly cleared walkway that led to the main building, a large domed structure. During the revolution the campus had sustained quite a bit of damage, but it had mostly been repaired since then.

The double doors let them into a large, echoing foyer with marble floors and a series of hallways leading away to what Lilya presumed must be classrooms. People milled the area. Immediately Byron spotted someone he needed to talk to and excused himself for a moment, leaving her alone near the doors.

"Lilya!"

She turned at the familiar male voice and saw Gregorio Vikhin striding toward her. "Gregorio, so nice to see you." He gave her a hug when he reached her.

"Where's Evangeline?"

"At home with the babies. They're only a little over a week old."

"Babies?" She clasped her hands together at her chest. "She had them? Two?"

His smile could've powered the building. "Indeed. Two girls. We named them Anastasia and Annetka."

"Ah, Annetka." That had been the name of Evangeline's one and only friend at Belai, who'd died when they'd been children.

Gregorio nodded and smiled. "Anastasia is my mother's name."

"As Nicoli was the name of Anatol's father."

"Yes."

Well, the threesome seemed to be working out fine between them. Lilya was very happy for them, if not just a little jealous.

Expectations, Lilya, she reminded herself. Such things were not for her.

"Planning on having any more children?"

Gregorio laughed. "If Anatol or I even bring up the topic it's cause for the sharp edge of Evangeline's tongue right now. None of us are getting much sleep these days."

Yes, she could see the dark lines under his eyes. Twin girls would keep the household hopping, but Evangeline was lucky she had two such supportive husbands to give her a hand. Evangeline was lucky in so many ways.

"We were actually thinking we might adopt after these three are a little older," Gregorio continued. "Angel House is full, especially after the revolution."

Lilya nodded and smiled. "That would be a wonderful way to

build your family." It had always seemed silly to her to bring more children into the world when there were so many already who needed families to love them.

"Gregorio." Byron greeted him as he came up to stand beside them. "It's good to see you." They shook hands.

Gregorio looked to Byron and Lilya, who were standing close to one another. "Did you come here together?"

"Remember when I said I was taking some time off from the project to have a houseguest? Lilya is that houseguest."

Gregorio's eyebrows rose into his hairline. "That's wonderful! I didn't know you two were so well acquainted."

"We've known each other for a long time." Lilya glanced at Byron and smiled.

"So what are you doing here today, Byron? There's nothing so pressing that needs your attention this moment. You didn't need to travel all the way from Ulstrat."

"Well, actually, there's the Aralynda matter."

Gregorio's face went serious. "Of course. You intend to try and sway her before she leaves?"

"It's our last chance."

Lilya frowned, looking between the two men and wondering who Aralynda was.

"Yes." Gregorio's gaze darted to Lilya. "Do you think—?"

"No." Byron's voice was firm and protective.

Gregorio's gaze shifted between them, his eyes lighting with some new knowledge about their relationship. "I understand."

"Uh, what's going on that I don't know about?" Lilya shifted impatiently.

"I'll explain as we go upstairs. I just need to gather her paperwork and we'll be off."

Someone across the foyer greeted Gregorio and he excused himself from them. "It was good to see you both."

"Give Evangeline a hug from me," Lilya called after him.

"I will," he called back. "I know she's anxious to see you. When you get back from Ulstrat, we'll come by for a visit."

"Sounds wonderful."

Byron took her elbow and led her up the stairs. "So, tell me about Aralynda," she prompted him.

"She's a woman who lives on the outskirts of Milzyr, a former J'Edaeii. She's had a very rough time since the revolution and she wants nothing to do with the new government, yet her magick is extremely powerful and could be of great help to the farmers of Rylisk."

"What's her magick?"

He glanced at her, grinning. "She makes plants grow twice as fast as normal."

"Ah. That would be a helpful type of magick to have at the state's disposal." She reached the top of the stairs. "Let me guess, she doesn't want to be at the state's disposal?"

He stopped outside of an open door and sighed. "She's an older woman and proud, very—"

"J'Edaeii?"

He nodded. "Life has been rough on her these past three years. She's spent time on the streets, she's starved, and she's been mistreated. She blames the new government for all that."

"She sounds like Evangeline once was." Lilya paused. "Considering her recent history, you know I'm the best person to talk to her, don't you?"

"*No.*" Byron walked past her into the room.

Frowning at his back, she followed him in and glanced around.

Desk, chairs, bookshelves. This must be his office. He walked around to the other side of the desk, pulled out a drawer, and began riffling through a pile of papers.

Lilya put a hand on her hip. "And why not?"

He glanced up at the tone in her voice. "I brought you into the city for pleasant things. I intend to drop you on Bergen Avenue with a purse full of money while I meet with Aralynda." Bergen Avenue was where all the finest shops were located. "I never intended for you to come with me to talk with an irascible, proud woman with a recent history so close to yours and so sharp it might full well draw blood from you."

She smiled and spread her hands. "And, yet, here I am, fully qualified and willing."

"*No.*" He stared at her in challenge for a long moment, then went back to riffling through the desk.

"Byron, you can't tell me what to do."

He looked up her. "I want what's best for you."

"That's very sweet and protective of you, but I'm a grown woman. I'm strong and resilient. I know what I can handle and, Byron, I can handle a lot."

"I know you're strong, it's just—"

"You want to spare me any unnecessary pain. I appreciate that. I want the same for you."

"Then you understand."

"I understand, but I don't agree. I can help you and I *want* to help you." She tilted her head at him. "Do you really think I'm the type of woman who'd prefer to go shopping when there's any opportunity I could take to aid someone?"

He studied her for a moment, then sighed as though relenting. "No, I don't."

She favored him with a winning smile. "Then it's settled, I'm coming with you."

His full lips twisted and she had a moment of all-consuming lust watching them. He had the most sensual lips of any man she'd ever known. "I guess it is." He dipped his head again, still searching for his papers on the woman, Aralynda, she guessed. Finally he came up with a fistful, then closed the drawer.

"Where is Aralynda going that it's so urgent to talk to her today?"

He came around the desk to stand beside her. "She's leaving Rylisk tomorrow. There's a small enclave of former J'Edaeii in Malbask." Malbask neighbored Rylisk to the north. "She's set on leaving, but I've talked with her several times and have glimpsed a way to get through to her. I just haven't been able to say the right things. This time, I go armed with a monetary offer from the government so maybe words and pleas to her sentiment won't matter."

"To a former J'Edaeii, the monetary amount matters greatly."

"Ah, yes, and the amount is not great. We only have so much money we can offer the former J'Edaeii as an incentive to join our cause and we must spread the lot out among them. It's not all that much."

"Let's go try."

He stared down at her for a moment, then dipped his head and caught her lips against his. She melted against him a little, inhaling the heady scent of his skin that mingled with the musky scent of the cologne he used every morning after his bath. She closed her eyes, drinking him in, enjoying the slow slide of his mouth along hers. Sweet Joshui, she could kiss this man forever.

"I . . . care about you very much, Lilya," he whispered against her lips.

He cared about her; he didn't love her.

Expectations, Lilya.

She smiled against his lips. "I care very much about you too. I'm happy to be spending this time with you and Alek."

He backed away from her and cleared his throat. "Alek is certainly enjoying your company."

Her smile faded. "Why is there an edge to your voice when you say that?"

He stared at her for a moment, then shook his head and gave a low, rough laugh. "Because I'm an idiot, Lilya, that's why." He pushed past her without another word. "Let's get going."

Aralynda lived in a small one-room apartment on the west side of town. Lilya followed Byron up a flight of creaking wooden stairs and down a chilly hallway to her door and knocked. Nothing happened for long enough to make Lilya think Aralynda wasn't home. Then a scuffling and muttering from the opposite side of the door met her ears and the lock snapped open.

The door creaked inward to reveal a tall, thin woman with iron-colored hair staring at them. She wore a threadbare gown and tattered slippers, yet she did it with such a rigid backbone and regal carriage that Lilya could easily imagine yards of silk and lace.

"You again," came Aralynda's tight voice as soon as her gaze met Byron's.

"Me again, Aralynda, yes." Byron gave her his most charming smile, a smile Lilya was sure no woman had the power to resist not even Aralynda Hansdaughter, formerly Aralynda J'Edaeii. "I wanted to come over, say good-bye, and make you a final offer."

Aralynda eyed Lilya. "Who is this?"

"This is Lilya Orensdaughter, a friend of mine."

Lilya inclined her head. "It's a pleasure to meet you."

Aralynda scowled at both of them and Lilya thought for certain she'd slam the door in their faces, but instead she opened it wider and stepped aside, allowing them passage. "I have time for one cup of tea, but mind the disarray, I'm packing."

They entered after her and Lilya took stock of the humble abode. A few pieces of worn furniture, tiny corner kitchen, boxes and clothing strewn on the bed. It didn't appear that Aralynda had much to pack. The apartment was quite spare, but it was spotless.

"Well, sit down, then." Aralynda waved at a couple of chairs, sounding put out, then moved into the tiny kitchen to make tea, presumably.

Lilya and Byron sank into rickety chairs near the fire and soon Aralynda brought them both weak tea in chipped cups. Then she retrieved her own tea and sat on the threadbare rouge divan opposite the hearth.

Looking at Byron expectantly, Aralynda sipped her tea. "So, talk. I don't have all day."

Byron shrugged in an easygoing manner. "Of course." He looked down at his teacup and Lilya stifled a snicker. She knew that Byron hated tea, especially weak tea, and the tiny, delicate cup in his massive hands looked ridiculous. "I come today with a monetary offer in hand, Aralynda." Well, he was getting right down to business. "An incentive to keep you in Rylisk. You won't like Malbask anyway, it's very cold."

Aralynda's straight back went a little straighter. "The government of Rylisk would offer me money to stay here?" She said *government* the way another person might say *maggot*.

"Yes. You mean much to us."

Her lips pressed into a thin line and her eyes took on a calculating expression. "How much?"

He glanced around her apartment. "Enough that you could afford a better, warmer apartment." He lifted the cup. "Dishes that aren't chipped. Food on your table and a new gown or two."

She studied him for a moment with hard, glittering dark eyes. "I accept your money and I'm beholden to the government, then? Bound to provide my magick whenever they ask it of me? A slave?"

He gave his head a sharp shake. "Never a slave. You would not be compelled to use your magick at any time, but we would hope you would take joy in helping your fellow citizens by using your gift. We could put all of that in writing, if you choose."

"Take joy?" she sputtered. "My fellow citizens?" She pointed a bony finger toward the window. "Those are the people who stripped me of my old life and set me on the street to rot. I froze. I starved. I was *beaten* by men in an alleyway once. Why should I feel any inclination toward helping these people? If I take this money from you I will be a prisoner of my enemies."

"Excuse me, Miss Hansdaughter," Lilya broke in, "but how is that any different than being J'Edaeii?"

Byron's face went from passively accepting of Aralynda's rant to alarm. Lilya calmly sipped her tea and waited for Aralynda's inevitable eruption.

Aralynda turned her icy gaze to her. "Before someone *cut it out* of me on the street, I had a jewel nestled at the base of my spine." She lifted her chin. "A diamond. It was there for over thirty-five years. I was widow to an Edaeii for most of those years."

"Did you love him?"

She scowled. "What an impertinent question! That's none of your business, young lady."

"It's a very simple question, Aralynda. Did you marry him because you *wanted* to marry him? Because you loved him? Or did you marry him because you were *forced* to marry him in an effort to infuse the Edaeii bloodline with your magickal talent? If the answer is the latter, you were a prisoner, no matter how many diamonds were embedded in your flesh or how many gorgeous gowns draped your body."

Aralynda's lower lip trembled and Lilya thought for a moment she'd made a horrible mistake. Then her face softened and she looked away. "He was horrid. Twice my age. Our wedding night was—" She shuddered. "I never bore a child because I couldn't stand his hands on me. Still, they threatened . . ." She trailed off.

Of course. She'd only been a broodmare.

After a several moments of silence, Lilya rose, set her teacup on the mantel and walked over to sit near Aralynda. "The J'Edaeii were wronged in the revolution. They were lumped together with the oppressors when they were really the oppressed. You were taken from your family at a young age, raised to think it was your birthright to become jeweled and marry an Edaeii. Then the revolution occurred and you were wronged again, this time by the people who should have sheltered you. The people didn't understand. They viewed you as a traitor and they did some horrible things." She paused as Aralynda turned her head to look at her. "Rylisk is a different place now."

"Is it? I don't believe that." Her voice came out cold and bitter.

"You've never had a chance to live as you see fit, Aralynda. Every moment of your life has been dictated by someone else. This is your chance to finally live as a free woman. You can do as you will with your power. The government hopes you will use it in service to others, as do I. Ultimately, however, the *choice* will be yours."

"And Malbask? I have people waiting there for me. My plans are made. The costs for travel paid." She waved a hand at the half-packed boxes scattering the floor.

"I'll cover your expenses personally," Byron cut in, "and give you an extra bonus for your trouble."

Aralynda gazed out the window, clearly deep in thought.

"You said you never loved your husband," Lilya said quietly. "But it's not too late to find real love. You have the rest of your life ahead of you to live as you choose."

"Find love?" She gave a sharp laugh. "I'm too old."

"No one is ever too old for that."

"Don't give me that clichéd dribble." Yet her voice lacked bite.

Lilya took a chance, reached out and covered the older woman's hand with hers. "It might be a cliché, but it's also true."

They left a short time later with Aralynda telling Byron she would take the afternoon and evening to think about it and would send word to the university when she'd made her decision . . . on Byron's coin, of course. Byron gracefully agreed and took his leave, his tea sitting untouched.

Eighteen

He pulled Lilya against his side as they walked down the hallway. "You said the right things, Lilya. I think you convinced her to stay."

She smiled up at him. "Aren't you happy you brought me with you now?"

"I'm always happy to have you at my side, love."

Those words made her heart skip a beat. She cursed herself.

They met Alek for lunch at an outdoor café not far from where her house was located and told him about their meeting with Aralynda.

Alek set his fork down on the table beside his plate of pasta. "I can't believe you convinced her to stay. She's a sour old biddy."

"You've met her?" Lilya asked.

Byron sat back in his chair and surveyed the busy street. "I think I've sent almost everyone out to see her, trying to talk her into working with us."

"Well, that job isn't done yet. We still don't know if she's staying." She pushed her fork around her plate, not very hungry. "And if she does stay, there's no guarantee she'll help Rylisk with her magick. She might just take the money, sit back, and do nothing."

"One step at a time." Byron looked at Alek meaningfully while Alek's head was down, munching his pasta.

She glanced at Alek too. She found it strange that Alek had agreed to go talk to Aralynda when he was such a reluctant magick user himself. Of course, maybe that's why Byron had sent him. Maybe it had been more for Alek's benefit than Aralynda's.

"Lilya was wonderful." Byron's voice held warm regard and she looked over to find his expression held it as well. Pleasure suffused her, making her cheeks warm.

"I'm sure she was magnificent, as always," said Alek in the same tone, looking up from his plate.

She smiled and caught a glimpse of a woman watching them from another table. The look on the woman's face reminded her of what she must have looked like watching the family at the teahouse while she'd been waiting for Evangeline to arrive. Envy. Longing. Hope. That woman saw in Lilya what she'd seen in that family—something she wanted.

Lilya looked between Byron and Alek and her own heart filled with the longing that it might be true, but she knew it was just an illusion.

Ivan waded through the drifts of snow at the back of Byron's home, the moon shining high in the sky above his head. He knew that as long as there were no strong winds or extra snow his boots would leave tracks that someone might find in the morning. That was fine. Preferable, really. Let them wonder and worry what stranger had come calling in the night. Let them wonder what the stranger had done and if he would be back. He *would* be back. This wouldn't be Ivan's last visit.

The back door was a heavy, expensive wooden frame filled with equally heavy, expensive colored glass. He supposed he could just break it, but he couldn't be sure that all the good little boys and girls would be sleeping at this hour and he wanted to remain unnoticed for the time being. Instead he extracted a set of lock-picking tools. They weren't the best set of tools in the world, not the finest that he owned by far, but they had sentimental value. He'd stolen them off his fuck of a father after he'd slit the man's throat. Ivan had been thirteen. These tools had given him his start.

He jiggled the lock and had it opened in less than five seconds. Apparently Byron wasn't all that concerned about his possessions . . . or his safety.

The open door let into the kitchen. Ivan nodded in approval. It was a nice place. A little palatial for his tastes, but this was the Andropov family's residence, after all. Nothing but the best for that family. It was amazing the peasants hadn't torched the house during the revolution, but he was aware that Byron's family had done a lot for the community here in Ulstrat. Apparently that had earned them a free ride during the upheaval. Byron was a lucky son of a bitch. Of course, a man who lived on luck had better hope he had a lot of it. By Ivan's measure, Byron was almost out.

The house was quiet and cold, though fires were kept burning low in the hearths of all the rooms to keep the home heated. They gave off a warm, merry light. Most likely everyone was in bed. He knew the bedrooms were upstairs, so he made his way out of the kitchen, through the foyer, and up the winding staircase.

The first bedroom he entered was Alek Chaikoveii's.

The man slept fitfully, blankets and sheets twisted around his legs despite the chill in the room. His pillows were a mess. Ivan moved closer to the bed and looked down at him. He was a handsome bastard. This man's father had never taken a knife to his face while his drunken mother looked on, laughing. No, this man had been born wealthy to parents that had cherished him, given him everything.

Well, he couldn't have Lilya.

Ivan had done his research on this man who was currently fucking the woman he owned. He didn't feel the same bone-gnawing hatred when he gazed down at him as he did when he looked at Byron, but Alek was going to have to die too.

But not quite yet.

He checked a few other rooms and eventually hit pay dirt—Byron.

His sleep wasn't troubled like his friend's. This bastard slept well in his huge four-poster bed, where Lilya had undoubtedly been spending a lot of time. It was lucky she wasn't there now; he wasn't sure he'd be able to control his temper and he wasn't ready to draw blood yet.

The fire sputtered in the hearth, casting shadows over his face. Ivan fisted his hands at his sides, glancing at the iron fireplace tools he could so easily use to bludgeon him to death in his sleep. He wouldn't even wake up. One solid hit to the head and Byron would *never* wake up.

Of course, what fun would that be? He liked to see the fear in his victim's eyes before they died.

Even so, he wanted to do it. He wanted to see Andropov's blood staining that white pillow. Imagining Lilya as she woke to find her lovers dead in their beds—both of them—would be very satisfying. But would she run back to Milzyr and take up her old life the way he wanted her to? Ivan wasn't certain. He needed to see her with these men in order to know how to proceed. How deep had her emotions been invested in them? He had to know that before he dealt with her. It was possible that he would have to break her again in order to put her back in her place.

His body eased. Byron was safe. At least for tonight. He regretted he couldn't take Andropov's life tonight, but the anticipation of that event in the future was sweet.

Leaving Andropov's room, he continued to explore the house.

At last he found Lilya.

He hadn't seen her up close in many years. She was older, though Lilya had never had that sweet, fresh bloom of youth that so many other young girls possessed. Her life had put wisdom in her eyes early on and Ivan had always thought her more beautiful because of it. She had fit him in so many ways. She had been able to match the sorrow he held as a result of his abusive upbringing. She was the only woman he'd ever loved.

Too bad she was a faithless slut.

Rage overcame him as he remembered what he'd seen in the hallway so many years ago, Lilya clinging to that man the way he'd remembered his mother drunkenly clinging to men that weren't her husband. That familiar anger rose up in him. He'd come too close to killing Lilya that day. She owed her life to him.

She should be grateful he hadn't simply slit her throat.

Now she lay serenely under the soft sheets and blankets, her thick, dark hair spread over her pillow. Yes, she was still beautiful, more so now that age had settled on her and good nutrition had filled her out. He reached down and fingered a lock of her hair. She made a soft sound in her sleep and turned over, pulling the silky tendril through his loosely grasping fingers.

He pulled a knife and let it glint in the reflected firelight for a moment. The urge to kill her passed quickly. He didn't want her dead, not if he had a choice. Hurt, maybe, but not dead. He just wanted her back where she'd been, where he could watch her.

She seemed far too happy here and that was not acceptable. This woman did not deserve happiness, not after the way she'd broken his heart. He'd thought he'd marry her. Gods, he'd wanted to have *children* with her. Then she'd defiled herself, made herself untouchable.

He stood for a moment over her sleeping body, hating the slight smile she wore on her pretty mouth. He wasn't even sure he could bring himself to scar her, though that was in his plans. If he scarred that beautiful face, every man would turn her away. Byron and Alek would turn her away. She'd be forced to stay at the Temple of Dreams taking whatever men threw her scraps.

Hovering over her for a moment longer, he made his decision. His knife swooped down and cut a tendril of hair, too small an amount for her to ever notice. Scarring, yes. Perhaps that would soon make his to-do list.

Turning, he brought her hair up to his nose and inhaled the scent of her. He'd be back.

*   *   *

Something woke Lilya from a sound sleep. Gasping, she sat up to an empty room and a flickering fire. Rubbing at one tired eye with the flat of her hand—she'd been painting until the wee hours—she flipped the blankets back, got out of bed, and quickly went for her robe and slippers.

There was no logical reason for it, but something felt wrong . . . *off* in the house. She walked to the window that looked over the garden. All she saw in the moonlit night was snow. Snow drifting. Snow falling. Snow covering very cold things.

Shivering, she turned and went to sit near the fire. The scent of the cologne Ivan used to wear hung very faintly in the chilly air. Her nose wrinkled and she frowned. It had to be her imagination. Maybe she'd had a nightmare she didn't remember. That would wake her up quickly and frighten her as well. Hugging herself, she stared into the fire. The years could pass, the physical wounds could heal, but the vestiges of that event would never leave her.

"Lilya?"

She jumped, startled, then turned at the sound of Alek's voice. He stood in the doorway. "You scared me."

He walked toward her. "Someone's been in the house. Are you all right? Did you see anyone?"

She leapt to her feet. "What?"

"Byron went down to the kitchen and found the door in the kitchen open and tracks leading to and away from the house."

Her eyes opened wide and she put a hand to her mouth for a moment. "No. I didn't see anyone. I woke up feeling disturbed and looked out the window. I saw nothing but snow. Then I came over here and sat down by the fire."

He nodded. "Come here."

She walked to him and he pulled her against his side, kissing her temple. "Byron's checking the house. You stay with me."

"Byron's checking the house alone?" She looked up at him, shaking her head. "No." Glancing around, she saw the iron fire poker near the hearth. She went to it and picked it up. "Let's go make sure he's all right."

He looked surprised for a moment, then grinned. "All right, let's go."

They found Byron in the kitchen, leaning against the table and frowning. It was extra cold in the room from the door being left open. "The house appears to be clear. It was just one man and he appears to have left." He looked up at them. "One set of tracks lead up to the door, but another set lead away. Same pair of shoes."

"Anything missing?" Lilya dropped the poker to her side.

Byron shook his head. "Nothing I can see at first glance. All the really valuable things are locked away in hidden safes."

"Why did he leave the door open?"

Alek shrugged. "Carelessness. Fear. Maybe the intruder heard Byron get up and he fled."

"I don't think so. The tracks leading away are calm and measured, not the tracks of someone running." He rubbed a tired hand over his face. "Maybe he wanted us to know he'd been here."

Silence descended.

"Bold for a thief," said Alek.

Byron looked at him and nodded.

"And disturbing. Well, that's it for sleep tonight." Lilya clutched the poker and wondered where in the house she could find a better weapon. Old street habits died hard and, at the moment, they were all reviving fast.

"Maybe not. You sleep with me. Alek can as well. My bed is big enough."

She let a breath. "I'd feel better if we were all together."

"Me too," Byron answered.

They walked up to Byron's room and crawled under his thick blankets. Lilya snuggled in with both men on either side of her, snug, warm, and feeling safe again. Yet the uneasiness of the way she'd woken still clung to her. The scent of Ivan's cologne made her shudder with revulsion, even though she must have imagined it. It had to be that she'd sensed something amiss in the house—heard a sound in her sleep—and it had spurred a nightmare about Ivan.

Either way, silly or not, in the morning she would tell Alek and Byron about the scent.

Even though she was comfortable and safe between the men she admired most in the world, sleep didn't come again until dawn lighted the horizon.

By the light of day, Byron inventoried the house and found nothing taken. It was an ominous thing. What had the intruder wanted if not valuables? The memory of Lilya's unease in the market-place was still fresh in his mind too. Was there someone in Ulstrat who meant him harm because of his noble blood or family name? Maybe a last hold out from the revolution? It was definitely possible. Crimes were still committed against the nobles who'd survived the revolution. Hatred died hard.

The morning after the break-in, Lilya had told him and Alek about the faint, lingering scent of Ivan's cologne in her bedroom. They were all of the opinion that Lilya's nerves had caused her to imagine his scent. Ivan had had nothing to do with Lilya for six years and they were far from Milzyr now.

Still, someone had broken into the house and Byron wasn't taking any chances—not with Lilya—so the next day, when the town had been a little more recovered from the storm, he'd gone in and hired men to go over the house more thoroughly. The snow was cleared away from the shops and streets, and the town of Ulstrat was partially running again. Those with sleighs had brought them out for use in the heavy ground cover. Since he'd returned he'd been watching the men he'd hired scour the house and improve the locks.

Alek and Lilya had secreted themselves in her painting room to get away from the commotion. After making sure the men had everything they needed, he headed up there. In the hallway outside he heard muffled talking and laughing. A jolt of jealousy went through him even though he was happy that Lilya and Alek were getting along so well.

He knocked, then entered when Lilya called.

"You have to sit still, Alek!" She stood in front of her easel with a wet paintbrush in her hand. "All that fidgeting has forced me to give you an extraordinarily large nose."

"A man is not meant to sit still for this long a period of time."

"Not even a scholar?"

"No."

Byron peered over Lilya's shoulder at the portrait. "Huh."

"Huh?" Alek asked from his chair near the window. "What does *huh* mean?"

Lilya took a step back and tilted her head to the side, studying her work. "See what I mean about the nose?"

"Hmm, yes." He pointed at the image of Alek's head. "And his head . . ."

"What's wrong with my head?"

Byron ignored him. "His head is a bit bulbous too, don't you think?"

"Yes, and it probably shouldn't be that shade of green."

Alek jumped out of his chair and came to look while he and Lilya laughed. He tilted his head to the side the way Lilya had. "My nose isn't too big, my head's not bulbous or green, but there's definitely something off about it."

Lilya nodded and sighed. "Apparently portraits are not my forte."

Byron glanced at the incredible street scene she was still working on. It was propped against a nearby wall. "Maybe not, but you're definitely good at other kinds of painting."

"It's not that bad," said Alek. "Better than I could ever do. Miles better than anyone could do without any formal instruction. I think you just need practice."

"Maybe when you go back to Milzyr you can find a teacher," Byron offered. "I'll even help you find one. There has to be someone close to the Temple of Dreams you can work with."

The small smile she wore faded. "Yes, maybe." She turned away, cleaning off her brush. "I'm done with portraits for the time being though."

Byron stared at her back. She'd gone cold all of a sudden and he had no idea why. "If you don't want me to help find a teacher, that's all right, Lilya."

She gave a short laugh and turned around. "Of course I want your help. Are the men gone yet?"

"They're almost finished. They better be since it's almost time for us to leave."

She nodded. "The crossball game." It had been rescheduled for that afternoon. She glanced down at her paint-smeared hands. "How much time do I have? I'm a mess."

"You look good to me," answered Alek. "And it's not exactly a formal occasion, by the way."

She waved her hand dismissively at him. "You're a man and have no idea what you're talking about when it comes to appearance. Which begs the question, will I be the only woman there?"

"No," Byron answered. "Many of the wives and daughters come to watch, though the majority of the fans are men."

She pushed past them both. "I need to get ready, then."

Nineteen

Lilya hurried down the corridor to her room. The back of her throat stung from the threat of tears. Needing to hurry to get ready had just been an excuse to leave the room. She crashed through her door, closed it, and only barely kept herself from locking it.

Walking over to the area where the bathtub sat, she stared at her reflection in the mirror above the water basin. She'd been a fool to think that she'd ever have a chance at ending up with Byron for the long term. He'd told her that every man she met fell in love with her, but instead he'd brought her here and she'd fallen in love with him.

And now she had significant feelings for Alek too. When she left this place her heart would break twice.

Maybe this was payback for all the hearts she'd broken over the years. It probably served her right.

She shook her head and tried to put it all out of her mind. That Byron had every intention of packing her back off to the city should come as no great shock. What had she been expecting? Declarations of undying love? A ring? An entreaty to leave the Temple of Dreams and stay here with him forever? Thinking on her ring drawer back in the city, she snorted. Funny how she would never get any of that from the one man she wanted it from.

And as far as the Temple of Dreams went, she was done with it. There was no way she could sleep with any man other than Byron or Alek now. Too much had changed as result of her trip here. That was all right. She had money.

She concentrated on getting ready to go watch Byron and Alek play crossball and tried not to think on stupid things like getting to stay here forever with these men. That wasn't going to happen and she needed to accept it, get her expectations back in the realm of reality. This was not like her at all. She guessed love must make women dumb. So perhaps it was better she was leaving them.

It was time she started protecting herself as much as she could, time to pull away physically and emotionally. She was probably too far past the point of no return to save herself, but maybe she could ease a little of the coming pain. She was headed for heartache no matter what.

Alek knocked on the door and she answered with a smile, with absolutely no trace of her turmoil visible on her face. "Is it time to leave?"

He nodded. "Snow's falling again, but a messenger came to tell us that the game is still on."

She gave him a head-to-toe appraisal and raised an eyebrow in appreciation. He wore a formfitting shirt that delineated every one of his muscles. The tight black pants he wore did the same for his derrière. "That uniform is . . . nice."

"I'm glad you like it." His arm came around her waist and his head dropped close to hers. "And you look good enough to eat, but there's nothing unusual about that."

She tensed, wanting to push him away, but she just couldn't make herself no matter her new resolution to keep her distance. Instead, she closed her eyes as his lips skimmed down the column of her throat. His teeth closed around the curve of her neck and goose bumps erupted all over her body. She slid her hands up his arms, appreciating every inch of hard muscle as she went.

His head dropped to the swell of her breasts and traced them as her head fell back. His touch was doing very nice, very dangerous things to her body right now. Tipping her head forward, she put her fingers under his chin and lifted his head. His eyes, dark with lust, met hers. "If you keep doing that, we'll be late."

He grinned. "You're right. Let's just consider this an appetizer. To be continued later."

Just then Byron rounded the corner and stopped, taking in the scene. He wore a similar uniform to Alek's. His body seemed to go rigid at the sight of them—*but why?* Joshui, she did not understand this man.

All the same, she straightened and backed away from Alek. Byron walked straight for her, cupping her cheek and kissing her hard. He pulled her against his body, slanting his mouth over hers and sliding his tongue past her lips. His tongue worked against hers in long, possessive strokes, while his hand at her waist rubbed her skin through the fabric of her dress as though he imagined she wore nothing. It made her knees go weak.

Very slowly, Byron broke the kiss. He backed away, glancing at Alek. "Ready?"

Lilya sagged against the door to her room. Just one of these men was enough to heat her blood, both of them together nearly did her in. She felt like she'd drunk one too many glasses of wine.

They took the carriage—now on sleds instead of wheels—down a snow-covered road and into the village. In the carriage, while the driver urged the two pairs of horses to follow the snowy streets, she stared out the window at the white world with her thick coat buttoned tight around her throat and the hood covering her head.

"You're very quiet this evening, Lilya."

She glanced at Alek sitting next to her who stared back at her with eyes that saw too much. Managing a smile, she took his hand. "Just a little tired, I guess." It was no lie. All the emotion pummeling her these days did leave her feeling fatigued.

A large building stood on the other end of town, the enormous crossball stadium. She'd heard of such places existing in Milzyr, but they were on the outskirts of the city and she'd never seen any of them firsthand. They entered and Lilya gawked in spite of herself. It was a long, wide building with a huge open area in the middle. On either side were chairs, set up for the spectators.

Alek and Byron found a place for her to sit in the quickly filling building and then left to join their team. She gazed out at the field, watching the team's players arrive and listening to the excited hum of the people around her.

She knew a little about the game of crossball, though she'd never seen it played. Typically it was considered more of a sport played in the country and was eschewed by the city nobility. The Edaeii family had considered it crass. Outside the city, even before the revolution, it was called the Great Uniter because men across the social spectrum played it side by side. Even the crowd as it filled the building was clearly of the mixed variety.

After some time, the players filtered onto the field and were greeted by immense cheering. The teams assembled on either end of the enormous area. Lines made of some substance that lay over the packed dirt field marked off increments of space in a way she didn't understand. She watched as Alek emerged onto the field, followed by Byron. A cheer went up from the spectators and Byron waved. Lilya wasn't sure if he was being cheered because of his expected performance on the field or if it was because his family was so well loved in this area for giving money to those in need.

A tall man dressed in a formfitting black uniform came out onto the field with a large black ball. Both teams lined up on either side in a diamond pattern. A pregnant silence descended over the building. Then the man in black tossed the ball into the air, a gong sounded, and total chaos broke loose.

Lilya sucked in a breath as the crowd swelled around her, seeming to almost explode with excitement. The two teams met head on, like two armies crashing together in battle. Clearly the object was to gain control of the black ball and apparently anything went in the pursuit of that goal.

For a moment she couldn't find Alek or Byron in the melee. Heart pounding, she half stood to get a better view, finally spotting Alek on the field going for the ball. A man on the other team grabbed him around the waist, trying to pull him down into the dirt. Alek collapsed, rolled, extricated himself, and was on his feet again in a heartbeat.

Now she saw that Byron had the ball. He fought off two players of the opposite team with the help of some of his teammates, who seemed to be helping him get to the opposite end of the field. Byron spotted Alek who'd managed to get himself relatively clear of opposing team members, and threw the ball to him. Alek caught it and ran flat out for the goal that, Lilya guessed, was at the other end of the field in enemy territory.

Lilya fell back hard into her seat, almost unable to watch. The crowd became loud, some screaming for someone to take Alek down, the others cheering him to the goal. One of the opposing team members tried to take him to the dirt, but failed as Alek's own team came to his defense. They formed a crescent around Alek's running body, Byron in the lead, pushing away or throwing down anyone who threatened to take the ball from him. In seconds it was over and Alek had run through the large black metal gate at the end of the field, arms wide, ball flying up into the air in victory. A huge cheer went up from the crowd around her. Melancholy momentarily forgotten, Lilya found herself on her feet, cheering along with them, breathless, and with her heart in her throat.

The game continued on that way with goals for both teams. The score remained close the entire time, one team scoring and then the other reciprocating. Ulstrat's team edged out the visiting team in the end by only one point and the fans went wild with cheering and celebrating.

The winning team on the field celebrated too, clapping each other on the back and ruffling each other's hair. If there hadn't been a fence separating the spectators from the teams Lilya was certain that all the fans would have joined them to dance on the hard-packed field.

Finally everything calmed and the players left the field and entered some area in the back, where she presumed they would wash up and dress. Around her the fans began to filter out as well, eventually leaving her in a nearly empty building with only a handful of remaining spectators—perhaps families also waiting for players.

She milled around, growing more and more uneasy.

When Lilya had lived on the streets of Milzyr, she'd lived by her intuition. Her ability to sense danger, or someone watching her, had saved her more than once. Now her intuition kicked in again, just as it had at the market. The hair on her nape rose and she felt the odd pressure of another person's close regard. Her stomach tightened in that old familiar way. It said *Go. Run. Get away from here.*

Like in the marketplace, there was no reason for it, but it made her skin crawl. Perhaps it was some remnant left over from the break-in and the lingering scent in her bedroom. She had reason to feel slightly paranoid. Either way, she wasn't one to take chances or brush things off. Standing, she turned in a slow circle, looking for the source of her unease.

Since the break-in, she'd secured a dagger in the bodice of her dress for easy access. She touched the cold iron hilt of it. It made her feel less vulnerable.

But there was no one threatening anywhere around her that she could see, only small groups of laughing and talking people left over from the game. No menacing-looking man staring at her and thinking about ways to harm her. No Ivan. She shook her head and turned back toward the field. It was only her imagination.

Alek and Byron eventually came out of the players' area at the back of the building. They were both scrubbed clean, their damp hair slicked back away from their faces, and each wearing clean pants and shirts beneath their heavy winter coats.

She reached up and smoothed Byron's damp hair away from his face, frowning. "You'll both catch your death outside." The feel of his hair was nice under her fingers, so nice that she dropped her hand and took a step away from him.

She was going to miss him so much.

Alek secured his bag over his shoulder. "Trust me, you don't want to be trapped in the carriage on the way home without us bathed."

She gave him a tight smile. "I'd *rather* you didn't catch pneumonia and die."

"We won't," answered Byron. "We're stronger than that."

She gazed out at the field. "So I saw. Now I understand why you both need to stay in shape. That game was amazing."

Byron took a step toward her, as if to touch her, and she involuntarily took a step back. His face went carefully blank. "I'm glad you were here to watch." His words came out uncertain. He'd sensed the reserve that had come over her, her desire to draw away and protect herself.

"Me too." She smiled to try to smooth over her obvious unwillingness to touch him. To touch him was to lose her battle. "It was very . . . invigorating." And it was. There wasn't much that didn't arouse her where these two men were concerned—more was the pity—but watching them compete on that field had definitely heated her blood.

Byron returned her smile, probably as confused as she was by the mixed messages she was giving him. But she wasn't the only one giving mixed messages. She had no idea what to think about her relationship with him—or with Alek—at this point in time. All she could do was hold on and try to survive their next week together. Then it was back to Milzyr with a heart broken twice and she'd have the long job of putting it back together again.

She looked at Alek, who was also studying her with questions in his eyes. She wished she could just talk to them, ask them what it was they felt in their hearts for her. Was she simply a plaything for them for these three weeks—surely that had to be the case. She was incapable of taking herself seriously, so why should they? And if that was the case, how silly would she feel for asking if they felt more for her? Too stupid. Too silly.

She had way too much pride for that.

Her head dipped and she closed her eyes for a moment. *Hang on, Lilya. Get through this.* When she raised it, it was with a smile on her face. "Shall we go? I had a fun evening, but I'm exhausted. You've both got to be weary as well."

Ivan watched, concealed partially around a corner in the crossball building, as Lilya conversed with the men. He studied every move the three of them made and he liked what he saw.

Lilya had always been awful at lying. Even in her role as a courtesan, she couldn't pretend. That was the reason he suspected she choose her clients so carefully, since she couldn't fake caring for them. Her emotions had always lain open on her face and in her body language, and right now she was revealing her feelings to all who were paying attention. Stiff, a little cold, and avoiding their touch, Ivan could see clearly that she was not having a good time. She wanted out. She wanted to go home.

She wasn't in love with these men. Far from it.

Ivan let out a slow, careful breath. Perhaps this situation

wasn't as out of control as he'd presumed. Perhaps soon, Lilya would be done with Alek and Byron and return to Milzyr to take up her old life again. Everything would return to normal. He'd still have to kill the men, of course, simply on principle, but maybe he could leave Lilya alone.

It appeared she was still broken. That was good. It meant he wouldn't have to break her twice.

He wasn't malicious. He just wanted Lilya back in her place.

Twenty

The three returned home to fires lit in all the hearths. Byron had ordered it done before they'd returned home so the house would be as warm as a house this large could be in the middle of a Rylisk winter.

He watched as Lilya entered the foyer and nodded at them both. She turned with her coat still on, strange shadows dancing in her eyes, and kissed them. "Good evening. I'm sure you'll both sleep soundly tonight." She laughed lightly and then hurried up the stairs.

Once she was gone, he met Alek's eyes.

"She's not good at masking her emotions, is she?" Alek asked with a smile.

Byron stared up the stairs. "No. I don't know what's going on with her. I wish she'd tell us."

Alek snorted and shook his head while he took his coat off. "You don't know what it is?"

He rubbed his chin, glancing at Alek in annoyance. "And you do?"

Alek only shook his head again and headed for the library. "I need a drink."

Byron pulled his coat off and followed him. When he entered the room, Alek was pouring himself a glass of scotch. He tipped the decanter up at him. "Want one? To celebrate our win?"

He didn't feel like celebrating anything with Lilya acting this way, but Byron waved a hand absently at him anyway and slumped into a chair near the roaring fire. Ah, that was better. He was beginning to defrost, despite the deep freeze that Lilya had thrust him into.

Frowning and staring into the flames dancing in the hearth, he took the glass from Alek and downed the fiery alcohol in one gulp. His head lolled to regard Alek in the other chair who was sipping his drink instead of tossing it back. "So, what is your great insight into the inner workings of Lilya's mind?"

Alek smirked into the lip of his glass before taking a drink. "She loves you."

This time it was Byron who snorted. He gazed into the fire. "No. Lilya loves no man, but all men love her. Like you, Alek. You love her. I can see it when you look at her."

Alek let out a long, slow breath and set his glass on the side table. "Lilya is very different from Evianna."

He stared hard at him. "No matter. You've still fallen for her."

"Maybe. I don't know what it is I feel." He looked down at the carpet. "I know I care very deeply for her. Maybe I'm starting to love her. I don't know. It's been a long time since I could say I loved a woman. And what about you, Byron? How far do your feelings go for our little blushing courtesan?"

He rubbed a hand over his mouth and chin. "You make her sound harmless when she's not. She seems soft, Alek, but she's strong."

"I know that. You're avoiding the question."

"You know how I feel." He practically snarled the words. "I've loved her since I nursed her back to health. Six years she's out of my life and I still love her."

"Why don't you tell her, then?"

He shook his head and smiled a cold little smile. "And end up another dead soldier in her ring drawer? You're not listening to me, Alek. All men fall in love with her, but she falls in love with no one."

"You may be different. Your relationship with her is different."

He shot up from his chair and began to pace the room. "Stop it. Down that path of thinking lies despair and disappointment for me." He stopped and speared him with a hard stare. "Didn't you listen to her tell that story about her life with Ivan? Didn't you hear what happened to her? All of that has made her incapable of trusting in one man, investing in him."

"She trusts you. I think she's beginning to trust me. You're not giving her enough credit. In fact, you're insulting her."

"Stop it. I would never insult her."

"You're telling me she's incapable of love, Byron. That she's too broken for it." He leaned forward in his seat. "I disagree. That bastard hurt her, but she's healed."

He shook his head. "You don't ever completely heal from something like that."

"Maybe not." Alek stared into the fire. "Maybe it's a little like grief. You never heal from the loss of someone you loved. You never heal when you lose part of yourself." He paused. "But you do learn to live with it. You learn to go on, live your life, and find happiness. You learn to identify the destructive patterns of behavior you have as a result of your trauma and move past them. You learn to risk yourself again because not risking yourself means a life lived in misery."

Byron turned away and looked out the window. Snow was falling again. He didn't want to listen to Alek. He didn't want to hope for Lilya. Hoping for her and then being denied her would be more than he could handle. He wasn't as strong as Lilya. Hell, he wasn't as strong as Alek. He wouldn't be able to stand the disappointment and rejection if Lilya pushed him away.

Behind him, he heard the chair squeak as Alek rose. "She's hurting and I'm going to her tonight." He paused. "Do you have any objections? After all, you did bring her here *for me* . . . right?" The end of the sentence was laden with sarcasm.

Byron closed eyes and his hands fisted at his sides. He wanted to turn and punch Alek in the face right now. He didn't want to imagine Lilya and Alek alone in her bed tonight. But he needed some distance. Needed to pull back away from Lilya to protect himself. He needed to let this happen however much it might hurt. "Go then," he said hoarsely.

Alek didn't move for a full ten seconds. Then he turned on his heel and walked out of the room.

"Ouch!" Lilya dropped the book she'd been reading into her lap and held her hand. She given herself a paper cut while turning the page.

Someone knocked on the door.

She held her hand, blood welling, and closed her eyes. She'd didn't want to see either of the men tonight. She wanted her pajamas, her bed, a warm fire, and a good book. Sighing, she relented. "Come in."

The door opened and Alek came in. "Lilya?" His gaze dropped to her hand. "What happened?"

She laughed. "It's nothing, really."

He went to the water basin, found a towel, and wet it. Then he walked over to her and sat down on the edge of her bed. "Let me see."

Hesitating for a moment, she gave him her hand. "See? It's just a dumb paper cut."

"Yes, well," he murmured as he wiped the blood away, "dumb paper cuts hurt like a son of a bitch."

She drew an unsteady breath as his hands held hers. His touch was becoming like Byron's, something irresistible to her. Why couldn't he have just left her alone for the night? Every time he touched her, she felt more for him. "Yes, they do."

"Byron went to bed. I just came in to check on you. You seem disturbed this evening." His head was down, examining the cut.

She didn't want to talk about this, so she changed the subject. "When you look at a wound, do you feel the impulse to heal it?"

He looked up at her, surprise in his dark eyes, making them seem a shade lighter. "Sometimes."

She placed her other hand over his. "Try it. Try it now. I know it's just a paper cut, but—"

He looked down and away. For a moment she thought he might bolt. Anything reminding him of Evianna made him want to run, she suspected.

Her unwounded hand closed over his. "Alek, please?" She only had a week to do the impossible thing that Byron had brought her here to accomplish. That meant she needed to push him a little.

He looked back at her, his eyes brimming with emotion. "I care about you, Lilya."

She tried to smile. "I know you do. I can feel it." She held his gaze for a long moment, then leaned in and pressed her lips to his. "And," she murmured against his lips, "I have come to care very much about you."

He increased the pressure of his lips on hers and pushed her back into the pillows. Alek was like a gathering storm, quiet, intense . . . then explosive. From the moment she'd leaned in toward him, she'd known what she was inviting.

Joshui help her, she knew she should push him away, demand that he leave—but she couldn't. She wanted his hands on her, wanted the sensation of his warm breath on her skin.

"Stay with me tonight, Alek," she whispered against his mouth.

In reply, he pulled his shirt over his head and she ran her hands down his chest and up his arms, over warm skin and bunching muscles. Dropping to his pants, she undid the button and zipper, urging him to be free of them. Her fingers closed around his cock and found all his sensitive places, making him groan her name.

He slid bare into her bed, his warm body against her silky nightgown. He grabbed fistfuls of the soft material and yanked it upward, working it over her head and off so that they were soon skin against skin.

He rolled her under his body, his mouth on hers, lips kissing and teeth softly nipping. She explored his powerful torso as his hands slipped over her breasts, between her legs, stroking, petting, making her wet with need. Her fingers curled around his cock and she caressed him until he gave a low groan of arousal, a sound that went right through her, making her shiver.

His head dropped to her breast as he speared two fingers deep inside her and thrust. Her back arched and she moaned his name, her fingers curling in his hair. Alek touched her the way Byron did—made her melt, made her senseless with want. Alek was rougher, more demanding, but he found all the places that made her purr, including the very sensitive one deep within her.

His tongue swirled around each nipple, making them wet with his saliva and hard as pink pebbles while he thumbed her clit, making her moan as he coaxed it into plump need.

When he'd made her mindless with the desire to come, he kneed her thighs wide and slipped between her legs, guiding the head of his cock to her entrance. He stayed that way, hovering over her, his gaze intense and hot on hers. Then he slid inside inch by mind-numbing inch as he stared into her face.

She gasped at the stretch of her inner muscles, her lips parting and her eyes going wide. Then he was seated as deeply inside her body as he could get. She licked her lips, her eyes fluttering shut.

He took her wrists and gently pinned them to the mattress as he began to move in and out of her. He stared down into her face the whole time, a strangely intimate act that heightened her pleasure. Keeping his pace slow, he thrust in and out of her body, letting her feel every single inch of his cock as it moved inside her. His body rocked against her clit, sending spasms of pleasure through her, making the world seem far away—as if only he existed, the play of his body on hers and the pleasure they gave each other.

"You feel so fucking good to me," he groaned, his eyes closing for a moment. "Like hot silk."

She pushed at him, urging him up. He rolled and she went

with him so she was on top, taking control from him. She sat on him, rolling her hips and taking him even deeper into her body. Flipping her head back, her hair cascaded down her spine as she sighed out his name.

He found her clit and petted it as she rode him. His hands roamed her breasts and stomach, explored the place where her sex and his cock met. Then it was back to the relentless pressure on her clit until she exploded in orgasm, bucking on him and moaning as her sex spasmed around his length.

Before she knew what was happening, she was on her stomach, hips high in the air. She clawed at the bedclothes for a moment, empty. Then he was there, thrusting into her from behind with a feral sound growling out from his throat. He held her hips in place and took her fast and hard. Their bodies slammed together, making pleasure race through her with every inward thrust. He moved a hand down past her abdomen, between her thighs, finding her orgasm-sensitive clit and stimulating it.

So much for taking control. Alek had all of it now.

She gasped, her fingers finding purchase in the comforter and holding on for dear life. He pushed her past the postclimax sensitivity in her body and straight back to teetering on the edge of ecstasy.

"Come again for me, Lilya," he growled.

She complied. It burst over her like a bomb, making her cry out. She shuddered and moaned, her internal muscles milking his thrusting cock. Behind her, he shouted her name and his cock jumped deep inside her as he spilled.

"Sweet Joshui," he groaned as he collapsed. He pulled her toward him, kissing the top of her head. "You kill me every time, Lilya. It's always so good with you."

She snuggled against him, her body humming in the aftermath. Her muscles would hurt in the morning, but it would be worth it. "We go well together, you and I."

"Like you and Byron."

She took a moment to answer. "Like me and Byron."

"We all go well together, don't we?"

She nodded. "I have never been with men who were your equals. Never."

He turned her to face him and kissed her lips slowly. "I know you're not lying when you say that."

She smiled, looking anywhere but at his eyes. "Are you really so sure of yourself?"

He tipped her chin up, forcing her to hold his gaze. "No. It's because you can't lie worth a damn, Lilya."

"Ah." Her smile slipped. "That's true enough. Never could. It's what made me a beggar on the streets instead of a thief. I'm honest by nature."

His fingers skimmed the shape of her cheek. "I can see almost everything on your face."

She returned his gaze steadily, silently daring him. "Can you?" Could he tell she was falling in love with him?

He kissed her forehead, tucking her head against his chest. The fight went out of her, postcoital satisfaction ringing the last bit of awareness from her body. She closed her eyes and slept.

When she woke, the sheets and blankets tangled and still warm from Alek's body, she caught a glimpse of her hand.

He'd healed her paper cut.

Twenty-one

◆

She came downstairs and into the kitchen, wrapping her robe around her midsection, her hair still damp from her morning bath. Byron sat at the table with a book and a cup of coffee.

Her stomach in a knot, she poured herself a cup and sat down beside him. "Alek used his magick last night."

He raised an eyebrow and glanced at her. "You thought it was magickal, did you?" He murmured it and it sounded a little antagonistic, though his voice lacked heat.

She dipped her head and blushed—it wasn't from embarrassment; it was from anger. "I meant his magick to *heal*."

He set his book down and looked at her. "Really. Well, I'm not surprised. Like I said, I thought you'd eventually draw it out of him." He paused. "He cares about you a lot."

"As . . . I care about him." *You too.* But she didn't feel comfortable saying that out loud right now.

He returned to his book. "He's gone for the day. Gone to the university."

She nodded and sipped her coffee in silence for several moments. Setting her cup down, she asked, "Are you upset with me for some reason?" When he looked up at her, she knew she had a glitter of anger in her eyes. "What is it you want from me, Byron? You brought me here to supposedly do the impossible task of getting Alek back in touch with his magick. Yet when I say he's beginning to show signs of doing just that you act like you're unhappy with me." Riled by her own words, she stood. "Perhaps it's time I left. I've done what you wanted. There's no reason for me to stay."

Whirling she went for the door. She could pack and be on a transport back to the city by late morning. It was better this way. She wasn't certain she could take another week under these circumstances.

Byron grabbed her arm before she reached the door. She figured he would, but his touch didn't make her melt or soften her resolve. Not today. It was time to stop this craziness and get back to her life—no matter how drastically changed that life would be after these men.

Apparently she'd received the same treatment from them that she'd given her clients for so many years. She thought again about the drawer full of rings. A part of her had always enjoyed rejecting men. It was hard to admit that to herself, but it was true. Since the attack, way deep inside, a part of her had hated men.

But not Byron, not Alek. Not even now.

She stood, her body leaning toward the door, his hand firmly on her upper arm. Her jaw set, she refused to look at him or give him an inch. She wanted him to let go of her so she could flee.

"Lilya, please stop."

"Release my arm."

"Lilya—"

"Let me go."

He released her and she went straight for the door.

"I care about you too."

She stopped, her hand on the doorjamb. She hated herself for pausing there. All she wanted was to push her way over this threshold, up the stairs and to her bags, but Byron had such a strong hold over her. It was magick the way a few loving words from him seemed to enslave her. In this moment, she hated the power he held.

"It's better if I go." Her voice sounded shaky to her own ears. "Better for all of us." *Especially me.*

"I don't want you to leave."

Her body sagged as if she'd been waging a physical fight and had lost. She leaned her forehead against the back of her hand that was braced on the door frame. "What do you want from me, Byron?"

When he spoke again he was so close she could feel his body heat. "I want to spend the day with you. I want to walk outside with you. Talk with you. I want to have lunch with you. I want enjoy your presence in my life." His chest pressed against her back and his arms came around her.

She leaned back against him and closed her eyes.

"You have done nothing wrong, Lilya. I'm not upset with you. Upset with myself, but never you."

"Why?"

He took a long moment to answer. "Because I want impossible things."

"What impossible thing do you want?"

He turned her to face him. She studied him in the shadowed light of the doorway, trying to read his expression and failing. For a moment it seemed like he was going to say something, but instead he leaned in and kissed her.

She frowned, pulling away from him and studying his face. "Byron?"

"Come," he said, turning and taking her hand. "We have a whole kitchen full of ingredients. Will you teach me how to make a decent breakfast?"

She watched him for a moment, wanting to press him. In the end she followed him behind the counter and tried to relax, torn between wanting to bolt and find somewhere quiet to wallow in her pain and wanting to stay and enjoy as much of Byron and Alek as she could.

Surveying the fresh eggs, tomatoes, cheese, and spices and she drew a steadying breath and gave him a shaky smile that she didn't quite feel. "All right, let's get busy, then."

Together they made one of the best omelets she'd ever tasted.

As they finished up their plates of hot, perfectly seasoned eggs, Lilya wondered why she didn't have the sense to run from him. Now she was trapped here for another day with a man she could never have.

Damned expectations.

Lilya looked outside at the piles of snow and the cold, gusting wind. "Doesn't look like a very good day for a walk."

"You're right." He leaned back in his chair, plate scraped clean. "How about skating instead?"

She laughed. "Skating? You mean on ice?"

He lifted a brow and grinned. "Do you know another kind?"

Shaking her head, she looked down at the remnants of her eggs. "I've never ice skated in my life. I have no skates and even if I did—"

"I have skates that I'm sure will fit you and you should try it at least once in your life. We have a pond on the property. I'm told it's been cleared of snow and its frozen clean through. What do you think?"

She gazed out the window. A day spent with Byron sounded good, no matter what they did. She looked at him and smiled. "Let's go."

Byron slipped the skates onto Lilya's feet while she sat on a bench near the frozen pond. He'd had it cleared of snow in the winter so the children nearby could skate and play games on it.

"You call this a pond?" Lilya asked, gazing out at the huge expanse of ice.

He stopped lacing her skates, to follow her gaze, his breath showing white in the cold air. "It's a really big pond."

"It's an ocean."

She shivered and he looked up at her. "Do you need a heavier coat?"

Letting out a burst of laughter, she cupped his cheek with one gloved hand. The action made his heart ache. "You've got me so bundled up that if I fall out there on the ice, I won't feel a thing. I'm fine. I was just shivering at the thought of using these tiny knives to move on the ice." She picked up one booted foot and examined the skate blade. "Who thought inventing these was a good idea?"

His breath huffed out of him as he finished lacing her skate. "According to Alek, the inventor of the ice skate was a people who lived in the far nor—"

She held up a hand. "I get it. All right, I'm ready. Can you help me up?"

He grasped her hands and helped her to stand. Taking baby steps, she walked to the ice and ventured a careful step onto it. Then she put her other foot on and immediately lost her balance. Shrieking, she fought for control, arms whirling, then went down on her rear.

"Lilya! Are you all right?"

She stared straight ahead for a moment, as if in shock, then started to laugh.

"Lilya?" He skated over in front of her. She was still just sitting there and laughing. "Are you all right?" he asked again. He laughed too. That's what happened when one heard Lilya laugh. Surprisingly for a woman who'd had such hardship in her life, she did it wholeheartedly and with her entire beautiful body.

She wiped tears from her eyes from the laughter. "Yes, I'm fine." Then she reached for him to help her up.

"Try to keep your weight directly above your skates. Don't lean back or forward too far."

Coming to a standing position, she looked up into his eyes. "I think I've got it now."

He smiled down at her, his chest filling with that familiar warm feeling he had whenever she was close. He leaned down and kissed her. "All right. Skate forward."

Slowly she skated out into the pond and turned in a slow

circle. "Hey! I think I've—*whoa!*" She went down and was laughing again.

It went on that way, Lilya making a little progress, falling, laughing, then getting up and trying again. Even when he thought they'd had enough and should go in, she wanted to stay and try to master the ice skates.

Finally she was able to stay on her feet and keep her balance. She skated around the pond with him with a huge smile on her face, her cheeks pink from the cold and her dark hair coming free around her face.

She was more beautiful than he'd ever seen her.

His heart swelled with emotion, joy mixed with the knowledge that he'd soon lose her. He wanted to savor this day, tuck it away in his pocket forever. They spent the afternoon on the ice and only went in when he insisted they needed to get warm.

They entered the house exhausted and happy, their cheeks burning from the cold. A fire had been lit in the library. Byron made coffee and carried it into the room on a tray. He sat down in the big chair in front of the hearth and when Lilya went to sit in the opposite chair, he grabbed her around the waist and pulled her into his lap.

She came to him with a yelp of surprise and a sigh of contentment, settling onto his lap and tucking herself against his chest with her head on his shoulder. He took the rest of the pins out of her hair, setting them on the table beside him one by one, and ran his fingers through the long, dark skeins wordlessly. Eventually Lilya's breathing grew deep and even and he knew she'd dropped off to sleep.

Deep satisfaction settling into his bones, he wrapped his arms around her and watched the fire while she napped. Today had been by far one of the best days of his life. Lilya was an easy person for him to be with, not only was she his lover, but a friend as well. Right now he knew without a doubt he wanted to spend his life with her, but if he asked her marry him, would he end up another abandoned ring box in her drawer of wealthy, besotted men? Odds were the answer was yes.

Twenty-two

❖

"S he's leaving in two days."

Hiding the way those words made him feel, Alek turned toward Byron. "I am aware." He returned to staring out the library window at the cold, starless night.

"So why are we down here and she's upstairs?"

Alek threw back the rest of his drink. He suspected he knew why, but it wouldn't do any good to tell Byron what he thought; he wouldn't believe him. "I don't think it's because she wants to be left alone. I suspect Lilya is sad to be leaving."

"I'm going up." Byron stood. "We only have a short time left with her."

"It doesn't have to be that way."

Byron let out a long, slow breath. "Yes, it does."

Alek ground his teeth together. Byron didn't know it yet, but there was no way he was letting Lilya go without telling her how he felt about her. Byron might have a problem doing that—but *he* didn't.

He glanced guiltily at his friend. He just didn't want to lose Byron over it. Byron was as close as a brother to him and that made this situation tricky.

"I want to see her. I'm heading upstairs." Byron walked toward the door.

Jealousy flashed through him. He knew he really had no right to feel that way. He had no claim on Lilya. No man did. And if there was any man who *did* have a claim on her, it was Byron. Still, he set his glass down. "Not alone, you aren't."

Byron stilled, anger flashed just briefly through his eyes and then settled into acceptance. "All right."

Together they mounted the stairs and knocked on her door. "Come in."

They entered the room and found her sitting near a fire in her nightgown, a heavy blanket draped over her legs and a book in her lap. She turned and smiled at them. "I'm glad you came up. I was just about to go downstairs and find you."

"We're not disturbing you, then?" Byron asked. "You seemed a little melancholy this afternoon. I just wanted to make sure you were all right." There were two more chairs near her and he and Alek took them.

She shook her head, then bowed it. Her smile faded. "I am a little sad. I've enjoyed my stay here."

Byron glanced at Alek. Alek held his gaze for a moment, acknowledging that Alek had been right about Lilya's depression. Now if only Byron would believe he was right about how Lilya felt about him—and about himself, he hoped.

Lilya rose, pushing the blanket off her legs and standing in front of the fire. The material of her nightgown was sheer and they could see the slim silhouette of her body through the fabric. Alek's body tightened at the sight. He imagined his fingers curling to lift the garment over her head and then immersing himself in the experience of her silken skin and lush body.

Lilya watched them as she stood in front of the fire, her body tightening from their mere presence in her room. Two days and she would be gone. Two days and she wouldn't know the hungry look in their eyes as they watched her anymore. Two days and she would be alone again.

She knew what they wanted. They were men and she knew men very well. They may have come up to her room because they were concerned about her state of mind, but they wanted her body.

That was fine. She wanted them too.

Her gaze drifted over them both. Alek's fingers were clenched tight on the armrests of his chair, as though holding himself back from getting up and coming over to her. Byron watched her with dark eyes, full of unmistakable desire.

The sight of them both in front of her, wanting her, made her body react. Ripen. Grow warm and wet. She pulled the nightgown over her head and threw it to the chair, standing before them completely naked with the fire warming the flesh of her back. Now there could be no mistake about what would happen between them tonight.

She wasn't sure which man she should go to. Going to one would slight the other. Instead she waited for one of them to make a move. It was Alek who rose first. Deceptively mild Alek, who

He slid his hand between her legs and found her wet and warm. Finding her clit nestled in the tangle of her damp curls, he stroked it past its postclimax sensitivity until she was incoherent with need once more. Then Byron picked up the lubricated object on the bed beside him and slid it into her cunt. It was thick, long, and studded with small protrusions that felt delicious when he pushed and pulled the object in and out of her. She cried out, moaning.

"I think she likes that," said Alek.

"Then let's see how she enjoys this." Byron picked up the second cylinder, this one was the elongated one, graduated in size, and it was also coated with a sticky lubricant. She'd known what it was for when she'd spotted it earlier, any courtesan would, though one had never been used on her.

He slid it into her nether entrance and gently pushed the object within. The walls of her rear stretched and gave as her body fought to accommodate the toy. She squirmed on the bed, panting in ecstasy as her body adjusted to having both objects inside her. The cylinder in her rear rode a confusing edge of pain and sweet pleasure, the slight pain playing counterpoint and deepening the pleasure. She could barely stay sane from the eroticism of having both her orifices filled. The two sensations blended together until she didn't know where one ended and the other began.

Byron worked one of the toys and Alek took the other. Together, they moved in unison, slowly thrusting the objects in and out of her. They slid in and out slowly at first, then faster. Her hands fisted the blankets and she tossed her head, the ecstasy rising quickly to an overwhelming level.

She came hard and fast, with no warning. It slammed into her body, stealing her thoughts and, for a moment, her very breath. She cried out, her body spasming in pleasure.

When her climax had ebbed once more, they pulled the toys from her and she collapsed to the mattress. Both men were pulling off their clothes. *Finally*. Byron slipped in behind her and Alek pressed against her front, his mouth finding and meshing with hers.

She pushed up and straddled Alek, guiding the head of his cock deep inside. Her back bowed as she sank all the way down on him, her hair cascading down her spine. She let out a shuddering breath. Alek felt bigger and better than the toy ever would.

Byron's hands roamed her breasts, petting her nipples and teasing them to hard little peaks, while Alek found her very sensitive clit and ever so gently teased it. She shuddered, amazed that her body was capable of holding this much pleasure at one time. Even now she felt her body responding to these men, though she'd come twice already.

Rolling her hips, she rode Alek, taking him in long, deep thrusts. Alek groaned her name and closed his eyes for a moment, his throat working as he swallowed hard.

Then Alek pulled her down against his chest and his mouth sealed over hers. Lips and tongue working, he kissed her senseless while Byron coated his cock in lubricant and straddled Alek's legs, setting the crown of his shaft to her nether hole.

He pushed in an inch and she stiffened, letting out a moan that was part pleasure, part fear. Byron was a large man in every way, larger than the toy had been.

"You can do this," he purred near her ear, his chest against her back. His words rumbled through his body and into her. "I'm going to take you in your rear while Alek takes your sweet cunt."

He thrust in another inch and she whimpered, finding purchase in the blankets. This time it was almost all pleasure, with just that luscious edge of pain to accentuate the ecstasy. Her muscles stretched to accommodate his girth as he slid in another inch and yet another.

Finally both men were seated root-deep inside her. After a moment they began to move.

Lilya saw stars. All she could do was hold on as the intense sensation of being filled this way overcame her. The three of them found a rhythm, each moving in time with one another, Lilya between them. She had never felt anything like this and she never wanted it to end. Their cocks tunneled in and out of her in unison, creating a perfect storm of sexual bliss that her body could barely hold.

Alek caught her nape and pulled her head down to kiss her, his tongue spearing aggressively into her mouth. She cupped his cheek with one hand and kissed him back just as forcefully—as if she could tell him how she felt using her mouth and body instead of words.

"Are you going to come?" he asked against her mouth.

She nodded, unable to form a verbal reply. Her body tensed and her third climax hit her, this one more powerful than either of the other two. She cried as it hit her, pulling her under for a moment in complete sexual rapture. The muscles of her sex milked Alek's thrusting shaft and he groaned hard, jerking against her as he came. Their climaxes triggered Byron's and he orgasmed in her rear, yelling out her name.

Sated, satisfied, and exhausted, the three of them collapsed to the mattress in a tangle. Tucked between them, Lilya breathed heavily. The muscles of her body would be sore in the morning, but it would be a glorious kind of sore.

Byron pulled her against him and kissed her temple, his arms winding around her. She sighed in perfect sexual lethargy. For now she would push aside her heartache and take this moment with Byron and Alek. Savor it. Memorize it so it could keep her warm on her lonely nights to come.

Alek curled up on her other side and nuzzled her neck. "I'll get up and run a bath."

Her arms tightened around him. "You're not going anywhere." She kissed the top of his head. "That was incredible."

"We seem to fit well together, all of us," Byron said, running his hand over her breast. Her nipple went hard against his palm.

"Mmm," she agreed. Forming words was fast becoming an impossible task.

After a few more moments of cuddling, Alek rose and ran a bath. Byron lifted her and placed her in it and both men climbed in after her. The bathtub was huge, but it just barely fit the three of them and water sloshed over the side.

Byron and Alek soaped their hands and washed her from head to toe, their strong hands working all the strain from her muscles until she felt like half-melted butter. Byron helped her dry off while Alek tended the fire and soon the three of them were under the blankets of her bed, bare skin against bare skin.

Feeling cherished and protected, Lilya drifted off to sleep warmed by the heat of both of them, their hands stroking over her still-damp skin.

Twenty-three

Byron looked up from his chair as Alek entered the room, lowering the paper he was reading to his lap.

"A messenger was just at the door," said Alek. "Sent by Gregorio. Your meeting with Aralynda went much better than anticipated."

"She's agreed to stay?"

"Yes."

Byron smiled. Lilya would be pleased by the news. He lifted his paper once more, but Alek was still standing in the doorway, staring hard at him. "Do you have something else you need to say to me, Alek?"

"I'm falling in love with her."

Byron said nothing in response. Stony-faced, he regarded his best friend in silence.

Alek walked toward him. "I know you're already in love with her and have been for a long time. What do you have to say?"

He leaned back in his chair. "Of course you're falling in love with her. I expected no less. That's the curse of Lilya." He paused. "She told me you used your magick to heal some small wound she had. You would not have done such a thing if you didn't love her."

"Is that all you have to say? You're not jealous? You're not worried that I might ask her to stay with me, even marry me . . . and she might say yes?"

Byron pushed away from his desk and stood. "I'm jealous every time you touch her, Alek." His voice came out sounding rough with emotion. "Because I want her touching me."

"I knew it."

"Go ahead and ask her to marry you. Be like all the others who've done the same. She'll turn you down. She turns all of them down."

"I'm different."

He walked toward him slowly, his eyebrows rising. "Do you really think so?"

"Yes."

Byron shook his head. "I think every man who has asked her has thought he was *different*, and she's said no to them all."

Alek turned away from him. "I haven't felt like this since Evianna."

Byron stared at his back. "Lilya is . . . *Lilya*. We can love her without forcing her to be someone she isn't. We have to be ready to let her go."

"Love her from afar, you mean."

"I've been doing it for years."

"You might be able to do it." Alek shook his head. "But I can't." He left the room. A moment later, Byron heard the front door slam shut.

He dropped his head into his hands, wondering what that meant. Was Alek gone for the night or gone for good? Was he fleeing the tension that had been growing in the house surrounding Lilya's departure?

Despite that tension, the day had been a nice one. They'd taken the carriage, still on sleds, into town. They'd had lunch and Lilya had come to watch them practice crossball. When they'd arrived home, they'd made dinner, the three of them, laughing, joking, and enjoying each other's company. Yet the unspoken had hung in the air—that tension.

Lilya was leaving tomorrow.

Perhaps Alek wouldn't be here in the morning. Maybe he couldn't take saying good-bye to her. Byron wasn't sure he could do it either.

He rubbed a hand over his tired face, wanting nothing more than to see Lilya. It was like she was a drug. He knew she was bad for him because he was about to be cut off, yet he couldn't stop himself from getting all he could until then.

Maybe it had been mistake to bring her here, although he had achieved his goal of getting Alek to use his magick. It had only been a small act, but it was a start. It meant the block that had formed at the time of Evianna's death was breaking down. Lilya had done that. And no matter how much pain Alek was in right now, that crumbling block was worth it. In time Byron hoped Alek saw that.

When he entered Lilya's painting room, she was so obsessed with her work that she didn't even hear him come in. She'd taken

off her gown and stockings and laid them carefully over a chair.
Her boots were on the floor near the fireplace. She stood barefoot
in front of the canvas wearing only her undershift.

His breath caught at the sight of her. Elusian crystal lights
blazed behind her, throwing the curve of her body beneath the
thin fabric of the shift into clear view. He could see her slim waist
and the flared heart shape of her hips and rear. Her full breasts
pressed through the bodice, nipples hard from the chill in the
room that the fire in the hearth couldn't completely banish. Paint
smears marked her bare arms and rosy cheeks. Her hair was
mussed—half up and half down—the way she looked after sex or
a day of ice skating.

Beautiful.

"Lilya?"

She jumped, startled, then turned and flashed a devastating
smile at him. Her eyes had been out of focus—like she was looking into another world while she worked—but now they were
clear and focused on him. "You scared me."

He walked toward her, looking at the canvas. The landscape
she was working on was a departure from the other paintings
she'd done while here. This was no street environment imagined
from her youth.

He frowned, studying it. "Where is that?"

She shrugged, smiling, her paintbrush still in hand. "I don't
really know. I can see it in my imagination. It's pretty, don't you
think? Wouldn't you like to go there?"

The landscape was lush green with hills rising in the background. A building that looked a lot like a cathedral rose on one
of the hills, a deep forest running down along its side. The sky
was a deep blue with perfectly painted clouds. "It's gorgeous."

She set her paintbrush down and stepped back to look at it, her back coming very close to his chest. "I wanted to abandon reality for a little while, I guess."

Yes, he knew about that all too well on this last eve they— *he*—had with her. He enveloped her in his arms and kissed the top of her head. "I want you to take everything with you tomorrow when you go."

"What?" She turned toward him, her eyes stormy and . . . hurt. "I thought you said I could come back here whenever I wanted."

He touched her mouth, searching her eyes. "And you can. I hope you do." His gaze lifted to the canvas. "But you have real talent, Lilya. You shouldn't go even a day without painting. Take all these supplies with you and use them daily."

She stared at him for a moment, then laid her head on his chest. "I'll miss you." Her voice sounded full of emotion and a little broken.

Not like I'll miss you. He closed his eyes, unable to answer. Instead he moved her head and dropped his mouth to kiss her slowly, as if trying to savor her. His tongue slipped between her lips and rubbed up against her tongue. He wished he could bottle up the taste of her for the long nights ahead. Finally he broke the kiss and set his forehead to hers. "I'll come into the city to visit you often."

"Why?" Her voice sounded full of tears. "Do you want to become a client?"

He stared down at her. Her eyes sparkled with something between anger and sadness. "Do you want me to?"

She pushed away from him, going to stand in front of the painting with her arms over her chest. "No. I'm not taking clients anymore."

He stepped toward her, frowning. "Lilya—"

Then she turned and came back into his arms, kissing him hard. Tears were running down her cheeks. Her body crushed up against his. Her breasts pressed against his chest and her fingers tangled in the hair at his nape as she pulled his head down to kiss him. His own body ignited, need flaring to life. His fingers gripped her shift and lifted it, pulled it over her head, and threw it aside.

He pushed her down to the floor of the room. Her hands pulled at his clothes, yanking his sweater over his head and then tugging at the button and zipper of his pants. Once his bare skin slid against hers, he kneed her thighs apart, his cock hard and throbbing with need. He dropped his head to her breast, pulling one small red nipple between his lips and then the other. She gasped softly, her fingers stroking through his hair.

Trailing his tongue down over her abdomen and her mound, he found her sweet little clit and licked it. Her back arched and the bundle of nerves immediately began to swell. He explored her with his tongue, leisurely driving her crazy and enjoying the taste of her and all the ways he could make her moan. When she exploded in climax, he clamped his mouth down on her as she bucked, drinking in every lovely jerk of her hips and committing it to memory.

Then, unable to wait even a moment more, he raised himself up, guided the crown of his cock into her, and sank deep inside her velvety hot sex. Her muscles clamped down around his shaft, rippling as they accommodated his girth and length. He tipped his head back, groaning her name. They fit so well together.

Her breath hissed out of her and she closed her eyes as he began to thrust into her. Her fingers found and clenched around his shoulders while he rode her faster and harder.

"Open your eyes," he murmured. "I want to watch your face when you come."

Her eyes fluttered open, unfocused at first, then slowly cleared and held his gaze, though they remained heavy-lidded with arousal. Her hair was a riot of darkness around her head, her pretty lips slightly parted.

He took her in long, hard, driving strokes, pulling out almost all the way before impaling her over and over. They were one right now, connected by body, if not by heart and soul—sharing pleasure.

Her body twitched and her back arched in the way he recognized meant she was close to her orgasm. He was close too. She moaned, her eyes drifting closed.

"Look at me," he commanded in a harsh, broken voice.

Her eyes locked with his as her climax hit her. They widened, her mouth opening with a silent rush of air. The muscles of her sex pulsed and rippled, her hips bucking. Her back arched and she cried out his name, her fingernails digging into the skin of his arms.

Pleasure bubbled up and exploded over him as well. His cock jumped deep inside her, spasming as he came. He groaned out her name as it washed through him just on the tail end of her orgasm.

"Ah, gods," he breathed, collapsing over her and rolling to the side. They both lay there, breathing hard. He pulled her up against him, and stroked his hands over her skin, unable to stop touching her. Forcing all other thought from his body, he immersed himself in this moment, trying to stay here with her forever.

She snuggled against him, her hands roaming his body as well. She kissed his chest, rolling over his body as if she wanted to feel the slip of his skin over hers, finding his mouth and sliding her tongue inside. Her hand stroked his flaccid cock, making it twitch and start to harden again. He rolled her over again, closer to the fire, his hand delving between her thighs and finding her sticky sweet with the remnants of their mingled bliss.

He used it to pleasure her again, stroking over her sensitive clit until she moaned and panted, then thrust up into her sex with his fingers while his tongue worked over her breasts. He felt obsessed, relentless in his need to devour every inch of her.

She came again, suddenly and softly, there on the floor, and he drank up every sound she made with his mouth slanted across hers, tongues tangled.

Finally they lay snuggled up against his each other, breathless and unable to speak.

Eventually they got up and went to his room. Alek still wasn't home. Lilya didn't ask where he was, though her gaze lingered on his door as they passed it as if she wanted to ask. She didn't and Byron was glad. Tonight he wanted her to be his alone.

He filled a tub and they washed each other. Then, naked, they crawled into his bed. Limbs entangled, they fell asleep, though it took Byron a long time to drop off.

Tomorrow she'd be gone.

Twenty-four

❖

Steam billowed from the transport at regular intervals with angry-sounding hisses. Lilya stared at it, bag in hand, fighting back an overwhelming melancholy.

"Are you sure you don't want me to come with you?"

She stared at the billowing steam while she answered. "No. You'd just have to turn around and come right back on the next transport. What a waste of a day. But thank you for offering."

In actuality she didn't want him to come with her because she wasn't going back to the Temple of Dreams. Not ever. She didn't want him to know that because he'd ask her why.

To change the subject, she asked the question she'd been suppressing with much effort since that morning. "Where is Alek?"

"Ah." He glanced away from her. "I think saying good-bye to you was a little too much for him."

"Oh." She wasn't sure how to interpret that. Emotion caught

at the back of her throat. Swallowing it down, she looked away from him so he couldn't see the sadness on her face. She'd definitely wanted to say good-bye to Alek.

The conductor called for all the ticket holders to board. She went very still for a moment, then she gathered her strength and embraced Byron. This was the moment she'd been dreading. "I hope I did what you wanted me to do, Byron. I feel like I failed. Good-bye." Then, before he could say another word, she hurried onto the transport without looking back.

As she made her way to his private car, she could see him out of the corner of her eye, following her down the length of the transport. She reached the car and slid into the seat nearest the window, only then daring to look at him. Hopefully he wouldn't be able to see the tears in her eyes.

But he wasn't there. He'd already left.

Blowing out a long breath, she stared ahead and mustered every ounce of her strength not to dissolve into large, self-pitying tears. Leaving Byron and Alek was the hardest thing she'd ever done and, in her life, that was saying a lot.

Her heart didn't feel broken; it felt crushed.

When the transport finally pulled into the station in Milzyr, she hired a carriage and had the driver load her luggage, including all of the painting supplies and her paintings. Instead of instructing the carriage to the Temple of Dreams, she had the driver take her to Byron's old house—her house now.

The driver off-loaded all her things in the entryway. She paid him, then turned to survey the damage. She hadn't been in here in years. Straight ahead of her were the stairs that led to the second-floor bedrooms. Down the hallway to the left of the stairs were the kitchen and a large dining room. Through an arched doorway

on her immediate left was a sitting room filled with furniture that she'd covered with canvas before she'd left.

Entering the musty-smelling room, she pulled the canvas off a couch, a chair, and an end table. Then walked over and threw open the heavy drapes of the front window to reveal a bustling downtown street. Light flooded into the room. She'd need to open all the windows and do a bit of cleaning. That was good; it would keep her busy and her mind focused on things other than Byron and Alek.

She was done with the Temple of Dreams, unable to ever bring herself to be with a man she didn't care about. Love, she'd always said, was the demise of a courtesan and she was suffering under the power of it twice-fold.

This was her new life.

She turned, surveying the large, empty house. It was going to be a lonely one.

Byron stood in the library, feeling the weight of his huge, empty house. Hands fisting, he closed his eyes and dropped his head. This day was going to be hard; it would probably be hard for a while. He was going to have to learn to live without her and that would take some time.

A part of him was sorry he'd ever gone to her in the first place, but he didn't regret the last three weeks. Despite the pain, it was good he'd had those days with her. At least he had the memories.

The front door opened and footsteps sounded in the foyer and corridor. He knew who it was because he recognized the cadence. Byron opened his eyes as Alek entered the room. He knew his expression looked stormy—it matched the way he felt. "She was sorry you weren't there to see her off. In fact, I believe she was quite hurt. Where did you go?" He couldn't keep the hostility from his voice.

"I couldn't say good-bye to her." Alek looked down into his hand. A ring box lay in his palm. "I *won't* say good-bye to her. I had to go get this. It was my mother's."

Byron stared at the box for a moment, then snarled. "You're a fool."

"I think you're just worried she'll agree to marry me and you'll lose her forever. You love her as much as I do. It doesn't have to be this way. You don't need to be shut out."

"What do you mean, share her?"

Alek closed his hand, his arm dropping to his side. "We both love her and I believe she loves us in return."

"You're crazy." Byron stalked to the fireplace and turned his back to him, his hands on the mantel. "She's got a whole drawer full of little boxes just like that. You're going to be rejected and come back here brokenhearted."

"I know that's what you're afraid of. You don't want to be like all those other men she's turned down. Is your pride really that strong, Byron? You'll let the one woman you love go just because you're afraid she'll tell you she doesn't feel the same way?"

His hand tightened on the wood. That would kill him. Destroy him. He couldn't bear to hear words like that coming out of Lilya's mouth. "*Yes*," he hissed.

"What if she says she loves you back, Byron? What then?"

"She won't."

"You don't know that. Come with me."

Byron whirled to face him. "You go and get your heart broken if you want to do that. If you're so certain you're somehow better than the other fifty men who have asked her to marry them, you go on ahead. I don't have any wish to hear the rejection you'll undoubtedly receive for your trouble."

Alek's face hardened. "I never pegged you for a coward, Byron."

Byron stared at him for a long moment, the silence of the house suddenly pressing down on him so hard he couldn't breathe. He tore past him, catching up his coat as he went. "I can't stay here anymore," he growled. "Good luck, Alek."

He turned as Byron barreled through the doorway and into the foyer. "Where are you going?"

"Away." His hand found the doorknob and he threw the door open. Cold winter air blasted him in the face. "For a long time," he finished, looking out at the drifts of snow. Then it was his turn to slam the door as he left.

Ivan slipped in through the back door with minimum effort. Byron Andropov had fortified his defenses since his last visit, but it still didn't take much for him to break in. He was the King of Crime in Milzyr; a few expensive locks meant nothing to him. He hadn't even had to break the lovely expensive glass.

Once in the kitchen, he felt immediately that something was wrong. He knew that Lilya had left for the city earlier that day; he'd seen her terse final exchange with Byron in front of the steam transport and noted with contentment that Alek had not even bothered to show up to say good-bye to her. But he hadn't known that the men had also left.

The house felt empty to him and all the hearths were cold.

Hell, even his breath showed white in the air of the kitchen. It seemed like no one had been in the house for a long time, though he knew that Byron and Alek had returned to it earlier that day.

Just to make sure, he made his way up the stairs and checked all the bedrooms, first Alek's and then Byron's.

"Fuck!" he bellowed into the quiet air as he stood next to Byron's empty bed. He took his dagger out of his pocket and slammed it into the pillow again and again, sending clouds of feathers into the air.

Then he turned, grabbed a vase from a nearby table, and hurled it against the door. He stalked around the room, destroying everything he could, ripping the pictures from the wall and smashing the end tables against the floor.

Breathing hard, but feeling a little better, he came to a stop in the middle of the shattered room and ran a hand through his hair. He'd been counting on the men being here tonight so he could slit their throats in their sleep. Now, with no sign they'd be returning anytime soon, that would have to wait.

He needed to get back to Milzyr and make sure Lilya was once again where she belonged.

Twenty-five

She wasn't at the Temple of Dreams.

Ivan turned the corner of the block where the building was located, only barely able to contain his rage. He'd even gone there himself. He'd never once personally set foot in that place until today. The woman who answered the door had recognized him right off and had paled. She'd paled even more when he'd asked after Lilya.

Clearly Lilya hadn't kept her history a secret from everyone.

But Lilya wasn't there. Hadn't even so much as stopped there when she'd returned from Milzyr and had sent word she would never return. She hadn't even sent for her things, according to the woman who'd answered the door, instead she'd donated everything to some of the other women who needed them.

How . . . fucking . . . *sweet.*

No, Lilya hadn't left a forwarding address, said the woman when he'd asked. That was fine. He knew where she'd be. She still owned property across town. Byron's old place.

And that's when the rage had set in.

Nothing he'd seen in Ulstrat had been what he'd presumed. He stood on a street corner, watching carriages drive past, a boy hawking newspapers on the corner, smoke curling from the chimney of a nearby cook shop. The snow in the streets looked grimy from the passing of carriages and the muck from the smokestacks.

Everything he'd watched between Lilya and the men replayed in his mind. The scene at the crossball stadium hadn't been Lilya being cold and removed from the men because she disliked them—it had probably been because she'd cared for them and it frightened her. The way she'd embraced Byron at the transport station and immediately turned to get onto the train hadn't been because she'd been ready to leave—it had been because she'd been ready *to cry*. And Alek Chaikoveii not being present? In his mind it suddenly became not a lack of caring, *but far too much caring.*

His hands fisted at his sides, fingernails digging into his palms so hard he nearly drew his own blood. Lilya wasn't going back to the Temple of Dreams because something had changed significantly in Ulstrat, something that made it impossible for her to take up her old life again.

And that made Ivan very unhappy.

Because of the way she'd left Byron at the station, Ivan presumed there was no happily ever after in the offing for them. Perhaps Lilya's broken heart prevented her from returning to the temple. Of course, add in Byron's absence at his home in Ulstrat and perhaps a happy ending *was* plausible. Maybe Byron needed to go off on some sort of business, making her sad he'd be away from her, and she'd returned to the city to get their love nest ready for his return.

Either way, Ivan wasn't getting what he wanted and he *always* got what he wanted . . . eventually, anyway.

This changed nothing for the men. They both needed to die as soon as he could locate them.

But . . . Lilya.

Well, this changed things for Lilya significantly.

It seemed he could no longer take the hands-off approach with her. No, it was definitely time to lay *hands on*.

"She's beautiful," Lilya breathed, moving the blanket away from the baby's face and gazing on the pout of her lips. "Both of them." She met Gregorio's gaze, the proud father who held the other little girl snug in his arms.

"Thank you." Evangeline sat on the couch in Lilya's living room, gently rocking the sleeping girl. "So, you were right. *Twins*."

Lilya sat down next to Anatol, who was wrangling their two-year-old son, Nicoli. Anatol looked at her. "Yes, gods help us," he groaned, catching the tot around the waist before he could bolt into the hallway.

Lilya laughed. "Don't give me that. You love it."

"It's just lucky there are three of us," said Gregorio in a low voice from across the room.

"I wonder if they'll be magicked." Lilya caught the scampering boy, who was chasing the stray cat Lilya had adopted only that morning, and gave him a quick kiss on the head.

"Time will tell on that score." Evangeline gazed down into her three-week-old daughter's face, smiling gently.

The glow of motherhood sat well on her. It was something that Lilya never would have been able to imagine for her when they'd first met. Evangeline and Anatol had been homeless and penniless J'Edaeii who'd been running from the mob of the revolution. As an added obstacle, Evangeline had suffered a terrible backlash from her magick, making her emotionless all her life. But the stress of her situation during the initial days of the revolution had broken all the walls she'd built to dam her emotion and uncontrollable raucous, raw feeling had poured through her. It had complicated an already bad situation.

Lilya was happy for Evangeline, but watching her with that babe in her arms, surrounded by the men who loved her, made her wistful too. It would take her a while to get over having Byron and Alek for those three weeks and then losing them. Eventually, she would be all right. She just needed to hang on until time taught her to deal with her loss.

She looked up to find Anatol looking at her in that way he had. Anatol's magick was shaping light into illusion, but there was a backlash to his magick too. While he could create lies for the eye, he could also see the truth of people.

"You're hurting really badly right now, aren't you, Lilya?" he asked.

She gave him a small smile. "I'd say no, but you'd know I was lying."

"I would. I can see what it is you need."

She laughed. "I'll never get what I need, Anatol." The words didn't sound bitter; they sounded truthful.

Just then someone knocked at her door. "I'm not expecting anyone." Frowning, she got up to answer it. Her heart skipped when she opened the door and found Alek on her doorstep.

"Hello, Lilya."

She gripped the door so hard her fingers turned white. "How did you know where to find me?"

"When you weren't at the Temple of Dreams, it wasn't hard to guess where you'd gone."

"What are you doing here?"

He smiled, peering into the house. "Can I come in?"

"Oh." She backed away from the door. "I'm sorry. Of course."

He entered the house just as Anatol was rounding his family up to leave. He leveled a meaningful look at her. "It's time we were going."

"You just got here! You don't have to leave."

Anatol shook Alek's hand. "It's nice to meet you. I'm Anatol, a friend of Lilya's. That's Evangeline and Gregorio." He motioned to Gregorio and Evangeline who were getting the babies ready. Nicoli ran over and took his hand, beaming up at Alek, making Alek laugh. "And this is our son, Nicoli."

"Gregorio Vikhin?" Alek asked.

Gregorio waved a hand clutched around a baby bottle. "I am."

Alek nodded. "Then all of you know my friend, Byron Andropov."

Anatol looked at Lilya, his eyebrows rising. She hadn't said a word to any of them about Alek or Byron, but Anatol was getting the shape of things from his magick. "Yes, we all know him very well."

Gregorio walked over with his infant daughter tucked against his brawny chest, the picture of fatherly protection. "Byron has been very active and generous in getting a magickal education program started both in the government and at the university. He's told us about you, Alek."

"You have healing magick," Evangeline said, approaching them with the other sleeping infant. "That's very strong and rare. Byron wants you to come into the education program and train it."

Alek's lips twisted. "I'm aware." He paused, looking at Lilya. "And I intend to do just that. Someone very special has convinced me that I need to stop being so selfish and share my ability with the world."

Lilya smiled at him, warmth blossoming in her chest. "I'm very glad to hear that."

A smile broke out across Evangeline's mouth. "That's wonderful news! We'll expect you at the university, then."

Alek nodded at her. "I'll be there."

They all said their good-byes and with a flurry of baby blankets, bottles, and a few toddler toys, they were gone. Alek watched them climb into their carriage outside. "They seem like a happy and loving family."

Lilya came to stand next to him. "They are."

"I want what they have." Alek turned to her and pulled a ring box from his pocket and opened it up to reveal a sparkling sapphire-and-diamond engagement ring. "With you, Lilya."

Lilya stared down at the ring, stunned. "What did you say?" She reached out and touched the box, thinking maybe she was imagining it. But, no, it was sturdy under her fingertips.

"I love you and I want to spend my life with you."

She glanced outside at the retreating carriage and imagined the happy family within. Pressing her lips together at the stab of pain in her chest and stomach at what would never be hers, she looked up at him. "I can't have children, Alek. Remember? I can't give you what you want." Unless they adopted. That was always a possibility.

He gripped her chin, staring down at her fiercely. "I know that, Lilya." He paused. "I love you. I want to be with you no matter what. Children or no children. Anyway, we can always adopt." There could never have been a more perfect response.

She dropped her gaze to the ring, smiling. It was the first one she'd ever seen that she wanted to accept. Her finger ached to wear it. She took the box from him carefully, her smile fading. "I love you too," she whispered. "But you're not the only one I love." She looked up into his face to gauge his reaction. "It wouldn't be fair to you if I accepted this ring with the weight of Byron still on my heart."

"I know that. He loves you too."

Something sparked inside her chest, then went cold. Her face twisted and she blinked away sudden tears. "Then why did he let me go?"

"He's afraid." Alek closed his eyes for a moment and let out a long, deep breath. "I was afraid too. Did you just say you loved me?"

She smiled. "Yes." Reaching up, she cupped his cheek. "I love you, Alek." Gently, she pressed her lips to his.

He offered the ring to her again. "So, do you accept?"

Her smile faded and she backed away.

He snapped the box closed. Despair clouded his face. "Lilya?"

"You must understand. Being that I also love Byron, this is complicated, Alek."

"Not for me. Byron is my best friend and I love him as the closest thing I will ever have to a brother. You love him, as he loves you. You also love me, as I love you. We all love each other." He motioned at the door through which Evangeline, Anatol, and Gregorio had just exited. "We wouldn't be the first to join in such a relationship." He shook his head. "It's not complicated."

She turned and walked into the living room. Alek followed. She went to the window and looked out. "But he's not here, Alek. *You're* the one who came. I need *him* to come to me, tell me what's in his heart. I need to look into his eyes and see it's the truth."

Alek pulled her against his body and she tucked her head beneath his chin. "He loves you so much that your rejection would tear him apart. He didn't want to end up another ring box in your drawer. You have to admit, he had cause to suspect he'd become one."

"What made you so brave?"

He didn't answer her for several moments. Then finally he said, "Evianna."

She pulled away from him, looking into his face with concern. Of course going through what he'd gone through with Evianna would make him brave. She guessed that once you faced the sudden death of someone you loved there wasn't much left to fear.

"I don't run from love because of Evianna. On the contrary, once I found it again, with you, I ran toward it since I know how precious, rare, and short-lived it can be. It would be a sin to push it away instead of embracing it. I understand that, but Byron doesn't."

"I'm glad you didn't run from me."

He touched her face. "I've never seen Byron this way, Lilya. He loves you very much."

"Where is he?"

"I don't know. He couldn't stand to be in his house without you there. We fought when I told him I was coming here to ask you to marry me and then he left."

"I was afraid too. I should have told him how I felt, but I never imagined he might feel the same way." She pressed her lips to-gether. "I need to go find him, Alek."

He shook his head. "I'll go find him. He needs to come to you, not the other way around."

"Do you have any idea where to look?"

He nodded. "I think I know exactly where he's gone. Now, can we stop talking about Byron?" He still had the ring box in his hand. "Let's talk about you and me instead."

Smiling, wanting to savor this moment, she took his hand led him over to sit next to her on the couch. "I want this piece of jewelry, Alek. I want it with all my heart." She took the box into her hands and opened it, admiring the way the light glinted on the shiny gems. "It's the first ring I've ever been given that I desire to wear."

He took the ring from the box and slipped it on her finger. It looked very good there. Then he touched the ring finger of her other hand. "Once we find Byron, you'll have one to go here too."

She stared at it. Could it be that her wish was coming true? She couldn't even imagine. . . . "Maybe."

He tipped her chin to force her eyes to his. *"Definitely."*

His mouth found hers and she wrapped her arms around him, pressing her lips up against his and closing her eyes. He pulled her onto his lap and kissed her harder, his mouth possessing hers.

She finally broke the kiss. "But don't leave until tomorrow morning, all right? I want to spend some time with you."

His lips curved into a smile. "Tonight you're all mine, *just* mine."

"Would it bother you to share me?"

"Sometimes. Our relationships won't be jealousy-free, but I think we can make it work."

She looked into her lap where her fingers were intertwined with his. "I think so too."

He eased his hand to the nape of her neck and compelled her mouth to his. He kissed her until her knees felt weak. Gently, she pushed away from him. Standing, she went to the curtains and drew them against anyone on the street peering in, then lit the elusian crystal lamp on a nearby table.

"What are you doing, love?" Alek asked from his place on the couch.

Smiling wickedly, she stood on the rug before the couch and began to unbutton the bodice of her dress very slowly, revealing the top bulge of her breasts and the lacy bra that cupped them.

Alek moved from the couch, as if to come to her, and she held up a hand. "Sit and watch," she ordered him. He slid back into his place.

She unbuttoned her gown to her waist, revealing her skimpy brassiere made of lace, silk, and pink ribbons. Catching his gaze, she slid her finger over the plump of one breast and then swirled it around her nipple. A shiver of pleasure went through her that made her catch her breath. Alek shifted on the couch, as if already becoming aroused by the game.

She continued with the buttons, releasing enough of them that her gown fell past her hips to become a pool of silk and satin at her feet. Today she wore black stockings, held up by a black silk garter belt and clipped with tiny black ribbons. Her panties were nearly nonexistent, a silk so thin he could clearly see the mound of her dark hair covering her sex.

Slowly, she ran her hand down her abdomen and under the elastic band of her panties to her cunt. She found her clit and worked it between her fingers, her head falling back on a moan as another ripple of pleasure went through her. Her panties were becoming damp.

"Lilya." The word came out hoarse and needy, clearly an entreaty to let him off the couch.

She gave a slight head shake. Then she reached around and undid her bra, throwing it to the side. Alek groaned as she cupped her breasts in her hands and teased her nipples.

A full-length mirror near the doorway reflected her image and she studied herself for a moment. Her face was flushed with passion, her lips slightly parted, and her eyes shiny with arousal. She barely recognized herself from the tightly controlled courtesan she used to be. Before sex was always for someone else, never herself.

This, *this* was for her as much as it was for Alek. A shared experience wherein they gave each other pleasure. It was totally new for her and she could see how healthy it was by just looking in the mirror.

Giving Alek a playful smile, she turned and bent at the waist, spreading her legs so he could see her breasts hanging through the space. Then she hooked her fingers through the waistband of her panties and shimmied them very slowly down her legs. She slid them down as far as the garters would allow and treated Alek to a full view of her pouting sex.

Alek lunged from the couch, pulling her up and around to face him. He reached down and ripped her flimsy little silk panties off her. She gasped and opened her mouth to protest.

"I'll buy you new ones," he growled. "I'll buy you a whole drawer full of them. Now, on the floor."

She sank to the carpet while he undid his trousers. Soon he was covering her body with his, roughly pushing her thighs apart with his knee and sliding inside her. The reflection showed their coupling. Her spread pale thighs against his slightly darker, hairy legs.

With fascination, she watched the way his thigh and rear muscles flexed as he thrust inside her. He came down over her and kissed her long and hard, the width of his cock tunneling in and out her.

"You made me crazy," he murmured against her lips.

She smiled. "That was the idea."

He took her that way for a while, then turned her to all fours and came behind her, his hand teasing her clit while he thrust.

Finally she fell apart under the force of her climax, back arching and body convulsing. He came too, then pulled her down to the carpet with him to cuddle before the fire.

Twenty-six

✦

They spent the rest of the day together and went out to dinner that evening. In the morning she saw him off as he left to go find Byron.

She pulled her shawl around her shoulders and waved as the carriage lurched off toward the steam transport station. Alek thought he might have gone to Middentown, where they had several good friends from their time at the university.

Turning to go back into her house, a building that was feeling more like home every day, she caught movement out of the corner of her eye. A tall man turned the corner. She glanced at him, smiling. She was in a fine mood this morning. He wore a dark, very expensive suit and a fancy hat. His face was narrow, handsome, his hair—

"Ivan." She stilled in complete and perfect shock, one hand on the door of her home. A violent shudder ran through her as recognition of the man slammed into her.

"Hello, Lilya."

His voice washed through her like a wave of arctic water, breaking her astonishment. She lunged up the last stair and past the threshold, turning and slamming the door shut. But it wouldn't close. She looked down to see Ivan's boot—he always wore heavy boots, good for kicking, never normal shoes—wedged between the door and the frame.

Through the colored glass of the window, she saw a huge man walk up beside Ivan. With massive hands, he pushed the door open. Knowing she had no hope of winning a physical contest with either of them, she whirled and ran down the hall, through the kitchen, and to the back door. She threw it open only to find another one of Ivan's thugs on the other side.

"You really shouldn't be so predictable, Lilya."

She closed her eyes, shuddering at the sound of Ivan's voice behind her. It was as if the last six-plus years had disappeared. Now here she was, confused and hurting—prey to Ivan all over again. Taking deep breaths, she fisted her hands until they hurt, trying to gain control.

She wasn't that woman anymore.

She wasn't vulnerable, or hurting.

She was strong enough to face this.

She was.

And she had a life to fight for now. A good life, one filled with love, laughter, and happiness.

Opening her eyes, she spied the knife she and Alek had used to cut up a melon for dessert the night before. They'd never got around to washing it . . . or eating the melon for that matter. She dashed to the side, grabbed the knife, and held it between herself and Ivan and his thugs. She still had the knife tucked into her bodice too. Every morning since the break-in at Byron's she'd made it a part of her wardrobe. That made two weapons she possessed.

"Get out of here, Ivan. Right now." Her voice came out sounding ten times stronger than she felt.

"Look at Lilya with the knife." Ivan seemed more fascinated than frightened. He took a step toward her. "You've changed."

She waved the knife. "If you think I won't use this, *think again*."

Ivan motioned at one of the goons with a finger. "Let's test that out, shall we?"

The thug moved without hesitation. Either he was really stupid, really under Ivan's control, or confident that the woman wielding the knife wouldn't actually use it.

If it was the latter, he was wrong.

Her heart pounding and adrenaline rushing through her ears like the ocean, she slammed the knife deep into the man's upper chest as soon as he got near enough. He fell back against the counter, screaming in pain, and then collapsed to the floor, whimpering and staring in alarm at the protruding handle of the knife.

One goon down, two to go. She grabbed for the knife in her bodice, but the handle was pushed too far down for her to grasp. Edging her way around the counter, she searched for something else to use to defend herself.

Too late.

The second goon was on her. His hands closed around her shoulders and she pushed at him with all her strength—it was like fighting a boulder. She twisted and fought him, screaming as loud as she could. She managed to turn in the man's grasp, reaching for anything she could grab and pulling it off the counter. Hurling a cutting board, she smacked the thug in the forehead, but all he did was grunt and hold on tighter.

Hands closing around her waist, the thug hefted her into the air and away from all possible projectiles. Now she faced Ivan. Fear turned to rage in her blood. Her hair had come down and she knew her eyes were wild. She reached toward him, grasping and scratching, wanting to draw blood. All Ivan did was step back. The thug tightened his grip on her.

"What do you want with me?"

His eyes glittered and he retained his cold, hard little smile, but said nothing.

"*What do you want with me?*" She screamed it at him this time. "You've already done your damage, just leave me alone!"

His smile faded. "Apparently I didn't do damage enough." He walked a little closer to her, just out of reach of her fingernails. The thug still had her around the waist. "You are mine, Lilya. You always have been, ever since the first day I glimpsed you peddling flowers on that street corner. No matter what you do, or who you're with . . . you're mine. And when you stray too far from the path I want to see you on, well, then it's time to set you back on it. You never knew I've been in the background, guiding your life these past six years, did you?"

Her body went rigid with a new flush of rage and fear. What did that mean? Did that mean he hadn't just dismissed her, forgotten about her as she'd always presumed? It sounded as if he'd been watching her from afar all these years and now she'd done something he didn't approve of . . . *going to Byron's house, coming back here to the town house instead of the Temple of Dreams.*

Ivan must know she'd developed feelings for Byron and Alek, and he didn't like it.

"Come on, then. Time to go." He walked to the back door and opened it.

She screamed and fought anew, but the goon had little trouble pushing her toward the exit. Outside she could see a fine carriage led by four matched black horses in the alley, the door open and waiting for her to be pushed in.

Ivan was so confident in this city, he wasn't even going to bother drugging her or knocking her out. He didn't care that her neighbors saw her being forced into a carriage, kicking and screaming. *Kidnapped.*

Behind her the man she'd stabbed yanked the knife from beneath his shoulder and threw it with a clatter to the floor. Then he rose, following them, with a look that promised her pain.

He needed to get in line if he wanted to her hurt her. Apparently Ivan was first.

The door to her town house slammed behind them.

Twenty-seven

✦

Alek threw open the door to the house in Ulstrat. "Byron!" he yelled. The call echoed through the empty home and he knew immediately Byron wasn't there. The enormous building felt like a frigid shell.

"Joshui damn it all," he muttered, heading through the foyer and into the library. The fire in the hearth was long cold and the glasses they'd been drinking from several days before still rested on a table.

He'd traveled to Middentown only to find Byron had recently left. Their mutual friends had said Byron was upset and hadn't told them where he was headed next.

Alek turned in a slow circle in the middle of the room. He'd figured Byron would have returned home, but there was no evidence that he'd so much as stopped here since leaving the first time. Byron could be anywhere in Rylisk by now. The stupid bastard. Alek didn't want to have to chase him all over the country.

He checked the house for some clue as to where Byron had traveled. Entering Byron's bedroom, he stopped short.

The room was a total disaster.

He stepped forward, nudging Byron's favorite vase with his shoe, now lying shattered on the floor. The pillow looked like it had been cut to ribbons and someone had thrown everything to the ground with the objective of destroying all they could.

He frowned as he took it all in. Byron in a fit of rage?

No. This was nothing like him at all.

His mind flitted back to the break-in. Someone meant them harm. Moving quickly, he checked the rooms where he and Lilya had stayed. No damage.

Frowning, he reentered Byron's bedroom, his shoes crunching on broken pottery. Judging by the looks of this room, the *only* room attacked in such a way—he'd say it was Byron who bore the brunt of this stranger's ill will. This seemed really personal.

He had no idea where to find Byron, but to get to Byron all one had to do was threaten Lilya.

Sweet Joshui.

Alek turned on his heel. He had to get back to Milzyr right now.

Byron headed up the steps to the door of Lilya's house and knocked. No one answered. She wasn't home? That was odd. It was so early in the morning. Maybe she'd gone somewhere with Alek . . . that is, if she hadn't rejected him.

He'd arrived in Middentown and had stayed for two days before realizing that he was making a mistake—maybe the biggest mistake of his life.

He'd been sitting there in a group of three happy couples and they'd been teasing him about finding a wife. Marta had told him he could have any woman he wanted and it had struck him—he would never want any woman but Lilya.

Not ever.

If he didn't take the risk of telling Lilya how he felt, he would end up alone until the day he died. Alek had been right; he was a fool. Lilya was all that mattered.

That evening he'd taken the first transport he could board to Milzyr, traveled all night, and gone straight to the Temple of Dreams to tell Lilya how he felt about her. If she rejected him, it would wound him deeply, but he couldn't live without knowing. He couldn't live with the regret of never having told her.

But she hadn't been at the Temple of Dreams, which had perplexed him at first. Then he realized what must have happened. She must have said yes to Alek and they'd both left for the town house. That filled him with elation, but also worried him.

What if she only had feelings for Alek and not for him?

He peered into the front window. The drapes were open and the coverings were off the furniture. That meant Lilya had taken up residence here for certain. But where was she?

Remembering the back door, he headed around the side of the building and tried the knob. It was open. "Lilya?" he called, entering the kitchen. "Alek?" He stopped short, seeing everything pulled off the counters and hurled to the floor. Signs of a struggle.

A knife. Blood.

Heart pounding, he bolted down the hallway and into the living room. "Lilya! Alek!" Nothing. Only silence met him. He ran up the stairs and checked the bedrooms. Everything appeared in order, but no one was home.

Something moved in the half-open closet, making him go on guard. He inched his way over slowly and eased the door open. A black-and-white cat strolled out, meowing up at him. He stared down at the cat, frowning for a moment, then picked it up. The cat purred when he petted its head and then jumped out of his arms and ran for the kitchen.

Byron followed, watching the cat pace in front of the counter, purring even louder. This cat was hungry. How long had Lilya been gone? Locating some food for the cat, he filled up a bowl and set it on the floor along with a cup filled with water.

Idly, he stroked the cat's back as it wolfed down food like it hadn't eaten in days. He stared at the knife and the dried smear of dark brown blood on the floor. "What happened here?" he asked the cat, wishing it could tell him. "Where did your mistress go?"

He had a feeling he knew.

Thinking back to the break-in at his house, the door left open like whoever had done it had wanted them to know he'd been there. Remembering the cologne Lilya had smelled that night, and the trip to the marketplace when she'd felt someone watching her. It seemed impossible after so many years, but could it be?

"*Ivan*." The word came out a low, animalistic growl.

He was the only one he could think of who would do something like this.

He knew where to find Ivan. Everyone knew where to find the most notorious crime lord of Milzyr since Ivan was so confident in his power he never bothered to hide it. He had the current law enforcement paid off, just as he'd paid off the Imperial Guard before them.

Yet Byron knew more than most people.

Ever since he'd learned that Ivan was *Ivan Lazarson*, he'd been gathering information on the man in preparation to punish him for what he'd done to Lilya. Thanks to a couple of contacts in Milzyr, Byron knew the addresses of all Ivan's residences, his regular haunts, his business associates, even the women he slept with.

He was also in possession of much personal information about the man. Ivan hadn't invited a woman to live with him since Lilya. It was a fact Byron had regarded as odd. Ivan had seemed to commit to her in his twisted way, so much that he'd never obligated himself to another woman that way ever again. Unbeknownst to Lilya or Alek, Byron had made a study out of the man for the last three weeks and had been plotting just how he would take revenge on Lilya's behalf.

In fact, he'd already started.

Those plans would have to be abandoned now. He couldn't wait for the slow wheels of financial ruin he'd put in motion to work. If Ivan had Lilya, Byron would deal with the crime lord the old-fashioned way.

"Lilya!" Someone yelled it from the front door, a fist pounding on the frame. The voice was muffled, but familiar. "Lilya!"

Byron bolted down the hallway to the front door. He knew that voice all right. He yanked the front door open to find Alek on the steps.

"You're here?" Alek looked confused for a moment, then plunged past him into the house. "Never mind. You obviously seemed so bookish and calm, but who was explosive and demanding in the bedroom.

He walked to her and pulled her against his chest, his mouth coming down on hers as his hand skated over her bare fire-warmed back, cupped her buttock, and then skimmed across the back of her leg, pulling her knee up over his hip so her sex pressed against his hard cock through his pants.

He pivoted her and lowered her into the chair she'd just been sitting in. Backing away a little, he began to undress. "Spread your thighs. Hook your knees over the armrests, and tilt your pelvis up. I want to see all of you."

She did as he commanded. Byron came over and knelt with Alek before her. Her breath came fast and hard as they examined her. She felt herself growing warm and swollen from their gazes—and they'd barely touched her yet. Her nipples went tight and hard and she held on to the back of the chair, completely spread and vulnerable to them.

"She has a very pretty cunt, don't you think Byron?" murmured Alek, stroking her folds until she closed her eyes and moaned.

Byron made a low sound of agreement and petted her clit, making it swell and pull from its hood.

Alek slipped a finger inside her and pumped, and then added a second, spreading her muscles until she whimpered. Byron continued to press and rotate her clit, and soon she was incoherent with need, poised on the edge of a climax.

Leaving her suspended in a state of teasing ecstasy, Byron dropped down and petted her nether hole. "You have taken men back here, haven't you?"

"Yes." Her response came out low and breathy.

"Good." Byron's voice sounded labored with need. He fingered her there, awakening all the nerves that slept until a man stimulated them. She moaned, closing her eyes as he pressed one of his long, broad digits slowly inside. "You're very tight," he breathed. "Before we can do this we'll need to relax your muscles back here."

"I want to make her come first," murmured Alek.

Byron backed away and Alek dropped his mouth to her. Her back arched and her breath hissed out of her as Alek's warm lips closed over her clit. His tongue nuzzled against the sensitive bundle of nerves as his fingers continually thrust in and out of her.

Alek flicked her clit with his skillful tongue while Byron watched them from a short distance, his eyes growing dark with arousal. Lilya's hands tightened on the armrests of the chair as her climax built. Alek's fingers found that secret spot deep inside her and rasped against it on every outward motion, pushing her toward the precipice of her orgasm.

It washed over her, making her cry out. Alek rode her through her it, intensifying it as the waves of pleasure racked her body. When the orgasm ebbed, Alek kissed her inner thigh and pulled away, letting Byron take her by the hand and help her to her feet.

He cupped her cheeks and kissed her, his tongue slipping between her lips. After he'd kissed her breathless, he set his forehead to hers. "You're so beautiful when you come, Lilya."

Byron led her to the bed where he'd laid out a few objects while Alek had had her in the chair. He pulled her onto the bed and rolled her to her stomach, hips elevated. His warm hand skated over her rear, making her shiver with anticipation.

Alek sat down nearby, letting Byron take over. "Now that's a pretty sight."

"Indeed," Byron growled.

haven't been home, have you? Did you see the mess in your bed-room?"

Byron frowned. "What mess?"

"Someone broke into your house again. This time they com-pletely tore apart your bedroom. It almost seemed—"

"Personal?" Byron's whole body seemed to feel a shade darker. So it *was* Ivan who'd broken in that night and left the door open. Of course. He'd probably been watching them from afar the whole time Lilya had been in Ulstrat. Ivan had probably been watching Lilya from afar for a long time now.

There was a reason he'd never committed to another woman—he was still in love with Lilya in some insane way.

Alek nodded and looked around. "Where's Lilya?"

"I think Ivan has her." He ground out the words as if they hurt.

Alek blanched. "What?"

"I'll fill you in on the details on the way. We need to go right now. Let's pray that we're not already too late. When's the last time you saw Lilya here?"

"Two days ago."

Fear clenched its icy fist in his stomach. *"Let's go."*

He never touched her. That was the only fortunate part of her captivity. It was almost as though she disgusted him. Instead his thugs touched her, but not in the way she most feared.

At least, not yet.

Dressed in a gown almost too fine to wear, she sat in a genteel sitting room. The garment was of dark blue silk and damask and she had on a pair of slippers that were so soft it was like going barefoot. She rested there endlessly drinking tea and listening to the grandfather clock in the hallway ticking off the moments of her imprisonment.

For the last two days it had been this way. She had been given a beautifully decorated room, clothes that seemed tailored to fit her body—and, indeed, she was beginning to suspect they were—the best food, the finest tea, and the run of the house.

Of course, she was not permitted to leave the house or walk the grounds and she had a shadow—several of them at all times.

Her prison might not seem like a prison, but it was one all the same.

Back in the kitchen, she'd anticipated a different sort of treatment. She'd expected a cell, beatings, and worse than beatings. None of that had occurred . . . yet. It was almost as if Ivan was watching her, studying her, deciding what to do to her. But why he was taking her measure this way perplexed her. Why did he care this much about her after so many years? She'd thought he'd just forgotten about her, had thrown her to the wolves as punishment for her imagined transgression like she was so much trash and then moved on.

After all, she'd moved on. Slowly. Painfully.

But, clearly, Ivan had not. Something about her still fascinated him. It was almost as if Ivan considered her his property and, as his property, she'd done something to displease him and was awaiting her punishment. *Again.* Dressing her up like a pretty doll and making her wait for her punishment without knowing when it was going to happen, that was Ivan's special brand of torture.

The swallow of tea in her throat went down hard. She'd come

back from such punishment once, but she wasn't sure she could do it twice.

At least she had a knife tucked into her bodice that screamed she would never have to. It was a comforting pressure against her skin.

They hadn't found it because even the thugs were being very circumspect with her. She was allowed to bathe and change her clothes in private, so they'd never located the thin stiletto she kept tucked down the front of her dress at all times. It was her way out of here, but she needed to use it carefully. If she drew it in the presence of too many of the thugs, she might wound or kill one or more of them, but then they would just take it away from her and she would be weaponless.

The careful way she was being handled unnerved her. If Ivan had immediately started treating her like trash, at least she wouldn't be so confused. As it was, she had no idea what was coming; she only knew it was going to be bad.

A storm was brewing on the horizon.

This morning he sat across from her, calmly reading a book while his minions passed through the room now and again, perhaps doing his evil bidding. This was one of the very few times she'd even seen him since she'd been abducted two days ago.

She took a sip of her tea and sat back, studying him. "So, Ivan, what is it you intend? Do you just want me to be a decoration for your parlor for the next twenty years? You want me to sit here and drink tea while you completely ignore me and force your goons to fetch and carry for me?"

Ivan said nothing to her for a moment, then he put his book aside and looked up at her. "I intend to do whatever I wish with you."

She knew her eyes were flashing. Her blood heated with anger. "You cannot treat me as though I'm property."

"Really? I can't? I have lots of money and muscle that says I can."

"Why do you even care about me, Ivan?"

Now his eyes flashed. "I care because I loved you once."

"Much to my misfortune. There are few women who can survive your brand of *love*, Ivan."

Red spots of color appeared on his cheeks and anger made his eyes bright. She was aware she was pushing him and that might turn out badly for her, but she couldn't stop herself. "I don't understand why you can't just leave me alone and let me live the life I'm lucky to have after what you did to me."

If there hadn't been five thugs in the house, she would have drawn her knife and stabbed him right then. She stared at him, her chest heaving and the blood rushing through her ears in her rage.

Ivan stood, threw the book down to the chair, and walked slowly across the room to her. Murder lit his eyes. She recognized it because she'd seen it before. She stared at him as he came toward her with not even a trace of fear in her body. At this point, she was beyond fear. She'd had more than enough of this man's presence in this world. Now all she wanted was him out of it.

She hoped he understood that she was going to kill him the first chance she got.

She almost thought he was going to get close enough to touch her, but he stopped short. Still . . . he was close enough to stab. The weight of the knife tucked into her bodice became acute, begging her to grab it and plunge it into this man. Just then one of his thugs caught sight of her proximity to his master and entered the room, watching them like a bulldog.

He leaned down and put his face near hers. "You owe me, Lilya. You owe me for wrapping me around your treacherous finger, making me love you, and then betraying me."

Her hands fisted. It was no use explaining that she'd been the one wronged in the hallway. Ivan saw what he wanted to see. It didn't matter anyway. Even if she had done what Ivan believed she had, there was no excuse for his reprisal. But, of course, he wouldn't understand that either.

She spit in his face.

He jerked in surprise and closed his eyes for a moment. Then he went very, very still. For the first time, a quiver of fear went through her. She'd pushed him too far and now he might hurt her so badly she wouldn't be able to escape. Her anger had gotten the better of her.

Ivan moved slowly, smoothly, picking up what was probably a priceless antique chair and heaving it into the air. He threw it around and held it aloft, above her, intending to smash it down on her. Lilya flinched, covering her head with her arms and closing her eyes—waiting for the pain.

Oh, she remembered this.

But Ivan threw the chair above her head instead, smashing it against the wall behind her. It splintered into a thousand pieces, raining down on her head. When the chair lay broken on the floor around her, she opened her eyes and brought her hands down into her lap.

Ivan paced in front of her, his face red. He stopped, drew a careful breath, and drew a hand through his hair. Without looking at her, he pointed. "You will dress in a manner that pleases me and join me for dinner tonight." Then he turned and pushed past the thug at the door, who stood watching her with a curl in his lip and a knowing, cruel glint in his eye.

She wondered for a moment if the thug knew what Ivan had done to her six years ago and hoped he might do it again.

Heart pounding, she tore her gaze away from the man and back down to her teacup, now with shards of splintered chair soaking in it.

She'd almost found happiness.

It had been right there in front of her, hers for the taking. She'd nearly had everything in life she'd wanted.

Ivan wasn't going to let her have it.

Twenty-eight

◆

S he's in there. She has to be." Byron's voice came out a dangerous growl.

Alek followed the direction of Byron's pointing finger and saw
a stately country home in a whole row of stately country homes.
They'd gone just outside the city to check this house after they'd
checked every single one of Ivan's residences in Milzyr. It had
taken them all day to get to this one; it figured the last one they
checked would be the only one occupied.

They'd parked the carriage a little ways down the road and
sat watching the place. Once in a while a servant or a thug dis-
guised as a servant would go around the back and, presumably,
enter the residence.

"It does look like it's pretty active," Alek answered.

"We can't waste any more time. We need to go in there and
get her out now." Byron had been fidgety, restless, and short-

tempered. Alek understood. He felt the same way; he just hid it better.

"I agree." His voice came out in a tense snap. "But we need a plan. We're only two men. Have you seen the amount of muscle going in and out of the house, Byron? Even if our will is strong, I don't think we can do this on our own."

Byron sat watching the house, his mind clearly mulling the problem over. "We need to go in *now*." His voice came out a snarl. "Anything could be happening to her in there."

"We don't even know she's in the house for certain."

"She is," Byron ground out. "I feel it."

Alek shifted impatiently. "So you just want to break down the front door and fight at least ten hulking guards without any weapons? You really think that's going to help Lilya? I think we'll be killed doing that and Lilya will have no hope at all."

"And if we wait, Lilya is dead." He paused, his voice lowering. "She could already be dead."

Alek closed his eyes, refusing to believe that was even a possibility. "We're only a few hours away from Ulstrat. Let's go get the team."

"What?"

"The boys on the crossball team. All we have to do is say the word and they'll come out here and help us. You know they will. We can go gather as many as we can, arm them, be back in seven hours."

Byron stared at the house. "Seven hours."

"It's Lilya's best shot. You know we can't bring the government down on him, the—"

"Gregorio!"

"What? Gregorio Vikhin?"

"He's a part of the government that I *know* Ivan hasn't paid off. Vikhin's been looking to catch Ivan for a crime ever since he was elected to lead the council." Byron climbed out of the carriage. "I'm taking one of the horses, you take the other. I'll have the driver rerig the carriage, hide it, and wait for us. You go to Ulstrat. I'm headed back to Milzyr to find Gregorio. He can find men to bring out here and we can take care of Ivan once and for all."

Alek nodded. It would probably take about the same amount of time for Byron to return to Milzyr and come back with Gregorio as it would for him to go to Ulstrat and back. "Let's go." He climbed out after him and they unhooked two of the horses, sheltered from the view of Ivan's house by a clump of evergreen bushes.

And they were off in two different directions, pushing their mounts as hard as they could go and hoping they wouldn't be too late.

All was silent but for the sound of clanking silverware. Mostly it was Ivan's silverware that was clanking, since Lilya wasn't eating. Lilya had done what Ivan had asked her to do, since defying him at this point didn't make sense. She'd dressed for dinner and arrived to the meal on time, escorted by not only one, but five burly guards.

One might almost think that Ivan was afraid of her.

She knew he wasn't. After all, she was one slight woman in a house of hulking men. What could she possibly do to him? He didn't know about the comforting pressure of the knife down her bodice or the vicious will she possessed. Ivan *should* be afraid of her. She was only biding her time before she killed him.

Although she was quite happy to remain underestimated. Being underestimated would only help her in the end. They'd even given her a knife to cut her chicken with. Imbeciles.

She stared down at her untouched plate of food. At least he couldn't make her eat. Across the table, he blissfully consumed the roasted chicken and vegetables as though they were merely a married couple with little to say to each other. Nothing at all wrong.

The gown he'd chosen for her to wear to dinner was flawless and exquisite, as was all the clothing he'd been forcing her to don. Gold-and-cream tulle, it possessed a fitted, strapless bodice and a dropped waist, with a full skirt gathering below her hips to fall in perfect flounces to the floor. She'd left her hair long and loose, since he wasn't forcing her to fix it and she wasn't going to do anything for him beyond wearing the clothing.

She'd even left the sapphire jewelry in her room, but all she'd received from Ivan was a flare of ire in his eyes as he'd assessed her as she entered the dining room. She would have gone barefoot too, if it wasn't for the fact she thought perhaps the heels of her shoes could be used as weapons.

"I have been watching you for the last two days." Ivan took a sip of his wine and looked up at her, his other hand on his fork. "Assessing how you've changed since I last stood in a room with you."

Remembering every detail about *the last time he stood in a room with her*, she raised her gaze to his, knowing full well how her eyes glittered with pure hatred.

"You are different than I imagined you would be. Very proud. Very strong. Much too proud, in fact. Defiant. Full of hope. Able to love." He shook his head. "This is unacceptable, Lilya. You are not supposed to be this way."

She smiled a cold little smile and raised an eyebrow. "Just how do you think I should be?"

"Broken." The answer came swiftly. He took another sip of wine and Lilya imagined all the things she could do with the shattered edge of his goblet. "Beaten. Unsure of yourself. Lacking self-confidence. Unhappy." He paused, looking at her over the rim of his glass. "After what you did to me, the way you continue to tie me in knots. . . . Me! Ivan Lazarson! You don't deserve happiness."

Ivan was a lunatic. Insane. She'd known it before, but this conversation was really driving it home. There was no way to reason with this man. He wouldn't understand anything she had to say. She *couldn't* reason with him—he *had* no reason.

"So you intend to kill me, then?" She wasn't going down without a fight, but if he chose to do it now, with so many of his men around, she didn't have much of a prayer.

Her mind flashed to Byron and Alek and her throat tightened at her loss. She should have known better—love was not for her. She'd known that from the start.

The problem had always been expectations. Hers were too high.

"Kill you? No, that's far too easy." He stared at her, his eyes going colder. "I want to destroy you, make it so you go back to your life at the Temple of Dreams and give up on happiness and love." He blinked slowly. "I know exactly how to do that."

One more attack like the one she'd had before would obliterate her. Her entire body went frigid as fear sucked all the warmth from her blood. "I will never, ever do what you want me to do, Ivan. No matter what you subject me to. I refuse."

He smiled. "But you already have been doing what I want you to do, my dear. At least, up until a few weeks ago."

"What are you talking about?"

"I've been watching you since you were lying in that alley six years ago. You haven't known it, but I've been managing you from afar. I was delighted when you took up with the Temple of Dreams and I've been monitoring your clientele. If a man seemed too likely to bring you love or happiness, I . . . *persuaded* . . . him to go quietly away."

Lilya pushed her chair away with a loud scrape against the floor and bolted to her feet. "You incredible bastard!"

All this time she'd been priding herself on being in control, choosing her clients and then carefully managing her relationships with them, but Ivan had been behind the scenes, directing and guiding her life from afar.

"I only want things back the way they were, Lilya." He spread his hands.

All of a sudden her life at the Temple of Dreams seemed like a cage. Dear Joshui, she'd been in prison since the day she'd met him but she hadn't known it.

The blood drained from her face and her body went cold and shaky. The room tilted and her vision went black. No. No, she couldn't pass out. Not now. Not ever in front of Ivan. It left her too vulnerable.

She swallowed hard and leaned down, gripping the table so she wouldn't fall over, and snarled into his face. "I will never, never give you anything you want, Ivan. I will die before I ever do anything you want me to do again."

He clucked his tongue and shook his head. "There's that pride. It's amazing that you should still have it." He paused. "I can make you do anything I want you to do, Lilya. Two words, *Byron and Alek*."

She straightened, her face going blank, and took a step backward. "Are you threatening me?"

"I'm threatening *them*, actually. If you go back to your life at the Temple of Dreams, tell them you care nothing for them, and force them to go away, I'll leave them alone."

"I don't think they'll be that easy to kill." Her voice shook with uncertainty.

Ivan laughed. "I could have done it in Ulstrat on any night of my choosing. Breaking into Byron Andropov's house was easy. I stood over all your beds, dagger in my pocket. Slitting their throats would have been a child's game."

Of course. He'd been the one to break into Byron's. She really had smelled Ivan's cologne that night. He'd probably been watching her at the crossball match that afternoon and at the market too. She just hadn't thought about it before. She shuddered.

"I've got men out looking for them even as we speak. Eventually they'll be located. If you refuse my terms, I'll order them brought here and I'll slit their throats right in front of you."

She swallowed hard. "You'd actually get your hands bloody, Ivan?"

His lips split in a mirthless smile. "Anything for you, love. Now what was that you were saying about not doing anything for my pleasure?"

Her mind whirled. If she killed him, they would all be free. Desperation made the back of her throat taste coppery. Her gaze flicked to the entrance of the dining room and the two monsters standing on either side of it. She knew there were more scattered around the house, stationed outside every entrance.

She looked at the knife lying alongside her plate and then at the one discarded beside Ivan's wineglass. Along with her dagger that was three weapons total. If she acted fast, maybe she had an opportunity.

Even in the three seconds it took her to calculate a plan and her odds, three of Ivan's men entered the room. That made six men total in her vicinity.

She wilted. Yet, now might be her last chance at trying to kill Ivan.

She hadn't given up yet, not by a long shot, but she had to appear as if she had. Bowing her head, she murmured, "I agree." She didn't have to fake the tears that plopped onto the floor. It was a lie—she was going to try and figure a way out of this—but the lie felt true. It confirmed everything she'd secretly believed about herself before Byron and Alek. Love and happiness really weren't for her. She wasn't allowed to have it.

Here was the proof.

"Good." Ivan nodded, a genuine smile splitting his face. "That's very good, Lilya. The men can live. I'll be watching you though. One little slip up and I'll slip them up. Got it?"

Miserable, she nodded.

"All right, boys, she's yours."

Her head snapped up and she backed away from them. "What? I thought we'd struck a bargain!"

"The bargain was for the lives of your lovers, not for your punishment. That is nonnegotiable."

"You bastard. You rotten, stinking bastard!" She grabbed up

the table knife and held it out between her and the six men who were now in the room. "I will die before I let them have me."

Ivan shrugged. "As you wish."

"I have a better idea, Ivan." She backed up a few more paces, away from the confident, smirking thugs who were clearly quite happy with their boss at the moment. "How about *you* die instead?"

She leapt onto the table, sliding across it using the table cloth. The cloth slipped over the edge, sending plates, food, and cutlery to the floor with a thunderous, clattering crash. Single-minded in her purpose, she ignored it all, driving the point of her knife straight for Ivan's throat.

Ivan's eyes grew wide and he threw up his hands to ward her off. No matter, she readjusted the blade's trajectory toward his chest.

A moment before her knife made contact, one of the guards slammed into her. She tumbled over the edge of the table, going down hard onto the floor amid the shattered plates and the remnants of roasted chicken. Her knife flew from her hand and skidded under the table.

"Nice try, Lilya," came Ivan's smug voice. "You can give up all hope now."

Her eyes closing, pain screaming through her, she rested for a moment against the floor. Give up? *Never.* She would fight until her dying breath. Coughing, she rolled onto her side, masking the movement of her hand going to the bodice of her dress. Pulling the weapon out, she hid it up her sleeve.

Shouting and crashing sounds came from another part of the house. "What? What's going on?" asked Ivan, glancing around him.

Chaos erupted. Men she didn't recognize rushed into the room and began fighting with the thugs. Shouting came from all over the house. Dazed from the fall she'd taken and her body hurting all over from the broken glass she'd landed on, she forced herself up, watching the battle explode in the room.

Suddenly Ivan was on her, snarling into her face, and raising the other table knife above his head. She threw up an arm instinctively to protect herself. Ivan brought his hand down for a killing blow. Using every ounce of her strength, she knocked his arm away and plunged her own blade upward, taking him in the throat. Ivan went motionless for a moment above her, his eyes going wide with surprise and shock. Hot blood pumped over her hand and dripped onto the floor.

Ivan slumped to the side, the knife limp in his lifeless hand.

Lilya fell back and closed her eyes, panting hard. Every part of her body screamed with pain. Around her the battle raged on. Men shouted. Things broke. For a moment she thought she heard Gregorio Vikhin's voice . . . but that was impossible.

Her heart ached for Byron and Alek.

Everything began to go black.

"Lilya!"

Her eyes opened to find Byron scooping her into his arms. "Lilya, what did they do to you?"

She smiled up into his face, wondering if it really could be Byron she was seeing now. If it was a dream, it was a good one. "This? I did this to myself."

"There's so much blood."

"Most of it is Ivan's." She paused, thinking about the broken plates and glasses she'd landed on. "Or maybe not," she amended.

Then everything really did go black.

Twenty-nine

T his is the second time I've found you broken and had to put you back together."

Lilya's eyes came open and she looked up into Byron's gently smiling face. Alek was beside him. The last thing she remembered was losing consciousness in Ivan's dining room. Now she appeared to be back at Byron's house.

"Not broken." Her voice came out rasping. "Ivan didn't manage to do that a second time." She smiled. "I'm just slightly damaged."

"Ivan is dead." Alek cupped her cheek. "He's not going to be hurting you ever again."

She leaned back into the pillows and let out a long sigh of relief. Closing her eyes, a tear squeezed out and dribbled down her cheek. The nightmare was over. Finally.

"The doctor says you need to rest. He pulled out several large pieces of glass from your back and legs and you've lost a lot of blood," continued Alek.

She'd come close to losing so much more than that.

Byron leaned over and kissed her forehead. "But never fear, Alek and I are here to pamper you until you're well."

She laughed. "That sounds like heaven."

"Alek has been using his magick to heal you as well. Thanks to him, your scarring will be minimal."

She reached out, took Alek's hand and squeezed. "Thank you."

He grinned. "I could think of better, far less scary ways you could have coaxed my magick from me, Lilya."

She smiled. "I'll try and remember that next time. How did you two know where Ivan had taken me?"

"When you revealed Ivan's identity, Byron began gathering information about him and had him watched. He'd planned to take him down for what he did to you. He knew about all of Ivan's properties. We just had to narrow it down. Once we did that, we gathered some reinforcements. Gregorio Vikhin was delighted to come out and arrest Ivan for kidnapping you, and the players from our crossball team were happy to come and crack a few heads."

She swallowed hard, remembering. "You came just at the right time."

"You killed Ivan, didn't you, Lilya?" asked Byron.

She was sure the rush of emotion she had at the memory made her face hard. "I did."

"Then the hard part is over. Alek and I are going to see that the rest of your life is easy and filled with love."

She closed her eyes, emotion making a hard lump in her throat. "I don't know if I deserve it."

Byron touched her face. She opened her eyes and locked gazes with him. "We're going to spend the rest of our lives proving that you deserve it." He pulled a ring box from his pocket. "Now you have two, one for each hand."

She gasped and reached out to touch the ruby-and-diamond ring. It didn't match Alek's ring, but it did complement it—just as the men themselves complemented each other. She took the ring from the box and slid it onto her right hand.

She held her hands at arm's length, admiring the way the gems caught the light. "They're the first rings I've ever accepted." She looked up at them each in turn. "And they will be the last."

Byron moved closer to her, cupping her face in his hands. "Lilya, I love you. I began to love you the day I collected you off the ground of that alley and my love only grew as I got to know what an amazing woman you are." He leaned in and kissed her softly. "I regret not telling you sooner. Can you forgive me for being afraid?"

She stroked his cheek with her fingers. "Only if you can forgive me for the same." She looked past him to Alek, who watched them with serious dark eyes. "I love you both more than I could ever have imagined I could love any man. How do you propose we handle this, the *three* of us?"

"We'll discuss that after you're well," answered Alek. "Until then, we're going to take care of you."

And she believed them.

Lilya looked up from her tea as Evangeline walked into the cook shop. Smiling, she rose. "You came without your babies?"

Evangeline returned her smile, though it was weary. "They're with Anatol and Gregorio. The men knew I needed an afternoon away. Thanks for dropping that note by and giving me the opportunity."

"It's been a long time since we've seen each other."

The serving girl came by and Evangeline ordered tea and a sugar bun. Evangeline peeled off her hat and gloves. It was unusually warm for early spring. "How are you feeling?"

"Much better. It took some time to recover from the injuries I sustained, but I managed to heal without any scars thanks to Alek's magick."

"You seem"—she studied her—"lighter, happier. In love?"

"I am. Twice over."

A huge smile split Evangeline's face. "And you said you never would be, but I remember the way you talked to me when I ran from Anatol and Gregorio. You wanted me to go back to them so much. You told me how much they loved me and wanted me."

"Ah." She leaned forward and cupped her chin in her palm. "And I was right, wasn't I?"

"You were." Evangeline paused as the serving girl set her tea and bun in front of her. "And I'm glad you were wrong about yourself. So, tell me, is it Alek Chaikoveii? That's what Anatol thinks."

"Yes, it's Alek and it's also Byron Andropov."

She set her teacup down on the plate with a clatter and clapped. "Two!"

Lilya felt her cheeks go crimson. "I wanted to ask your advice . . . about how you, Anatol, and Gregorio handle everything. I mean, a relationship between one man and woman is hard enough, add an extra partner and it's that much more complicated."

"It's not as complicated as you might think. Love seems to

iron out the wrinkles. Not that there aren't any. There will be jealousy from time to time. It's only natural. You three will be a family, with ups and down, happiness and sadness." She smiled. "You'll find your way if it's meant to be. Do you think it is?"

This time it was a huge smile that split her face. "Yes. Yes, I do."

Thirty

That evening Lilya stood at the window of the library in the house in Ulstrat admiring her rings in the evening light. She was smiling and she was certain she looked silly. She *felt* silly. Silly and content beyond belief.

"How did I get so lucky?" she murmured to herself.

Wonderful, she mused, now she was talking to herself. Maybe that's something women in love did.

"We think we're the lucky ones," whispered Byron, coming up behind her to pull her back against his chest. "I thought I would never have you in my life and now here you are."

She turned in his arms. "I never thought I'd end up with the men I love either."

"Love has its way, I guess."

"Thank Joshui, apparently it does. Of course, you and I owe a lot to Alek."

Byron nodded. "He was braver than us both."

"Who was?" asked Alek, walking into the room.

"You," Lilya and Byron answered together.

Lilya pulled away from Byron and went toward him. "We were just saying that we three wouldn't be together if it weren't for you."

"Ah." He gave her a saucy head-to-toe perusal. "And what sort of thanks will I be getting?"

"Oh," Lilya replied, turning her walk to a saunter and her voice to warmed butter. "I can think of a couple things."

"Can you now?"

She reached him and began to unbutton his shirt. "Mmmm, very interesting things." She leaned in and nipped at his lower lip. "Things that involve my mouth and my hands and my—"

"What are we waiting for?" he growled, making her laugh. He dragged her up against his chest and slanted his mouth over hers, easing his tongue between her lips.

He kissed her breathless before Byron scooped her into his arms and carried her upstairs to his bedroom. He set her down in the middle of the room and both men began to carefully undress her, their tongues and lips following in the wake of slowly re-vealed skin.

She worked at their clothing too, pulling Byron's shirt over his head and unbuttoning Alek's pants. Soon all three of them were skin to skin.

Kneeling on the plush carpet in the fire-warmed room, she drew Byron's cock into her mouth while stroking Alek's from base to tip with her free hand. She'd become adept at handling two men at once in recent days.

Byron groaned and tipped his head back as she ran her tongue along the ridge of his crown, finding the tiny bundle of nerves just along one side that she knew was extra sensitive. She sucked him back into the recesses of her mouth and his fingers tightened in her hair.

Soon she switched, giving Alek the same attention. It wasn't long before she had two very aroused males on her hands.

Alek eased her to the floor and positioned her so she half-sprawled in his lap, his hand roaming her breasts and teasing her nipples. "You have some work to do, Byron. Her pretty little cunt needs some attention."

"My pleasure." Byron lowered himself to the carpet and spread her thighs. Meeting her eyes, he petted her, his finger slipping between her folds and over her clit.

Her breath hissed out of her and her back arched. He speared two fingers inside her and she moaned, digging her heels into the carpet and shifting her hips impatiently. They loved to tease her until she was nearly incoherent with need. It was almost a competition between them.

Still holding her gaze, he dropped his mouth to her clit and sucked it between his lips. She bucked in Alek's arms when he pinched her nipples just enough to make her pant.

"I do believe she likes that, Byron," he murmured.

Byron's dark head bobbed between her thighs as he licked her, his fingers thrusting in and out of her. Pleasure poured through her, making her fidget. The men pushed her right up to the edge of a climax and held her there, making her insane with need. More than one time they'd made her beg and it appeared they were going to do so again.

Byron pulled away from her, nearly making her sob. "On your hands and knees," he ordered.

Alek helped her to roll to her stomach. She raised her rear in the air while the men sought the toys they liked to use on her. Soon she felt the pressure of a lubricated ridged cylinder against the entrance of her sex and another pushing against her nether hole, each of the men controlling one of them.

Byron used his free hand to stroke her clit as the men began easing both cylinders inside her at the same time. She cried out at the sensation of being so filled and stretched. The cylinder they pressed into her rear had a purpose, it made her ready for the girth of their cocks. The cylinder inside her sex they used just because they wanted to use it.

Soon both toys were seated deep inside her and she was a mess of sexual need. While Byron stroked her clit with the pad of his finger, they began to thrust the toys in and out of her.

Her climax hit her hard and fast, crashing over her body in waves of indescribable sexual bliss. She shuddered and bucked, crying out and digging her fingers into the carpet. The muscles of her sex convulsed around the toy as it went on and on until she was nearly hoarse.

Then the men were pulling the toys out of her and lifting her up. She could barely walk from the powerful orgasm she'd just had. They guided her to a rope they'd had placed in the ceiling. It had a bar set in the dangling end for her to hang on to.

She gripped the bar and hung for dear life as the men positioned themselves—Byron facing her and Alek behind her. Then she felt the press of their lubricated cocks against each of her entrances and they both slowly thrust inside her.

Holding on to the bar, she kept perfectly still, their hands bracing her waist as they hilted within her body at the same time.

"Oh, sweet Joshui," she breathed.

Having her rear stimulated this way brought to life all sorts of new pleasure she'd never before imagined. Having Byron so deep in her sex at the same time was an inexpressible ecstasy. It was pure sensation, and once they started to move, she wouldn't know one from the other—it would simply be an endless arc of perfect bliss.

They began to thrust and her fingers tightened on the handle of the rope that steadied her. The men found a rhythm that made her head fall back on Alek's shoulder and a moan rip from her throat.

Soon all that could be heard was the coming together of their three bodies. Sighs, pants, groans, and the gentle slap of skin on skin.

Another orgasm rose within Lilya, flirted with her, and then crashed over her. Her back arched and she cried out as she shuddered her way through the waves of it. It wasn't long before the men followed her, their cocks jumping deep inside her body almost in unison.

It was usually this way, one of them came first and the eroticism of watching it happen triggered the other two.

She could barely move. The men pulled from her body and Alek eased her into his arms and lifted her to the bathtub, where Byron was already drawing hot water.

The three of them bathed and then snuggled into Byron's huge bed, exhausted and satisfied. She snuggled between the two men, their skin still damp. Alek rolled her to face him and kissed her softly. "We love you so much," he whispered.

She reached out and cupped his cheek, Byron's ring glimmering on her finger. "And I love you both more than anything."

Byron snuggled against her back. "I'm so grateful for this cold snap," he murmured. "Gives us a good excuse to stay close all night."

She gave a low laugh. "We don't need an excuse for that anymore. We'll be married soon."

The date was set and the celebration was planned. She'd worried what people would think, Byron and Alek, both sons of wealthy houses, marrying a former courtesan.

But Byron and Alek didn't seem to care.

Byron's hand slipped over her abdomen and up to cup her breast. His fingers skated back and forth over her nipple, making her shiver.

"Stop that," she chided gently, "you'll make me want you again."

He rolled her to her back and dragged her under his body. "Oh, no. Not that."

Alek moved on her side, lazily moving his hand over her breasts. "Yes," he said drily. "I couldn't *possibly* have enough stamina for another round."

She chuckled. "You have enough stamina for sixty rounds."

He saucily raised an eyebrow. "Why, yes, I do." Then he leaned in to kiss her.

It looked like it was going be a long, luscious night.

The next morning someone knocked on the door. She answered it to find a well-dressed man carrying a sheaf of papers on her doorstep. "Miss Lilya Orensdaughter?"

"Yes."

"I'm the executor of Ivan Lazarson's last will and testament." He paused, peering past her to the two men who had entered the foyer to see who it was at the door. "You're named."

She went very still, her hand on the solid wood of Byron's front door. She used the sensation to ground herself as her mind hared off in several different directions. "I'm . . . named?"

"I know it's strange. It's a matter of public knowledge it was your hand that killed him."

"In self-defense," came Byron's rumbling voice from behind her.

"Yes, of course, self-defense. Yet this fact doesn't change that you are named in Mr. Lazarson's will." He stood on the step looking expectant for several long moments. "Uh. May I come in?"

She shook her head and forcibly broke the state of shock she'd been thrown into. "Of course, I apologize Mr. . . ."

"Mr. Emil Corbinson."

"Mr. Corbinson, please come in." She stood aside and allowed him to enter. "Please meet my intended husbands, Byron Andropov and Alek Chaikoveii."

The executor's eyebrows rose into his thick black hairline. "Ah." Arrangements of three in a marriage or relationship weren't unheard of and were becoming increasingly common. Still, it wasn't the most ordinary arrangement in Rylisk. "It's a pleasure to meet you both."

After the introductions were finished, she led them all into the library, offered the executor something to drink, which he declined, and they all sat down and settled into business.

He shuffled the papers he held. "In short, Miss Orensdaughter, Ivan Lazarson has left all his holdings and wealth to you. You are the only named person in his will."

Her eyes went wide and her hands clenched in her lap. How incredible that Ivan had done such a thing. He truly had been insane.

"Now," continued Mr. Corbinson, "some of that wealth is tied up in legal complications while the new government sorts through what due is owed various people wronged by Mr. Lazarson. Even so, when all is said and done, you will be an incredibly wealthy woman."

"No," she answered immediately. "I will take not one penny from Ivan Lazarson's estate."

The man blanched. "But, Miss Orensdaughter, this is a very substantial sum of money."

"I understand that. Mr. Corbinson, are you available for hire?"

He blinked. "Available for . . . Yes."

She folded her hands in her lap. "Then I would like to hire you to keep tabs on the progress of the estate. When the government has taken its share on behalf of Mr. Lazarson's victims, I want you to give the rest in its entirety to Angel House."

"Ah." He paused. "As you wish."

She stood. "Thank you for coming by, sir."

The executor stood and gave her a large smile. "It was my pleasure. Have a wonderful day."

She followed him out of the house and closed the door behind him, resting her head against it for a moment. She still couldn't believe that Ivan had left everything to her.

Byron cupped her shoulder with his big, warm hand. "Are you all right?"

She turned and smiled at him. Alek stood near the stairs, watching her with worried eyes. "At least Ivan's presence on this earth is finally doing some good."

"Yes, my love, because of you." Byron held out his hand to her.

"Let's not talk of Ivan anymore." Alek stepped toward her, took her hand, and led her back into the library. "We have something we want to talk to you about."

She took a seat on the couch and frowned at the serious note in his voice. "What is it?"

Byron grunted. "It's too early, Alek. I thought we agreed."

"It's just a discussion, Byron. Nothing more."

She looked between the two of them. "All right, you two, tell me what's going on."

Alek sank down next to her. "We were thinking that one day, not tomorrow or even next month, but one day . . . we should consider adopting a child, or maybe even *children*, from Angel House."

She went very still for a moment, then exhaled slowly, closing her eyes. "Lilya?" Alek touched her arm. "Are you all right?"

Opening her eyes, she launched herself at him, kissing him soundly. "Yes, I'm fine." She embraced Byron, then sat back and wiped her eyes. "I'm just perfect, actually."

Byron pulled her against him and kissed the top of her head. "We'll talk it about more after the wedding."

"Yes, let's do that." Her voice held a quaver and her throat still felt choked with tears of happiness and optimism.

Expectations, Lilya.

Yes, she could keep them *high*.

Alek cleared his throat. "I know you've been working on something upstairs, Lilya. I saw the covered canvas. Can we see it yet?"

She smiled and took his hand. "Yes, it's almost ready."

Together, the three of them mounted the stairs and entered her painting room. Walking over to the easel, she pulled the drape off to reveal the canvas. She'd been planning to wait until their wedding day to give them this, but now seemed an even better time. Stepping aside, she held her breath, waiting for their responses.

The men stood motionless, taking in the picture she'd painted. Seconds ticked off and she grew more and more nervous. She hoped they liked it.

Alek was the first to speak. "But we didn't even sit for this." His voice held a mystified quality.

"I thought you said you couldn't do portraits." Byron's gaze met hers.

She shrugged. "Apparently after those rings were placed on my fingers, the ability came to me. I just closed my eyes, pictured the three of us, and . . ." Her breathing hitched. "Do you like it?"

"We don't just like it, Lilya," answered Alek.

"We adore it. Just like we adore you." Byron held out his hand to her and she went to stand by his side.

It was a portrait of the three of them. She sat in a chair, dressed in one of the gowns Byron had bought for her and wearing a comb that Alek had given her. Her hands were folded in her lap and both rings were visible. Alek and Byron stood side by side behind her chair.

The painting had come very easily to her. It was the by far the easiest one she'd ever done. She didn't think there was any coincidence in that.

Alek stepped forward and carefully took it from the easel. "Let's put it up downstairs."

"Good idea."

The three of them went back downstairs and the men hung it

up above the mantel in the library. She hadn't been thinking about matching the colors in the painting to the room, yet everything complemented.

The three of them stood back to admire it. "It looks wonderful," she murmured with one arm around Byron's waist and her head on Alek's shoulder. "It looks like it was made to hang there."

"Of course it does," answered Byron. "Because we were meant to be together."